# Time *Will* Tell

## Scarlett Wells

# Dedication

*I dedicate this book to authors everywhere.*
*Thank you for sharing your stories with me and giving*
*me the courage to share my own.*

# Time *Will* Tell

# Prologue

## Viola

Today is my first day at kindergarten. Mama put me in my favorite sundress. It's pink with purple butterflies and has lots of ruffles. I also got to wear my white patent Sunday shoes. She pulled my long, messy auburn hair into a ponytail because she said I wouldn't be able to learn nothing if I couldn't see the chalkboard. My older brother, Carlyle, walked me to school. He's in fifth grade and was none too happy about me hanging around. But Mama told him he needed to make sure I got to and from school. He left me at the door to my classroom and told me to wait for him at the swings after school. So that's where I am right now, crying.

The big dummy had to go and pick a fight on the first day of school, so now he's in the middle of the schoolyard surrounded by all the other students, punching the class bully in the stomach. And I'm here watching. I'm too scared to leave. If I show up at home without him, Daddy will tan both of our hides. But I don't like being here all alone. Watching the other kids cheering and yelling is making me upset.

I shut my eyes and plug my ears, trying to block out the fight. I jump when someone puts a hand on my shoulder. I open my eyes, expecting to see Carlyle, but it's someone I've never met before. He's older than me. He's got light brown, curly hair and eyes that my mom would call hazel-colored (they look greenish-brown to me). When he smiles, I can see he's lost some of his baby teeth. His smile makes me want to smile.

"Are you okay?"

I tilt my head to the side to look at him for a moment, wondering if I should trust him. Mama told me never to talk to strangers. But he seems like a nice boy, coming all this way to check on me.

"My brother is fighting. He's supposed to walk me home. I'm too scared to go home alone, but I don't want to wait here," I tell him.

"How about I walk you home? And I'll tell your mama what's going on, so you don't get into any trouble. Okay?"

"But... I don't know you. I shouldn't go anywhere with a stranger," I mutter.

"My name is Emmett Davis. I turned 7 in July. My dad is the new football coach at Washington-Wilkes High School. We just moved here. And I'd like to be your friend," he says, smiling, showing big dimples in his cheeks.

I look at him for a minute. "Well, Emmett Davis,

I'm Viola Callaway. Everybody calls me Vi, but I don't like it. I live over on Lexington Street at the big ole house with all the pecan trees. I guess we're not strangers no more."

He laughs. "No, I guess we ain't. Now, can I walk you home?"

I smile a real smile then. "Yes. Yes, you can."

He takes my hand and helps me down from the swing I'm sitting on. When I have my feet on the ground, I figure he would let go, but he doesn't. He starts walking and keeps holding onto my hand, swinging our arms back and forth between us.

He tells me that he and his daddy just moved here from Texas. His mama had the cancer and went to heaven a few months ago. He misses her a whole bunch. It's just him and his daddy now, and his daddy spends almost all his time working. If there ain't things to be done, he's got the boys who play getting in shape or reading and things, so he can make sure the boys don't mess up their grades because when they go to the state champeens - and they will - he wants to make sure they all have good grades to get into the best colleges, even without football scholarships.

I ask him if he's lonesome. He says he is but they have a housekeeper looking after them, making sure clothes get clean, they get fed, and the house is picked up. He says she's a nice colored woman named Alma. I tell him I'm glad he has someone to look after him. And I really am. I dunno what I'd do if I lost my Mama.

He asks me about Washington, Georgia, where

we live. I tell him the little bits I know, which isn't much. Instead, I start pointing out all the big, old houses and tell him what I know about those. My Mama and Daddy both grew up here in Washington, so did both of my Grannies and Gramps. They know all about who lived where, when the houses were built, what crops used to grow where.

After the fourth house I tell him about, Emmett looks at me and says, "I thought you said you didn't know much about Washington!"

"I don't," I tell him, shrugging. "I just know about the big houses because I love 'em. One day I want to have my own big ole house and drink sweet tea on the porch swing at night."

"Then you will," he laughs.

We finally hit the dirt road leading up to my house. It's about a quarter-mile long, and has big oak trees lining both sides. It's really pretty at this time of day when the sun's getting lower and the light is coming through the leaves. It makes pretty patterns on us as we walk toward my house.

Our house is really old, but it's still pretty. It's white with big black front doors and shutters. It's got columns that go all the way from the floor to the roof two stories up along the front of the house. The porch is as long as the house and there's a balcony up on the second floor with an iron railing to keep us from falling off. The driveway goes in a loop in front of the house and there's a small fountain in the middle.

When we get to the house I see Mama on the front porch, wringing her hands. Daddy's car isn't in the driveway, which can only mean one thing: the school called. Mama runs down the steps to hug me.

"I was so worried! The principal called and told me that Carlyle was in a fight and that you were nowhere to be found! Heavens, child! You took ten years off my life!"

"I'm here, Mama! I'm okay! Emmett walked me home!"

Emmett clears his throat, "Hi, Mrs. Callaway. I'm Emmet Davis. My father is the new football coach at the high school. Carlyle asked me to make sure Viola got home because he was going to be late."

Mama looks at him like she looks at me when she knows I'm fibbing, but then she nods and smiles and says, "Well, thank you so much, Emmett. Why don't you come in for some lemonade and a cookie."

"I don't mean to be a bother, Mrs. Callaway," he says.

"It's the least I can do after you brought my baby girl home safe and sound. As a matter of fact," Mama goes on to say, "I'd be happy if you made sure she got to and from school every day, if it's not far out of your way. Apparently it's too much to ask of her own flesh and blood."

"That'd be fine, Mrs. Callaway. Viola's my only friend here in Washington." Emmett squeezes my hand and gives me a wink.

"Well, it's settled then! Come on in and have a sit and tell me more about you."

After our peanut butter cookies, ice-cold glasses of lemonade, and a lot of questions for Emmett from

Mama, I take him out to the yard to the big old oak tree to swing on the tree swing. We swing and have fun until I hear Daddy's car pull into the drive. Carlyle looks like he took a good beating and Daddy's got him by the collar, leading him up the steps to the front porch. I can't say as I feel sorry for him. Mama always says you reap what you sow. I'd say picking a fight on the first day of school instead of bringing his sister home, he's in a heap of trouble.

When Daddy sees Emmett and me, he turns around.

"Well, baby girl, I'm glad you got home. We were worried about you, weren't we, Carlyle? And who is this?"

"Emmett Davis, sir. Carlyle asked me to bring Viola home for him."

Daddy looks at Emmett like he's fibbing, just like Mama did. He asks Carlyle, "Is this true, son?"

Carlyle, knowing it'll ease up on his punishment and chores, nods his head so fast I'm surprised he don't hurt himself. "Yes, sir! I certainly did."

"Well, if that's the case, you are only grounded for two weeks instead of three. But we still need to discuss your other punishment."

Daddy turns to Emmett to shake his hand. Carlyle mouths a "thank you" and Emmett smiles at that. I'm surprised and happy that Carlyle isn't going to be in more trouble. I smile at my new friend, knowing he's the reason for that.

"Thank you, for bringing my baby girl home, Emmett. It's a pleasure to meet you."

"Nice to meet you, too, sir. I should get home. I'll walk you to school tomorrow?" Emmett turns around to ask me.

"Yes, please! I'll see you tomorrow morning," I answer giddily.

He smiles, the right side of his mouth lifting higher than the left. "See you tomorrow, Lola." And then he turns and walks back down my driveway.

I tilt my head to the side and watch him walk down the dirt road, hands in his pockets, whistling a song by a band my Mama won't let me listen to.

*Lola.*

Daddy, still hauling Carlyle into the house, turns back to me and says, "Are you coming, baby girl?"

I take one last look at Emmett Davis as he strolls down my lane. I may be 5, but I know that something big just happened in my life. I don't know what just yet, but I do know it's got everything to do with that boy.

"Coming, Daddy," I tell him, turning around and marching up the porch steps.

# Emmett

Maybe Georgia isn't going to be such a bad place to live. Texas just wasn't the same after Mom died. Dad wasn't either. He doesn't spend much time with me anymore. I think it's because I look a lot like her: same brown curly hair, same eyes. I'm only 7 but I know that it is hard for him. I only wish he knew that it is hard for me, too.

I am glad he hired Alma the day after we moved into the big white house by the high school. She's definitely not my mom, but you wouldn't know it if you saw how she treats me. She gives me a big hug every day when I get home from school, she bakes me cookies and brownies (but since Dad has us on the same eating plan as the football players, she hides them so it's our little secret). She also gives me what-for when I don't do as I'm told. Yup, she's not Mom, but she'll do.

And then there's Lola. She may be younger than me, but that little girl has me wrapped around her little finger. She's not like the girls in Texas. Sure, her mama has her dressed all prim and proper and she knows her manners and all, but she will play in the mud, go fishing at the creek, or climb trees in her pretty dresses, not caring that her mama will give her heck when she gets home. She's something else.

As long as I live, I'll never forget the look on her face when I called her Lola for the first time and then just walked away, her head tilted to the side, chewing on the inside of her cheek, just looking at me with those big green eyes.

*When I went to pick her up that first morning, I showed up at 8:02 a.m.*

*"You're late, Emmett Davis," she huffed. "I don't like to be kept waiting."*

*I laughed. "Lola, it's two minutes after 8:00! We're not going to be late."*

*She cocked her head to the side. "That's the second time you've called me Lola. Why?"*

*"Well," I drew the word out, "Yesterday, you told me you didn't like it when people called you Vi. And your full name sounds too much like an old lady, so I thought that - to me - you could be Lola. Do you like it?"*

*She thought about it for a minute and then nodded. "I like it! And I'm going to call you Mutt!"*

*I couldn't help but laugh. When I finally calmed down enough, I asked, "Why Mutt?"*

*"Well, your name is Emmett and with that shaggy hair and those big eyes, you look like a puppy dog. So...Mutt!" She smiled at me and I couldn't help but smile back.*

*"Then I'll always be your Mutt."*

That was two months ago. Since then we have walked to and from school every day. Every day when we get to her house, I come in and have a snack, and then Lola and I head back outside and play. Her favorite thing to do is play Hide and Go Seek in the pecan trees. She's got some pretty good hiding spots in those trees, let me tell you. Or we climb or swing on the big oak tree in her yard. We spend hours in that tree.

Sometimes we play with her friends Kevin and Deedee. Kevin's a year younger than me, but he's in kindergarten with Deedee and Lola because he mixes up his letters and numbers and stuff. He and Deedee live next door to each other and have been friends since birth. They know everything there is to know about each another.

But we never play with Carlyle. He says he's too cool to hang around with us babies. It seems like he doesn't like his sister very much. Maybe it's because she's a girl. But if he took the time to figure it out, he'd know that underneath all those curls and ruffles she's just a big ole tomboy.

I am excited to go trick-or-treating with Lola, even though she says I'm dumb because I won't be a lamb to her Mary, or the white rabbit to her Alice. My Dad got me a Dallas Cowboys jersey when he was back in Texas at a conference so I'm going as Danny White. Her folks are dropping her off at my house so we can trick-or-treat together.

I'm pacing by the front window, I'm so excited. When I see her daddy's car pull up, I open the front door. When she gets out of the car, she runs up and gives me a big hug. She's dressed up as Dorothy from *The Wizard of Oz*. Her hair is in two braids; she's wearing a cute little blue and white dress and sparkly red shoes. She's even carrying a toy dog in a little basket. I don't think I've ever seen anything so cute in my entire life. Alma, my Dad, and her folks all gush about how adorable we are and take too many pictures.

My dad comes with Lola and me. We walk all over Washington, talking, eating candy, and having fun.

Lola has my Dad wrapped around her pinky finger, too. The first time she came over to my house was after church one Sunday. Dad turned on the Cowboys game and she asked him all kinds of questions about football during the commercials.

After the first few commercial breaks, he started explaining the game to her as it went along. Now she is one of his favorite football buddies. She even gets to hang out with me during the high school games, as a water boy (well, girl). We are a great team. She fills the cups, I line them up, and hand them out.

Having her around has made things better with my Dad. Lola makes him almost as happy as she makes me. It's like he forgets to be sad or cranky when she's around. But I notice she does that with everyone. She's special, my Lola. She's my best friend. She's my girl.

Lola's sixth birthday is the day after Halloween. I think maybe that's why Carlyle doesn't like her so much - because her mama and daddy had to go to the hospital on Halloween and Carlyle didn't get to go trick-or-treating. I think he got something much better than candy. Lola's awesome.

I'm nervous about giving Lola her birthday present. Alma helped me pick it out when we went to the big department store in Augusta to get me some new shirts and pants. It's Saturday and she's having a big party. Her Daddy set up a petting zoo and pony rides in the yard. There are streamers and balloons everywhere in pink and purple, her favorite colors. I haven't seen her yet, but I see Kevin and Deedee so I hang out with them. After a few minutes, she comes out onto the front porch with her mama. She's wearing a pink and white dress with a puffy skirt and pink shoes. Her hair is down and curly, just the way I like it. She runs over to us and gives us all hugs and thanks us for coming.

We have a lot of fun playing with the goats, chickens, and pigs, and riding the pony, which is Lola's present from her parents. She couldn't be more excited. Deedee got her a new Barbie, Kevin got her a car for her new Barbie, and she got all kinds of games and toys from all the other kids. I keep my gift until all the others have been opened. My hands are sweaty, and I can't seem to stop swallowing and gulping down air. I hand over the box that Alma gift-wrapped for me. She looks at me with a big smile and then starts opening the wrapping paper. When she sees what it is, her smile gets even bigger.

"A jewelry box! Does it have a ballerina inside?"

"You'll have to open it and see," I whisper.

She opens the box and finds a ballerina spinning around to music from *Swan Lake*. Then she sees the present that has my tummy in knots: the locket with her picture and mine. She picks it up and stares at it so long I think I'm going to pass out. When she looks up at me, her eyes are full of tears.

"It's beautiful, Mutt. Thank you so much. Will you put it on me?"

I nod and take the necklace from her hands. She pulls her hair out of the way and I somehow manage to get the locket around her neck and the clasp done up, despite how badly my hands are shaking.

After it's on, she looks at the pictures again and

smiles. She grabs my hand and doesn't let go for the rest of the party.

I look down at our hands, our fingers twisted together, and I know that, as sure as I know the sun will come up tomorrow, my life will be twisted together with Lola's until the day I die.

# Part I

# Chapter 1

## Viola

My world is ending. I know I'm only twelve and it may sound melodramatic, but that's how it feels. Mutt and his daddy just came over to tell us the big news. Since Coach Davis got the Washington-Wilkes Tigers to the state championships, his work here is done. A private school up in Albany, New York has hired him to take their team all the way. They'll stay here until the new year and then move so Coach can get started doing his research and recruiting in the off-season.

I can't listen any more. I race out of the house to our tree. Mutt isn't too far behind. He climbs up on the branch with me and hugs me tight. I feel him crying, but I don't have it in me to look at him because it will kill me. He forces me to look at him by putting his finger under my chin and lifting my face so he can look me in the eyes. His voice sounds funny when he finally speaks.

"I don't want to go, Lola. I asked him if there was any way that I could stay here in Georgia. He told me that because of his job, I get to go to this school for free. It's one of the best private schools in the Northeast. It'll help me get into a better college if I don't get a football scholarship. Like I care. I only want to stay here and be with you, Kevin, Deedee, and Alma."

"Alma! Won't she take care of you?" I ask, grasping at straws.

"Don't think I haven't already asked. Because we're leaving, she's out of a job. And since there aren't a lot of folks who can afford to have a housekeeper around here anymore, she has to move back to Augusta to be with her family."

"I'll beg my Mama and Daddy to keep you here with us! You've become the son they never had!"

Mutt chuckles. "Lola, they already have a son. You remember your brother Carlyle?"

"Yeah, well, he's a big jerk. But you, they adore you! They are more proud of you than they are of Carlyle."

Mutt smiles at me, wiping the tears from my cheeks with his thumbs. "I know your parents think of me as another son. They have become family to me, too. Dad has promised me he'd ask your parents if I can stay here. He'll pay them room and board. But he's not hopeful. Taking care of someone else's kid is a big deal."

"Mutt, I...you're my best friend. How am I going to live without you?"

"How am I going to survive without you? You, Kevin, Deedee, your folks, Alma... You're the family I never had. It's just going to be my Dad and me. I'm going to have to start all over again and I know there won't be anyone there like you. Maybe your folks will send you to private school up in Albany with me?"

"Ha! You think my Mama's going to let a future member of the Daughters of the American Revolution go to school north of the Mason Dixon line?" I snort. "That'll be the day."

"Vi? Emmett? Where are you two?" Daddy shouts.

"Up in the tree, Daddy. We'll be down in a minute," I say, wiping another tear away.

My heart feels like it has been torn in half. When Emmett leaves, that is pretty much what will happen. The other half of my heart will be moving about a thousand miles away from me and there is nothing I can do about it. Why does this feel like the beginning of the end?

We climb down and head to the house. Coach Davis, Mama, and Daddy are sitting around the dining room table. Daddy and Coach have tumblers of scotch and Mama's got a glass of white wine. Normally they only drink on special occasions. But it doesn't seem like that kind of occasion.

Daddy waves me over and pulls me up on his lap like I'm a little girl. He wraps his arm around my shoulder and gives me a squeeze. I don't like the look he is giving me. Before he even opens his mouth, I know all hope of Emmett staying is lost.

"We've discussed the option of Emmett staying here in Washington. While I know it's going to be difficult for you two to be apart, we feel that it's best for Emmett to stay with his dad," Daddy says.

"No, Daddy! Please, please let Emmett stay with us! We'll both do chores, and help out more, and do our homework and go to bed whenever you tell us to and... and... I don't know, but you have to let him stay," I sob.

Daddy kisses the top of my head.

"Sweetheart, I know this is difficult and it seems incredibly unfair. Your Mama and I couldn't love Emmett more if he were our own. But it's in his best interest to be with his father. One day, I hope you can understand."

I look over at Mama through watery eyes. She gives me a sad smile.

"Can Emmett and Coach come and have Thanksgiving and Christmas with us again this year?"

She nods and says, "Of course, baby girl. They're always welcome in our home."

"Thank you, Luanne. Spending the holidays with you, Jack, and the kids has helped Emmett and I get through the past few years without Grace," Coach says. He is looking down at his glass and I can tell by his voice that he is sad talking about Emmett's mother.

"Well, I think this has been a hard night on all of us. Why don't we all get some rest and get together tomorrow after church? Does that sound good?"

Daddy asks looking at Coach and my mom because he knows I'm about to burst into bigger tears I think.

"Sounds great. Thanks again, Jack. Luanne, always a pleasure," Coach says as he gets up to leave.

I hop off of Daddy's lap and run to Mutt and hug him as hard as I can. My best friend is leaving me soon. I need to spend every possible moment with him before he goes, to get my fill of Emmett Allan Davis before he leaves and takes my heart with him.

"If you can't stay here then we'll have to make every minute until you move count. Don't you dare go make any plans that don't include me, you hear?"

He chuckles softly in my ear while twirling one of my curls around his finger. He gives me a big squeeze and says, "Like I'd ever do anything without my Lola."

# Chapter 2

## Emmett

It's New Year's Eve. Dad and I head to Albany the day after tomorrow. I have spent every spare moment of the last seven weeks with Lola. Sometimes we let Kevin and Deedee hang out, but mostly it's just the two of us. We've talked about the past, we've talked about the present, and we've talked about the future. And one thing has been made abundantly clear: there is no future that doesn't include the other one of us in it. I may only be 13, but I know that there will never be another girl who will hold a candle to Lola. She is beautiful inside and out. She is my best friend and knows everything there is to know about me. She is the other half of my heart. And one day, I'm going to come back to Washington and ask her to marry me.

Lola's parents are hosting their annual New Year's Eve party. My Dad and Alma are here celebrating with about 100 other adults from town.

Lola's parents relented and told Lola that I could sleep over. We haven't done this since she was eight and I was ten; we were told we couldn't anymore because of something about boys and girls and birds and bees that I didn't understand at the time. I understand what they mean now, but they know I want to spend every single last minute by my Lola.

We're up in her room, away from the party and the adults. We've hung more sheets up over the canopy on her bed so it's like we're in a tent. We're both lying on our sides, facing each other. Since it will be a long time before I see her again, I'm doing my best to memorize every little detail about her: the number and pattern of freckles on her nose, how incredibly long her eyelashes are, the exact shade of green of her eyes. I trace the shape of her face with my fingertip. She closes her eyes. My eyes focus on her mouth. I trace her lips and lean over and kiss her. Her eyes snap open and fix on mine.

I've kissed her almost every single day for the last few years, a peck on the lips or the cheek before I leave for the night. We hug, we hold hands... but something about this moment is very different.

She puts her hands on either side of my face and tells me what I want and need to hear.

"I love you, Emmett Allan Davis."

I hug her to me, putting her head on my shoulder, kissing the top of her hair. We fall asleep clinging to each other like our lives depend on it.

She wakes up before me and tries to wiggle out of my grasp, but I hug her to me for a few more minutes.

Not that she minds. If she did, I know darn well she would have been able to get free. I don't want to let her go, but I know by the way she's squirming that she needs to get up and pee, so I let her go.

I get dressed while she's in the bathroom. When she comes back, I go to do my morning routine while she gets dressed. We head downstairs to have one last breakfast with her family. Her parents try to make it fun, reminiscing about the past few years. Lola nibbles on her bacon and pushes the eggs around on her plate. I know she's really going to have a hard time after I go. It kills me to know I'll be the cause of her pain.

I head home to finish packing up with Dad and Alma. We're finished by the time the movers come to load the truck at one o'clock. And that's when Alma loses her grip and bursts into tears. I know she's been crying for the past two weeks. I hear her running the tap in the bathroom to try and hide it.

I rush to her and throw my arms around her.

"I'm going to miss you, Alma. Thank you so much for taking care of Dad and me. Thank you so much for being there for me. Thank you for all of the cookies and brownies that Dad didn't know about. But mostly, thank you for loving me."

This last sentence has her needing to sit down, so I help her over to one of the kitchen chairs and hold her hand until she finally gets the crying under control.

"Emmett, child, you will always be my boy. You go make me proud at that fancy school in New York.

And if you miss our monthly call, so help me, I will take the bus up there and break a wooden spoon over your behind!"

"Yes, ma'am! Understood," I say, with a mock salute. "I love you, Alma."

"I love you, too, child."

She says goodbye to Dad and hugs him so hard his eyes bulge out of his head. When she's done, we head out to her car. I open her car door for her and make sure she's all buckled up before closing it. She rolls down the window and blows me a kiss before she starts her car, puts it into gear, and, giving us one last wave, drives off.

Dad claps me on the back and tells me to head over to Lola's. He will meet me over there for dinner later.

I run over there as fast as I can, a gift for Lola in my hands. I have to take a few moments to catch my breath and calm my nerves. I don't want Lola to see how much this is hurting me. I have to be brave. For her.

I let myself in the front door, as I have every day for the past six years. I find her in the kitchen, helping her mama peel potatoes for dinner. I ask what I can do to help and get handed a bowl of peas to shell. I sit down at the kitchen table and get to work. We don't talk. We don't even look at each other. It's too hard.

My Dad is knocking at the front door within an hour of my arrival. Lola still hasn't looked at me or said anything to me. We help her mom get everything onto the dining room table and sit down to eat after a quick grace.

Being a growing boy, I eat everything on my plate quickly and help myself to seconds. Lola hasn't eaten anything and is pushing her peas into her mashed potatoes, making polka dot patterns. After I've finished my second helping, I ask if Lola and I may be excused. Mr. Callaway tells us to clear our plates and come back in a bit for some dessert. We take our plates to the kitchen, rinse them off, and place them into the dishwasher.

Without a word, I grab Lola's hand and the box I left on the kitchen counter and walk her out into the yard to our tree. I help her climb onto our favorite branch, put my arm around her shoulder, and pull her to me.

I open up the box and take out the ID bracelet Alma helped me pick out. I take her hand in my lap and put the bracelet on her wrist. I bring her hand up to my lips and kiss the back of it. She looks down at her bracelet and begins to cry.

"I'll always be your Lola," she says before a big sob escapes, and I pull her to me.

I squeeze her as tightly as I can, trying not to cry. But I can't hold it in anymore. I let the tears fall. She can feel my body wracking with every sob, my tears wetting her hair. I can feel her shaking and hear the keening noises she makes when she tries to keep quiet while she cries. It makes me cry even harder. My heart hurts so much. I can't do this. I'm about to ask her to run away with me when we hear her daddy telling us that we missed desert and that Dad and I need to leave soon. Time always seems to slow down when you don't want it to and speed up when you need more of it.

I get myself together and pull her face up so I can see it. Even after crying for as long as she has, she's still the prettiest girl I've ever seen. She knows everything about me: my hopes, my dreams, my darkest secrets. But there's one thing I haven't flat out told her.

"I love you, Viola Ann Callaway. I will come back for you. I promise."

"I'll be here waiting, Mutt. I love you, too," she manages between sobs.

Still holding her face, I lean in and gently brush my lips over hers. She shivers and then pulls back to look at me. I kiss tears from her cheeks. She smiles at me and pulls me in for another big hug.

We climb down from the branch and I go over to the tree trunk. I pull out my pocketknife and start to carve. The end product is a heart with "Mutt + Lola 4 ever" in the middle.

"Don't ever forget, Lola. You're mine. Forever."

She nods and smiles through her tears.

We walk back to the house slowly, trying to make these moments last as long as possible. But it doesn't last long enough, and the reality hits both of us as our parents and Carlyle hug, shake hands, and say goodbye. I pull her to me, never wanting to let go, but my Dad wants to say goodbye to her too, so I have to.

"My little Vi. I'm so sorry that I'm taking Emmett away from you. You've been his best friend and you're like a daughter to me. I love you, darlin'. Now, make an old man happy and give me a squeeze and some sugar."

She leaps at Dad, wrapping her arms tightly around his neck. She's crying again and, although my Dad isn't what you'd call a touchy-feely type, he's got tears rolling down his cheek.

"Don't go," she whimpers.

Dad kisses her on the cheek and whispers something only she can hear. She nods, gives him a big kiss on the cheek, and separates from him, wiping the tears in her eyes.

Her mama's in tears, hugging me fiercely and telling me not to forget them. She gives me one last squeeze. Carlyle gives me an indifferent handshake. I turn to Mr. Callaway and hold out my hand for a shake. He surprises me by giving me the bear hug to end all bear hugs.

"Take care, son," he says in a gruff voice. "You go be the best that you can be. Make us proud."

"I will, sir."

I find Lola for one last long hug. I don't want to let go because it means I'll be letting go of the last six years of my life. And they've been the best ever.

As I pull back, she grabs my hand. I touch the engraving on her ID bracelet: *Forever My Lola*. I make sure she looks me in the eye as I say, "Don't you ever forget it."

She manages a weak, watery smile before she vows, "Never. I love you, Mutt."

"I love you more."

She starts to cry harder and I know if I don't let go now, I never will. I release her hand, give her one last kiss on the top of her head, and get in the car.

I see her drop to her knees, her head in her hands, as we pull down their drive, heading to the motel for the night.

"It'll be all right, son," Dad grumbles. "I'm going to miss her, too."

I don't think he has any clue how badly I already miss her and we're not even a mile away yet. I want him to stop the car so I can get out, run back, and just stay with her. I don't care about Albany. I don't care about the future if she's not right there with me.

But I can't say any of this. Instead, I turn up the sports station, turn my head, and look out the window as the world turns blurry.

# Chapter 3

*Viola*

After Emmett kisses me goodbye and gets in the car, I watch the tail lights get farther and farther away down the drive. My knees give out, and I can't control the violent sobs that come out of me. Daddy picks me up and carries me up to my room. Mama gets me out of my dress and into my nightgown, then she spends the night cuddling and soothing me until I finally cry myself to sleep.

I don't get out of bed for another four days, except to do my business. Mama brings me meals and leaves them, only to pick them up later with only a bite or two missing. I just cry, sleep, and dig through all the photos of Mutt and me, reliving every memory. Kevin and Deedee come over every day after school to check in on me, but Mama always politely tells them I am resting.

On the fifth day, I get out of bed, have a shower,

get dressed, and go down for breakfast. Mama and Daddy do a poor job of hiding their shock, but they don't say a word. Carlyle doesn't even notice; or, if he does, he doesn't show it. Mama gives me a plate stacked high with hot blueberry pancakes, bacon, and strawberries and kisses me on the forehead. I know she is proud of me for joining the land of the living again.

But something told me it was *the* day to get up and out of bed. Mama calls Kevin and Deedee's moms and asks if they want to come over, since it's Saturday. About twenty minutes later, Kevin and Deedee knock on the front door. The mailman comes while we are sipping lemonade on the porch swing. He calls me over, smiling while he tells me that I have mail. It's a postcard from Mutt, sent from their first stop on the ride North. The postcard is cheesy: the word Kentucky in big letters, with pictures of various Kentuckian things inside the letters. But the part on the back is what matters most:

*Lola,*

*I can't even tell you how sad I am right now. It feels like a whole circus is sitting on my heart, not just the elephant. I miss you a lot already. The day driving was long, and we have to get up in a few hours to keep going, but I wanted to write to you and tell you I miss you and I love you.*

*Forever yours,*

*Mutt*

Every few days, there is another postcard from somewhere else, until finally there is a full letter from Albany with his return address. From that day forward, I write Mutt a letter and tell him that I miss him and what went on that day, every day. I get one back from him every few days, telling me about the new school, a new friend—a boy named Cooper—and learning to ice skate and play hockey.

After a few weeks, the letters come farther and farther apart. He starts calling me once a month on Sunday nights, explaining that he is training hard to get onto the hockey team next school year and doesn't have a lot of time to write anymore. It makes me sad, but I am happy that he has something to fill his time. I tell him I am happy with a phone call and the odd postcard. I can hear the smile in his voice when he says, "I'll see what I can do, Lola."

The last six months have been hard for me. Every time I walked out the front door to go to school and didn't find him waiting on the front porch for me, my heart hurt so bad I almost asked Mama to take me to the doctor. I thought it would get easier as the days went by, but it didn't because I had that same disappointment again at the end of the day when he wasn't standing next to my locker, grinning at me, waiting to walk me home.

Kevin and Deedee have done their best to try and make up for his absence. But how do you replace a giant void in your life? How do you fill in a gaping hole in your heart?

I spent a lot of time in our tree. I'd go up there and listen to music and read. I tried getting active in after school clubs, anything to keep my mind off of Emmett, but anytime I was alone, my mind always went back to him. And the hole would open up all over again.

This is going to be a very long summer break. Kevin and Deedee swear up and down they'll make it great. Kevin is excited because his cousin, Chase, is coming to spend the summer with him.

"So, when does Chase get here?"

"The day after tomorrow," Deedee answers. "Why, are you interested in him?"

"Please," I roll my eyes. "I see him for three hours every Thanksgiving. I barcly know the guy."

"Well, I'm just glad to have another guy to hang out with," Kevin says. He sees the glares coming at him from both Deedee and me and starts to sputter, "I mean, I'm totally lucky to have the two prettiest girls in Wilkes County on my arms every day, but sometimes it's good to have some guy time."

"Nice save, Butler," I giggle.

Deedee doesn't give him much slack on that remark, instead choosing to pinch his upper arm.

"Ow! Deedee! You know there's no one else I'd rather spend my days with. I'm just saying it's nice to hang out with different people every now and again, *with you."*

"That had better be the case, Kevin. Don't forget, I know where you sleep," she growls.

Two days later, I'm at Kevin's house for a barbeque to welcome Chase. He hasn't changed much over the years: he's our age, short with curly black hair, blue eyes behind thick-rimmed glasses, and chubby cheeks. Yup, he's still nerdy.

I steel myself and put on a smile because a Southern girl is nothing if not polite and gracious.

"Hi, Chase! It's great to see you! How have you been?"

"Hi, Viola. You're even prettier than I remembered," he gushes.

"Thank you. I'm really sorry to hear about your folks."

"Thanks. It's really for the best, though. They couldn't make it through a day without fighting anymore. I'm just glad to get away for the worst part," he says, suddenly finding the grass incredibly interesting.

I pick up his hand. He looks up at me. I smile and say, "We're going to have a great summer here in Washington. Okay?"

He smiles back at me and nods his head. His hand is all sweaty, so I give it a squeeze under the pretense of confirming what I just said, and then drop it and excuse myself so I can go and wipe the sweat away in secret.

That was how 'the summer of awkward' began. I love Kevin and Deedee to bits; always have, always will. Everyone— even our parents— have been trying to get Chase and me to bond, and it's driving me insane!

Chase is a nice boy. He's crazy smart; he should be two or three grades ahead by now, but his parents didn't want him to be socially stunted or something like that, so they didn't make him skip. And he is very sweet to me. The plain truth is that he's just not Mutt.

Even though I talk about Mutt all the time, I just don't think it's sinking into that smart brain of his that I don't like him the way he likes me. Maybe his brain is too full of math or something. Regardless, he keeps trying every single day; trying to hold my hand, trying to compliment me and work his way into my heart, but there's only one person my heart has room for— Mutt.

I've heard from Mutt twice over the summer break. I was expecting him to call or write every week, but he says he's been busy. I don't push, I'm not that kind of person. So I just try to enjoy every minute of his phone calls. And then I go and hide in our tree and cry because I miss him so much.

Summer is almost over and Chase is heading back home to Atlanta today. I go over to Kevin's house to say goodbye. Chase, Kevin, and Deedee are sitting in the wicker chairs on the porch with Mr. and Mrs. Butler and Chase's dad. Chase stands up and comes down the steps to meet me.

"I'm so glad you came to say goodbye. I am really going to miss you, Vi."

"Me too, Chase. Oh, I have something for you!" I pass him the gift bag I brought along with me.

When he opens it, he laughs. I put together a collage of photos of the four of us being silly and framed it. "Vi, this is the best gift ever. Thank you."

And that's when the most awkward moment of the whole summer happens. He gives me a big, sloppy kiss and hugs me tight. When he hugs me, I feel something poking me in the hip.

Not knowing what else to do, I give him a pat on the back, pull away, and excuse myself to go and get some lemonade, mumbling about being thirsty from the walk over. I run up the porch, say hello to the Butlers, and then go inside to get myself a drink.

Deedee is in hot pursuit. "Vi, what the heck was that all about? I know you don't *like him* like him, but at least you could be a little less obvious than running away."

"Dee, what I'm about to tell you goes no further than you, me, and the walls of this kitchen. You got me?" I look at her for confirmation before proceeding. She nods. "When Chase hugged me, I felt his 'thing.'"

"Noooooo!" Deedee squeals.

"Yes! I didn't know what else to do, so I just told him I was thirsty and ran inside. Please stop laughing."

"I can't, Vi! This is too funny," she gets out in between belly laughs. "Is this honestly the first time you've ever... felt it?"

I groan. "Yes, Dee. It is. Why does that seem so amusing to you?"

"Well, I just assumed that you would have felt Emmett's at some point in time." Her voice gets softer with every word.

"Are you telling me you've felt Kevin's thing?" I shriek and immediately shudder and say, "Ewww!"

"I haven't seen it since we played doctor in the second grade. I've felt it on my leg a few times when we are lying on the sofa, watching TV."

"Dear Lord, this is more than I need to know. And no, I never felt Emmett's thing," I huff.

"Oh. Well, maybe he didn't feel that way about you," she muses.

What? Hold the phone. Does he not love me like I love him? He certainly kissed me a few times like that before he left. Was it only because he was leaving me? What's all that business about me being his Lola forever and coming back for me? Is he ever coming back for me? I am now in a snit, and I need to go home and make a phone call.

"Excuse me, Dee. I need to go," I say, making my way out to the front porch to say goodbye to everyone.

I make an excuse about forgetting that Mama needed me to help with dinner. Mr. and Mrs. Butler look baffled, and Chase's dad looks at his watch. Kevin looks at me like I've grown another head, and Chase looks a little sheepish and hurt. But it's too late to back out now, so I just wave at everyone and run until I'm out of sight.

# Chapter 4

## Chase

Spending the summer with my cousin while my parents battled their divorce out in court was a blessing. Not only because I was away from all of the drama, but because I got to spend it with Kevin, Deedee, and - most importantly - with Viola Callaway.

I have known Viola almost all of my life, and I have been in love with her just as long. I know that she doesn't see me that way. She's always had Emmett. But maybe, just maybe, with him now living in Upstate New York, I can finally get her to see that I'd do anything for her.

I had big plans to try and woo her, but my efforts always failed. She was so sweet, always handling my awkward behavior with such patience that it just made me love her even more.

As Dad drives us back to Atlanta, I look at the photo collage that Vi made for me and smile, remembering all the amazing memories from my summer in Washington. Well, apart from the embarrassing moment when she said goodbye. That was something I hope to forget soon.

My favorite memory from the summer is the four of us lying on our backs on a blanket in the middle of Downtown Square, watching the fireworks going off above us. Well, I was watching Vi. Watching her stare up at the sky, her eyes smiling, listening to her giggle, ooh, and ah with each firework. After a particularly large firework went off and startled her, she reached out and clutched my hand, then turned her head to look at me, laughing.

"That was a sneaky one! I didn't see it shoot into the sky."

She turned her head back to watch the show, continuing to hold my hand, squeezing it with every bang and boom.

We did so much this summer. It certainly was one to beat.

My aunt and uncle rented a cabin for a week up in the Blue Ridge Mountains and took us all up there. We were right on a lake, so we spent most of our time swimming and fishing.

One afternoon we went horseback riding. Another afternoon we went to Denton Branch Falls and had a great time jumping off the boulders into the pool, skipping pebbles, and lazing about on the hot, smooth stones.

Nights were the best, though. We'd all sit around the fire pit, roasting marshmallows to make s'mores, telling jokes and stories, and just having fun.

She talked to me for hours about architecture and literature. She showed me how to bait a hook and fish – even took a picture of me holding up the first fish I caught. It wasn't much larger than the minnow we used as bait, but she was told me she was proud of me. She was curious about learning photography, so I taught her what I knew about composition and light. She was a very quick study, preferring landscape portraits over photographing people (although her candid shots were amazing).

She also spoke to me at length all summer about Emmet. I can't say that I enjoyed that but my father always told me that patience is a virtue. My mother preferred to say that good things come to those who wait. And I know that I am willing to be patient and wait if it means that Viola Callaway will be mine.

I wasn't beyond trying to hold her hand or put my arm around her shoulder while we watched TV. I had no clue what I was doing. The thing about Vi is that she is always so gracious. Even though she was completely uninterested, she would delicately remove her hand from mine to scratch her nose. Or if I had my arm around her shoulder, she would excuse herself to use the powder room and then come back and sit on a cushion on the floor. Never would she show any sign of impatience or disgust. She always handled it with a smile. And while it hurt, I couldn't help but adore her for not being rude about it like some of the girls I've seen.

I know that she sees me as a friend, but I'm not

going to let that stop me. I won't push, but I won't stop until Viola Callaway is my girl.

# Chapter 5

## Emmett

Cooper Forsythe was picked to be my "buddy" for the first week of school; help me get around to my classes, introduce me to people, that sort of thing. I am sitting on a bench in the office, looking at one of the pictures of me and Lola that I keep with me when he comes in and introduces himself. I try to put the picture away quickly, but he pulls it out, takes a peek, and whistles.

"Emmett, please tell me you won't be offended if I go after your baby sister. She's hot!"

My jaw clenches a few times before I spit out, "She's not my baby sister. That's my girl, Lola. She's not up for grabs. This is the only warning you'll get about speaking about her like that."

"Hey, man! It's all good! I was just trying to lighten the mood a bit. I was totally jerking your chain. Except the fact that she's gorgeous; she is something else." He puts out his hand for a shake.

"Forgiven?"

I take his hand and pump it a few times. "Yeah, man. Sorry. I'm just really stressed about school and I miss her something fierce."

"I can relate. My folks sent me to board here a few years ago after I got into trouble. I've got a girl or two back home," he says with a wink.

And with that, Cooper and I become friends.

After the first week is over, Cooper asks me if I want to play some shinney. He must have seen the perplexed look on my face because he quickly adds, "A few of the guys from my dorm are going to the outdoor skating rink to play a pickup game of hockey. Are you up for it?"

"I'm from the South, man. I've never been on ice before," I laugh.

"Well, you're in the North now, you rebel! Dress for the cold, and meet me at the dorm in 30 minutes."

And that is how I discovered hockey. After getting the basics of skating from Coop, I skated around the rink in a spare pair of his skates while the other guys played hockey. A week later we met up again, and I learned how to handle a stick and a puck. A week after that, I was playing with them. Now I spend any time I can on the ice, making up for years of living without hockey.

I am such a quick study that I catch the attention of the Academy's high school coach. He wants me involved in the junior high team, not playing yet but training with them. He says he's never seen someone with talent as natural as mine and he wants to foster it.

I let him break the news to my Dad, begging him for permission to have me train and try out for the hockey team next year.

"Em, I'm not going to lie. It's like your kid has been doing this his whole life, not just two months. As a coach, I know you know how rare this kind of talent is."

"I understand, but he's been raised on football."

"He was raised in the South. He never had the opportunity to try hockey down there. Listen, I'll get him hooked up with the junior team. He can train and run drills and study with them. We run our hockey teams like you run your football teams: eat, sleep, breathe hockey and schoolwork. If he doesn't make the team next year, I'll back off. But please just at least give him the chance to try."

My Dad rubs the stubble on his jaw. "All right, Dan. Let's see what happens."

I've made it to the end of the summer. Instead of being in football camp, I am at hockey camp with Coop. Team tryouts are in another week and all I have done since the day Coach Smith showed up at my house is train, drill, and do homework. And then I sleep, and I dream of Lola. I feel bad because I can't keep in touch as much as I'd like. But she has to know that I think about her every day and miss her more than I can tell her.

It's early on Sunday night. School starts up again the day after tomorrow, and I'm already exhausted. Ever since I moved up here, started at the Albany Academy and met Coop, my life has been all about hockey.

I'm getting my hockey bag all packed up for the first practice at school when the phone rings.

After a few mumbles, I hear Dad come to the bottom of the stairs. "Emmett, Vi's on the phone for you!"

I am surprised I don't break my neck flying down the stairs to grab the phone from Dad.

"Lola? I'm so happy to hear from you," I gush.

"Don't you Lola me, Emmett Allan Davis!"

Oh crap, she just middle named me. Did she somehow find out what I do at night when I think about her? How could she possibly know?

"I'm at a loss here, Lola. What'd I do... or not do?"

"Do you or do you not like me?" she asks calmly.

"You know I like you, Lola. I love you."

"Are you sure? Like, *love me,* love me?" Her voice softens, and I hear her take a deep breath.

"Lola, you are the only girl for me. The only things I think about are you and hockey."

"Oh, well then..." she seems like she's thinking about something and I'm not going to interrupt her. "Are you absolutely sure I'm the only girl you like like that?"

I chuckle, "I go to an all-boys school and live for

hockey. There are no other girls. And even if there were," I add quickly, knowing she's in a fragile state right now, "it's always only you."

I wait patiently for her response. I can almost see her with a big grin on her face. "Good. Did you get your birthday present yet?"

"Oh my gosh, yes! Thanks so much! I've been wearing my Rangers jersey at camp! The guys are jealous."

"Well, you can thank your Dad, too. He picked it up after I sent him your card and some money. Is he doing all right? He didn't sound like himself earlier."

"He's been really busy trying to start from scratch with the new assistant coaches and the new team. I think he's just tired. And he misses you and Alma and your folks a lot."

"Well, we miss him too. Now, tell me all about hockey camp," she prods.

We talk for another hour, and then I hang up and crash for the night, dreaming of her long auburn hair, emerald green eyes, and her pouty lips.

# Chapter 6

*Viola*

"Deedee, I think I'm coming down with something," I whine.

"Viola Ann, you will get your butt dressed and get to the salon in thirty minutes or I won't be your friend anymore!"

"Drama queen," I mumble. "FINE! But you let Chase know that I will *not* kiss him! He's my friend, not my date!"

It's our first school dance—only for eighth grade students. It's a big deal. And since Emmett is too busy with hockey to come down and escort me, Kevin volunteered Chase, who jumped at the chance. There's no way I would let any of the other boys at school escort me to the dance, although I had a number of offers. None of them even compare to my Mutt.

I put on a long-sleeved dress and some flat shoes

and have my Mama drive me over to the salon to get my hair and fingernails done. Normally I love to do girly things like this, but today it is wearing on me. Perhaps because I've been 14 for about two weeks and I still haven't had a phone call, card, present, or any sign of life from Emmett. I know he's on the high school hockey team now and it's a big deal for him to get a lot of ice time as a sophomore, but that's no excuse to forget your best girl's birthday! If I even am his best girl anymore. Sometimes I just don't know.

Julia, my stylist since birth, greets me with a big, "Hey Sug!" and a hug.

"Now what are we going to do with this pile of hair after we get it all conditioned and tamed, hmmm? I think we should put some of it up and leave the rest down your back. What do you think?

"I think that sounds great, Julia. Go ahead, I trust your judgment." Because I do. I wouldn't put my hair in anyone else's hands.

One of the manicurists gets to work on my fingernails as the conditioning treatment works its magic on my hair. I've only had my nails done one other time in my entire life on a mother-daughter date. I choose a pale pink polish to go with the beautiful strapless dress Mama picked out. I've even got matching pink strappy sandals with a 2-inch heel that I've been practicing walking in for a week now. Mama said I should look like a lady for this first special dance and she knows I wish Emmett would be here, so she's tried to make it as special as possible for me.

Julia has been twisting and curling and brushing

and back-combing for what seems like hours when she finally stops, smiles, and spins my chair to face the mirror. I am stunned at how incredible my hair looks! She has taken the hair from the front and pulled it gently back and pinned it up, making some soft curls. The rest flows down my back in cascades of auburn. My hair looks and feels soft to the touch, and it is incredibly shiny. There are a few tendrils at the front, gently framing my face.

"I'd put on a bit of mascara, a hint of pink blush on your cheeks, and a little pink lip gloss to round the look out," Julia says, admiring her work.

"Julia, it's amazing! Thank you so much," I gush as I give her a big hug.

"My pleasure, kiddo! You go and enjoy your first dance!"

It's 7:30 p.m. when the doorbell rings. Right on time (Chase is always on time, a trait I admire). I wait upstairs until Mama calls up to tell me that Kevin, Deedee, and Chase are here. I check myself in the mirror one last time. The dress is strapless with a sweetheart neckline. It is fitted at the top and flares out down to just past my knee with some layers of crinoline underneath for extra pouf. It's pink satin with a black lace overlay and a big pink satin sash, accentuating my waist. My boobs have grown and I've started noticing that my hips are getting broader. Hourglass shape is what they'd say back in the day. All I can say is that this dress makes me look much older than my 14 years.

"Here goes nothing," I mutter at the mirror.

As I step down the stairwell, the chatter between the parents and friends dies down and all eyes lift up to see me.

"Baby girl, you look beautiful! And you certainly don't look like my baby anymore!" Daddy says.

There's a chorus of "oohs," and "aahs," and "beautiful," as I make my way down.

Chase is standing at the bottom of the stairwell with my wrist corsage in hand. He chose a beautiful magnolia. I've got to give him bonus points for that. I hate roses.

He's so nervous, his hands are shaking and he can hardly get the corsage over my wrist. When it's finally in place, I take his hand and give it a squeeze. When he finally looks up at me, he says, "You're so beautiful, Vi. I think I'm the luckiest guy in all of Georgia."

I blush and say thank you.

The next thing I know, all of our parents are snapping pictures. We're asked to stand in couples on the stairwell, we're asked to stand on the porch, we're asked to sit in the parlor. About 20 minutes later we're finally allowed to leave the house.

Mr. and Mrs. Butler drop us off at the high school. We hand over our tickets and walk into the gym. It's been transformed into a blue and white wonderland, thanks to me and the rest of the gang on the dance committee. It took a lot of work but you'd never know this place was a gymnasium, except for the basketball court outlines on the floor.

Principal Stewart comes over to say hi and thank Deedee and me for our hard work putting the dance together. After he leaves, we find a table to sit at and the boys get punch.

Deedee's got her long, blonde hair in a twist and is wearing a beautiful blue floor-length spaghetti strapped gown. She's really tall and the cut of the dress flatters her form; her body hasn't hit womanhood as mine has, but her body is already showing signs of what is to come. She's so stunning, I'm often jealous. I tell her this and she snorts.

"Right, like you fell out of the ugly tree and hit every branch on the way down! You're gorgeous and you know it, Vi. Don't ever feel insecure about yourself. Are you feeling like this because you haven't heard from Emmett in a while?"

I mull this over a bit before responding, "I suppose."

The boys are back with plates of finger food and glasses of punch for us. We sit and eat and talk and laugh. I'm actually having fun, although I'd like for the other girls to stop coming to our table to talk to Chase. Yes, we get it. He's fresh meat. But he's here with me.

Chase has had quite a growth spurt since last Thanksgiving. He's considerably taller and his chubby cheeks have thinned out. His hair is a bit longer, more wavy than curly. He's definitely getting cuter. And he's not quite as gawky as the last time I saw him (I had conveniently been busy for a Thanksgiving or two after the 'summer of awkward'). But he's still not Emmett.

He asks me to dance. I smile and hold out my

hand to him as I gently push my chair back. We're about the same height with me wearing heels. He leads me to the dance floor and puts one hand around my waist, the other holding my hand up. He stands close, but not too close. He is very nervous and keeps looking around.

I giggle. "Chase, it's okay. I'm still me, Viola Ann Callaway. No need to be nervous."

"Vi, I don't think you know how beautiful you look tonight. I mean, you're always beautiful. But tonight... I can't even find words. It's kind of intimidating," he whispers the last bit.

"Hey now. Don't be intimidated. Did you forget the lineup of eligible bachelorettes vying for your attention earlier? It seems you're quite the looker yourself, mister."

"Yeah," he chuckles. "I guess so. But none of them are even half the girl you are, Vi. Thanks for asking me to be your date. I'm truly honored."

"Well, thank you for coming out a week before Thanksgiving to be my escort," I reply and give him a kiss on the cheek.

For the next week, Kevin, Deedee, Chase, and I are inseparable. When it's time for him and his Dad to head back to Atlanta, I'm really sad to see him leave.

"I probably won't see you for a while. Dad and I are heading to Hawaii for Christmas and then next year I have to do the holidays with my Mom's family," he says.

"Oh, that's too bad. I was kind of looking forward to seeing you again," I tell him, surprising myself with my honesty.

He smiles and raises his eyebrows in surprise.

"I'm finally starting to grow on you after all these years."

"Yes," I chuckle. "About that... I'm sorry for being a b-i-t-c-h. I really hope you can forgive me."

"You never were a b-i-t-c-h," he mimics me. "You were always perfectly polite and cordial. A true Southern belle. But I'd like to keep in touch. That is, if you want. We can call or email."

"I'd like that. I'm just going to grab a paper and pen from inside so we can swap contact info before you leave."

I turn to go upstairs and into the house when I hear Kevin softly singing, "Chase and Vi, sitting in a tree, K-I-S-S-"

"Butler, you'll zip that lip quick if you plan on giving Deedee the five babies she wants," I warn. There is nothing but silence as I walk into the house.

Victory is mine.

# Part II

# Chapter 7

## Emmett

I can't stop staring at the pictures Lola's folks sent with the annual Christmas newsletter. Her school picture is amazing. No one ever looks good in those, but she's perfection in her cream colored cashmere turtleneck sweater, auburn hair falling all around her in wild waves, green eyes blazing, and that smile. There's a glint in her eye like she's got a secret to share. I love that smile. I miss that smile. I miss her, period.

I haven't been a saint. Hell, I'm fifteen. I go to all the secret parties, I've kissed girls and fooled around with them. I even almost went to third base with a junior the other night. But her boyfriend found us making out in the closet, and that's why I'm sporting a shiner today.

The other picture, my God. I haven't seen her whole body since I left her in her front yard a few years ago. She has filled out in all the right places, and

I can't help the reaction my little buddy has to her. Any red-blooded male would have the same reaction looking at this picture of her.

Who is the ass clown with her? I'm going to rip that smug smirk off his face if I ever see him. Did she kiss him? Has she let him feel her up? Has she—oh God, I can't go there. *Don't even think about it, Emmett. You know she's a good girl. You know she'll wait for you.*

But how long will she wait? I haven't exactly been there for her. I even forgot her birthday. I sent her two-dozen roses last week. She hasn't called or written or anything. I think I may have blown it.

I pick up the phone and dial her number. Her mama answers.

"Hi, Mrs. Callaway. It's Emmett."

"Emmett, honey! How are you doing? Last we spoke to your dad, you were doing really well on the hockey team. It's not football, but I knew you'd be great at whatever you set your mind to. Are you keeping up with your studies?"

"Yes, ma'am. It's a requirement. I'm a B+ average right now," I tell her.

"Good boy, keep it up! College scouts are going to start sniffing around sooner than you think!"

"I know. They've already started making inquiries. Is Vi there?"

"Let me check and see, honey. I haven't seen her since this morning." I hear her put down the phone and shout, "Vi! Emmett's on the phone for you!" I smile, knowing exactly where she's standing in the hallway to get that perfect echo. I'm stunned when I hear Vi shout back, "I don't want to talk to him, Mama. Can you tell him I'm not here?"

After a few muffled comments, Vi picks up the phone.

"Hi, Emmett," she says, sounding less than pleased. "Thanks for the roses. They were nice. How's hockey going?"

I wince at her tone. I am an asshole. And I open my mouth to tell her exactly that.

"Lola," I drawl. She shuts me down.

"You don't get to call me that right now. I'm mad at you, Emmett," she spits out my real name. "I realize that you've got a whole life up there in Albany. But you don't get to call me Lola after promising me that you love me, that you'll be there for me and then never call or write, *and* you forget my birthday. It doesn't work like that!"

"I know, Lola. I'm so sorry. I'm the worst. I should treat my best girl with the respect she deserves. And you deserve respect. And so much more. And I'm an asshole for not putting forth the effort. I don't think I can apologize enough."

"Well, I'll consider forgiving you. And just for future reference, I hate roses," she says, lightening up. I can picture one side of her mouth turning up in a smile.

"Duly noted. Your mama sent pictures of you. You're so beautiful. But I've got a question. Who's the clown in the tuxedo?"

Her laughter does funny things to me. Good, but funny.

"That's Kevin's cousin, Chase. You probably met him a time or two when you were here. Someone—I'm not naming names—was too busy to come down to escort me to my first dance, so I needed a plan B."

"I'm pretty sure you could have had any boy in your class begging to take you to the dance, Lola," I state.

"Oh, I had offers, Emmett Allan Davis. But I didn't want to go with just anyone," she pauses and then lowers her voice. "I wanted to go with you."

I groan. She hit me where it hurts: right in the guilt trip.

"I know, Lola. I promise to make it up to you at some point. Things have been crazy here with hockey. And I'm trying really hard to keep my grades up, just in case I don't get a hockey scholarship. And, well, Dad and I haven't been getting along. Like for the last couple of years. Right now he's starting the search for another job because the Academy's team already won the state championship and we're arguing because I want to finish out high school here in boarding, and he wants me to come with him, although I don't know why. We never see each other anymore, and when we do, all we do is fight."

I sigh. "Lola, I really wish you were here. I miss you. I... I love you."

The silence that follows has me scared.

"I love you, too, Mutt. I wish I were there, as well, so I could hug you and kiss you and make everything better. Just... promise me you'll write or call more, please?"

"I'll do everything I can to make that happen, Lola. I've gotta go. Dad just got home. I love you."

"I love you, too. Tell Coach I miss him."

"I will," I promise. "Bye, Lola."

Even before I hang up, I hear her start to cry. And I curse myself for being an idiot.

# Chapter 8

*Viola*

I hate Deedee right now. Thanks to her, I have my first hangover. A select few sophomores were invited to go to a bonfire at a senior's house last night. It's not like we don't know these kids. We've all grown up together. Washington, Georgia isn't *that* big. But I had no idea that they partied hard.

It was a Halloween party, so Deedee determined we'd unofficially make it my birthday party as well. She decided we'd be angels. We picked out these cute, fitted white tank dresses and we managed to find gold wings and halos, too. We topped the look off with white go-go boots we bought last year for our 60's costumes. I had to admit that we looked hot.

And every male at the party also had to admit it, too. To our faces. Lucky for Deedee, Kevin was also invited. He spent the entire night threatening any guy that even looked at Deedee the wrong way. But I didn't have constant protection. So it was up to me to put my foot down, which was hard after my world got all blurry. As I understand it, Kevin narrowly saved me from being molested by one of the seniors on the football team. He got a bit of a beating for it, but as he said last night, my virtue is still intact so he did his job.

Note to self: bring your own sodas and waters to the next party, no matter how dorky that may seem.

My head is throbbing when I hear Mama tell me that Emmett's on the phone. He remembered my birthday this year! I throw off the blankets and race downstairs to pick up the phone.

"Happy birthday, beautiful! Your mama said you were still in bed. I hope I didn't wake you."

"No, Mutt! I miss you! Thank you for remembering this year!"

"Now, what kind of idiot forgets his best girl's birthday," he jokes. "But, I think the surprise I have for you is going to make up for last year."

"There's a surprise?! Where is it?!" I'm jumping up and down, giddy with excitement.

"Well, it's not going to be there for another few weeks, but I hope you can wait. Because your surprise is me."

I sure hope Mutt was smart enough to hold the phone away when I start screaming.

"Ohmigosh, ohmigosh, ohmigosh! Mutt, that's the best birthday present ever! Tell me how is this happening?"

"Well, the Tigers have now gone to the state

finals for four years in a row, as I'm sure you know. And to thank my Dad for making it happen, the Rotary Club decided to hold a banquet in his honor. He's driving over from Missouri, and I'm going to fly down from Albany to Atlanta. It's going to be the weekend after Thanksgiving. Are you excited?"

"Does a bear shit in the woods? Oops! Sorry, I never cuss! I'm just so excited, Mutt!"

"I couldn't tell," he laughs. "I can't wait to see you. I don't know if I'll be able to recognize you after all this time."

"Emmett Allan Davis, if you can't pick me out of a crowd, you'll be in a lot of trouble!" I giggle. And then I ask him, "How long do we have together?"

"I get in on Friday afternoon, and I have to fly out on Monday morning. I have a game on Wednesday night and a test I can't miss on Tuesday."

My heart aches a little, but I'm finally getting to see him after five years. "Well, we'll just have to make every minute count, won't we?"

I can hear him smile when he says, "You know it, Lola."

The next few weeks pass in a blur of excitement and shopping. Mama took me to Augusta to buy a whole new wardrobe. She said it was more birthday presents, but I know she's just as excited about my reunion with Mutt as I am. Today is finally the big day. He doesn't know it, but I've taken the afternoon off of school so I can pick him up at the airport with my parents.

It took me about an hour to get ready. I had to do something with my hair, put on a little makeup, and finally figure out what to wear. Nothing seemed right. I am so nervous and scared about seeing him. I want to make sure I look absolutely perfect. I settled on a cute off-white lace A-line dress with brown cowboy boots. I stare at myself in the mirror for another 15 minutes, wondering how much he has changed, if he still thinks I'm beautiful... If he still loves me. I have definitely changed in the past four years. Will he notice? Or will he just see his little Lola?

Mama and Daddy drop me off and head off to circle the airport a few times until they spot us outside. I check my reflection in the window once more before I take a deep breath and head inside the terminal to wait for Mutt. I check the board and his flight landed a few minutes ago.

My heart is beating out of my chest and I can't stand still. I start pacing back and forth until the doors open and people start filing out. I can't breathe when I finally see him.

He's no longer the adorable boy with shaggy hair. He's all man. And a gorgeous one, at that. He's six feet tall, his body all muscle, each ridge and ripple emphasized through the tight black t-shirt and worn jeans he's wearing. His face is chiseled and his dimples pop out when he finally sees me and smiles.

He picks up his pace to get to me and then stops a foot in front of me. His eyes take me in, from the top of my head to the tips of my cowboy boots, a pleased smile on his face the entire time. He drops his duffel bag and opens his arms and says, "So, what do I gotta do to get some love?"

And that's all it takes for me to break out of the spell he has on me. I squeal and run over and jump up to hug him. He catches me and holds me tight to him, smelling my hair and squeezing me every now and then. After about a minute, we hear people giggling around us and decide to head out to the car before we embarrass ourselves.

The whole ride home, my parents grill him about school and hockey and college prospects. He's sitting in the back seat with me, holding my hand. He gives me a wink and squeezes my hand every few minutes.

When we get back to our house, we see Coach Davis sitting in his pickup truck. The car barely stops rolling before I'm out and running to see Coach.

He picks me up and gives me a big hug and a kiss on the cheek. "If I had known I'd get a hug and a kiss from such a beautiful girl, I'd have come back sooner! How are you, Vi?"

He puts me down and greets my parents fondly. And then he gives Emmett an awkward hug.

Coach is going to stay at a hotel in town. After much begging, my folks agreed to let Mutt stay with us so we could spend as much time together as possible. After dinner, Coach heads to the hotel and my folks head to bed, leaving Mutt and I sitting on the porch swing, getting caught up.

I tell him about school, how I am now tutoring

because my grades are so high, about all the after-school activities I'm involved in, about Kevin, Deedee, and Chase. Mutt takes it all in, smiling the entire time.

During a pleasant lull in the conversation, he puts his arm behind me on the back of the swing and rests his head against mine, rubbing my shoulder with his fingers. I hum at the familiarity of it, even though he's changed so much since the last time I saw him. He hums, too, and then we both laugh.

He uses his other hand to turn my head toward him. My heart starts pounding so hard, I'm pretty sure he can hear it. When he licks his lips, I close my eyes and lean forward. It feels like the air crackles between us before I feel his lips brush against mine. I whimper, feeling him smile against my lips in response. He chuckles before he does it again, sending a shiver down my spine.

"Open your eyes, Lola. Look at me. Let me see you," he says, his voice low. "Tell me what you're thinking."

I open my eyes and gaze into his.

"I... I think you should definitely do that again," I breathe.

He does. This time, his lips are more forceful. He tilts my head to the side and then runs his tongue across the seam of my lips. I open my mouth to gasp, and he gently puts his tongue in my mouth. I've never made out with a boy before so I have no idea what I'm doing. I'm pretty sure he knows this, so he gently explores my mouth with his tongue, then rubs it against mine before retreating. We're still kissing, so I experiment with my tongue, running it along his lower lip. He groans and shifts his body so that he can pull me on his lap. His breathing is heavy and uneven, just like mine. I can feel him starting to stir underneath me. For some reason, it makes me bold. I pull my lips away from his and start to kiss his jawline, traveling from chin to ear. When I get to his ear, I gently bite his earlobe. He bucks underneath me, his breath coming out in sharp pants.

"Lola, I am going to kick myself in the ass for saying this, but I think we should stop. I don't want to take this too far, too fast with you. And if we go any further, I don't think I'll be able to stop myself."

"Are you sure?" I ask between kisses and licks. "I've been waiting for you for four years. I don't think I want to stop."

"Oh God, Lola. I dream about this every night. You have no idea how bad I want this. But, I think we should cool it down for tonight."

"Are you turning me down, Mutt?" I pull back to look at his face and ask, incredulous.

"No, just delaying gratification. Shit, Lola!" He grabs my hand as it starts to wander down his abdomen, toward his belt buckle. "What the hell have you been doing while I've been gone?"

I bolt upright, my sexual haze immediately gone. "Excuse me? Did you just ask me what I think you just asked me? I haven't kissed anyone since I kissed you the last time, when you left me. And if you don't believe me, you can ask Kevin, Deedee, Chase, and every single boy I go to school with. They will all tell you that all I do is go to school, participate in my after school activities, hang out with Kevin and Deedee and pine for you!" I stand up and stomp to the front door, stopping in my tracks when I hear him start to talk. *The dang nerve.*

"Lola, come back. I'm sorry! It just—you are really good at everything we were doing. I just assumed. I'm sorry. I should know better."

"Goodnight, Emmett. I'll see you in the morning."

# Chapter 9

## Emmett

Christ almighty! How did we go from 60 to 0 so quickly? Oh yeah! My big, fat mouth is how.

I close my eyes and throw my head back onto the back of the porch swing. After I bang it there a few times, hoping to smack some sense into myself, I lift my head up and rub my hands over my face. My dick is so hard I'm going to have trouble walking.

That girl was made for sin. I believe that she's been holding out for me. I should have known that given her reaction to my tongue in her mouth. But then she just started to roll with it and take control, it was so damn hot that I almost blew my wad. I hope that I didn't mess this up so much that we can't explore some more this weekend.

But I definitely can't have sex with her. She's only 16; she's too young. Definitely willing, but way too young. I also don't want to take her virginity and run.

I want to be with her; hell, I still want to marry her, as corny as that sounds.

I head upstairs to the bathroom and take a cold shower. It's not as effective as I need it to be, so I lean my weight on one hand against the shower wall and use the other to jerk off. It doesn't take long—I'm still insanely turned on by what just happened on the porch swing.

God, Lola is beautiful. But it's not just that. She truly is the whole package. She's incredibly smart, she's funny, she's kind, she's caring—and her body! God, I'm getting hard again just thinking about how she felt against me. This time, though, the cold water takes care of things.

I head back to my room, throw on some pajama pants, and crawl into bed. I had secretly switched out one of the pillows in the guest room with one of Lola's earlier; she just smells so damn good. I'm definitely going to have some sweet, sweet dreams tonight.

I wake up to Mrs. Callaway knocking on the door, telling me we have to leave in 30 minutes to meet my Dad for brunch. Crap—I had completely forgotten about him. Although, that's not entirely inconceivable.

A year ago, when the Academy's team won the state championship, Dad passed the proverbial torch to his assistant coach and made him head coach and then resigned and started looking for his next job. One came up pretty quickly in Missouri. I was one of two sophomores to make the high school hockey team, and I was even getting ice time, which is practically unheard of. Dad wanted to take me with him. Coach Smith fought really hard with the schools' board of directors to grant me a full ride, with room and board included, so that I could stay and finish out high school at the Academy.

He and Dad fought. Dad and I fought. In the end, he couldn't deny that my potential was in hockey, so he relented. But he didn't like it. We talk once a week, but it's a formality at this point. I haven't even spent the holidays with him.

Instead, I spend any school vacations with Cooper and his family, who have taken me under their wing. They gave me a job at one of their luxury car dealerships. I even have my own room at their estate. They have taken me to their compound on Maui a few times in their private jet. Yeah, Coop's family is loaded.

We meet Dad at the diner and get our orders placed. Dad raises an eyebrow when I have my second cup of coffee. I snort. I'll be able to vote in a few months, old man. Nothing you can do about it now.

Dad gushes over Lola. It's obvious he hasn't forgotten how much he cares about her. But I don't hold it against her. It's just another thing that makes her amazing. Watching her and Dad talk about what's going on in the NFL this season makes me smile. I notice Mr. Callaway looking at me funny, so I clear my throat and pick up my coffee again.

Our food comes and I'm pretty sure everyone in town will know exactly how much I can pack away. I train hard and burn a lot of calories, so I need lots of fuel coming in. Even the waitresses and line cooks have their mouths open, catching flies. For the first time this morning, Lola looks at me and smiles fondly. I squeeze her thigh underneath the table. She jumps a little, but then continues to eat while her cheeks turn the most beautiful shade of pink.

After brunch, we head over to the high school where they are throwing an exhibition game for my father. It seems like the whole town has turned out for it. The marching band has gotten better since we lived here. And the cheerleaders are... not anything I am going to look at while I'm sitting next to my Lola, I remind myself. I pick up her hand and place it in both of mine. She rests her head on my shoulder until some jerk behind me nudges me really hard. I am about to stand up and give this dickweed a beating, when I see it's Kevin.

I get up and give Kevin a bro hug — you know, shake one hand, throw the other arm around and slap on the back. Then I give Deedee a hug and a kiss. Kevin's one lucky dude. Not as lucky as me, but he's lucky all the same. We scoot down a bit to make room for them. I grab Lola's hand again, and the four of us chat and laugh and kind of tune out the rest of the world.

After the game, we head back to the Callaway's house to get showered and dressed for the dinner tonight. Coop loaned me a badass gray pinstriped Hugo Boss suit, paired with a starched white shirt, and charcoal gray tie. I gotta admit, with my hair slicked back and this suit on? I look good. I take a few more minutes to check myself out. "Davis. Emmett Davis," I goof, making a gun with my fingers. I bark out a laugh at my absurdity and then head downstairs. Mr. and Mrs. Callaway are ready and waiting. They ask me to go up and see how long Lola is going to be.

I hop up the stairs and knock on her door. She doesn't say, "Don't come in," so I turn the handle and step into her room. It is definitely not the room of a little girl anymore. There's still an abundance of pink—I don't think that will go away, even after she gets married. But it's more mature. I think the term is "shabby chic." I hear a rustle and then see her step out of her walk-in closet, putting one of her earrings in.

I'm pretty sure I just died and went to heaven. Her hair is down in shiny, loose curls. She's wearing a black, sleeveless cocktail dress—it reminds me of the one Audrey Hepburn wore in Breakfast at Tiffany' (don't revoke my man card; Lola used to love watching old movies). And she's wearing these high-heeled shoes that make her legs go on forever. When she looks up and sees me, she stops and licks her lips as she gives me a once over. My dick instantly hardens, and I gulp a world of air—it's all I can do to keep myself from attacking her while we are alone.

I know she notices my condition, and she's not embarrassed by it. *Interesting.*

She clears her throat as she turns around, "I just need to grab my wrap and my clutch, and I'll be down in a minute."

I adjust myself in an attempt to calm down what

is blatantly obvious, so that her folks don't know that their daughter just made me harder than steel. "I'll wait and go down with you."

When we head downstairs, I see her mom has the camera ready to go, so we stop on the steps so she can take photos. I ask Mrs. Callaway to please send me copies. I want to have pictures of her. Of us.

We get to the Rotary Club's dining hall and head inside. Dad's already there, chatting with Mayor Butler, Mr. Walker, and a few of the other dads he got to know while we lived here. Kevin and Deedee are sitting at a table, heads together. It amazes me those two are still together after all these years. I shake my head and chuckle. Lola squeezes my arm.

"What's so funny?" she asks.

"Kevin and Deedee. Do you think they'll ever break up?"

"Hell no! Their parents will kill them! But it's not just that. They've known each other so long that it's like they are two halves that make a whole. You know what I mean?"

I look at her sparkling eyes and say, "Yeah, I think I do."

She immediately casts her eyes down and blushes. And that does evil things to my man downstairs.

We're asked to be seated so they can start the presentations. Mayor Butler gives a big speech explaining how a decade back it seemed Washington was falling off the map; businesses were dying out, people were moving away, and there just wasn't much to keep up the town morale. After a few meetings, it was decided to try and hire someone to help revitalize high school football, reasoning that if we won a state championship, it might garner up some interest in our little town.

They came across Dad's name after making some inquiries. In fifteen years, he had taken three high school football teams from last in the league to the state championships. His methods may have seemed a bit drastic to some, but the hard work put in during training and practices built character, and his insistence that grades be maintained and elevated, if possible, couldn't be ignored. Neither could his successes. He came to Washington, got rid of the dead wood, hired a fresh team of coaches, and set about watching film and learning where the other guys went wrong. He made each and every player tryout, even if they'd been on the team awhile. If he didn't like what they had to offer, they got cut and could try out again next season. Those who made the team were expected to work hard on the field and in the classroom. And six years later, Coach Davis had another success to add to his resume. The Washington-Wilkes Tigers won the state championship. He handed the team over to the coaches he had hired under him, and they continued to use his methods to foster state champs. Each and every boy on one of those teams has gone on to college, either on academic or athletic scholarship.

When Mayor Butler asks him to stand up and be recognized, even I get off my chair and give him a standing ovation. I know all this about my father because grew up with him. But it's pretty amazing when you hear it from someone else. I'm proud of him. But we're still at odds, and I'm not sure if the rift that has grown between us can be repaired.

After the speeches and the dinner, there's a band and an open bar. We excuse ourselves to go and hang out with Kevin and Deedee at a house party nearby. When I walk into the place, I swear I hear the record scratch as the entire party goes silent. And then I get all kinds of slaps on the backs and welcomes from people I vaguely remember. The entire time, I've got a tight grip on my Lola. Until some asshole tells me not to bother, she's a frigid cow. Before I even realize I've done it, I've cold-cocked the bastard and he's down for the count. Everyone cheers while Lola pulls me into the kitchen to get ice for my hand.

I growl, "Do you mind explaining to me what he meant by that, Lola?"

"Kevin, Deedee, and I were at a senior party on Halloween. Kevin had his hands full trying to keep guys off Deedee. I stuck close by, but every time I went to go and get a soda, it tasted funny, and I was getting dizzy. The next thing I know, Brad was trying to take my dress off. Kevin pulled him off me and tried to hit him, but Brad's bigger and beat him pretty good. Their fight drew attention, so Brad let me be. But he's been spreading rumors about me at school."

I hug her to me and kiss her temple. "Baby, why didn't you tell me about this?"

"So you can do what, exactly? You can't keep him

away from me up in Albany, Emmett."

"I'm just failing miserably, aren't I?"

"No," she sighs, rubbing her temples with her hands. "It's just not what we thought it would be when we were younger, is it? But I still love you, Mutt. Why don't we just go home and get into our pajamas and watch a movie or something?"

"You don't need to ask me twice. Let's go find Kevin and Deedee and tell them we're heading out."

Kevin offers to drive us home. On the way home, we make plans to have lunch together tomorrow, and then they head back to the party. Mr. Callaway's car is in the driveway but the house is dark, so I guess they've retired for the night.

We go and get into our pajamas and meet back downstairs in the family room. Lola makes some popcorn and grabs a couple of cans of soda while I check what's on HBO. Frankly, I don't care what we watch as long as she's by my side, so I turn on a horrible romantic comedy. She snuggles up to me and it takes all of about 5 minutes before I lose all control to the devil on my shoulder.

I move her hair away from her neck and start kissing her collarbone. She leans her head away from me, so I take advantage and kiss every inch of bare skin on that side. Then I slowly work my way over to her mouth. By the time my lips meet hers, she is panting. I try to keep it relatively tame, but when she moans and parts her lips, I can't help but explore her mouth with my tongue. She slides hers along mine, and I groan and pull her to straddle my lap. She fists her hands in my hair and I fist my hands in the back of her already too-tight tank top. I shift under her to ease some of the tension on my dick. I'm guessing from the deep moan I got that it hit her on her sweet spot. I move my hands down to her hips and slowly help her rock against me.

She breaks our kiss and just stares into my eyes, panting. It is, by far, the hottest thing I have ever seen. My dick gets harder, if that's even possible. I move one of my hands from her hip, and she continues the rhythm we've set. I glide my hand slowly up her side and then gently fondle her breast. She's not wearing a bra underneath her tank, so I feel her nipple get hard at my touch. She grinds into me a little harder while she grabs my other hand and puts it on her other breast and then leans forward to hold onto my shoulders, then throws her head back. Her breath hitches when I lower my mouth to her breast.

This is getting really hot and really intense. If it were any girl but Lola, I'd throw her on her back and dive right in. But it's not. I can't do that to her. So I continue to tease her nipples through her tank top and enjoy the quiet moans and pants coming from her as she rubs herself against me. I'm seriously close to coming when she gasps and stops. She grinds against me again and then picks up the intensity and the pace until she bites my shoulder to keep from screaming. I feel her whole body shudder a few times, and I blow my load, crying her name.

We spend a few minutes kissing and catching our breath. She looks at me with so much love and adoration, I want to do anything I can to keep that look there. I grab the remote and turn the TV off, and then I tell her to wrap her legs around my waist and I carry her upstairs to her room. I lay her down in bed and kiss her one last time saying, "Sweet dreams, baby. I'll see you in the morning."

# Chapter 10

*Viola*

The second Mutt shuts the door to my bedroom, I turn my head into my pillow and squeal. I cannot believe I just did that! I am pretty sure that was an orgasm I just had. And if that's what they feel like, I want to have more. It felt like my whole body exploded, in the best way possible.

I know that we didn't really have sex, but now I really want to. I don't think he will this weekend, though. God, please let it not be another four years before I see him again! I don't think I can take it.

I am exhausted and I fall asleep only to have very naughty, yummy dreams of my Mutt.

In the morning, I get up and have a shower, then get dressed. Mama and Daddy are downstairs and Mutt's door is still closed, so I knock and wait for an answer. I don't hear one, so I'm guessing he's probably still asleep. I decide to go in and wake him up.

He's on his back in just his pajama pants, his arm covering his eyes, the covers tossed to the side. I can see his erection straining against the brushed cotton of his pants. I go over and sit beside him on the bed. Curious, I reach my hand out and gently run my finger along his length. I'm startled when it twitches. I see his body shaking in silent laughter before I hear him say, "That means he likes you."

I smack him on the stomach. He's quick and grabs my hand, and before I know it, I'm on my back, staring up into his eyes. Today they are more green than brown, and definitely more pupil than iris.

"Good morning," I say, shyly.

"It really is," he murmurs back, while slowly lowering his head to mine.

That's when my Mama decides to knock on the door.

"Breakfast is ready. And since you're both older, no closed doors with both of you in the room! We'll see you downstairs."

"Well, that certainly ruined the moment," I say, pushing him off me.

"I think your mom's new nickname is going to be Cockblock Callaway," he mutters.

I snicker and throw a shirt at him. "Have your shower and get dressed. I'll go and diffuse whatever situation this has brewed downstairs."

When I get downstairs, Mama and Daddy both raise their eyebrows at me.

"Don't look at me like that. I slept in my bed, he slept in his. I was already showered and dressed and I saw he wasn't up yet, so I went to wake him up!"

Daddy's clearly fighting laughter... or the urge to go and strangle Emmett.

Mama points a spatula at me and says, "Well, for the rest of the trip, no being alone behind closed doors. You got me, missy?"

"I understand, Mama."

"Good," she says. "Now, is he a good kisser? He looks like he'd be a good kisser."

I say, "Um, eewww," as my Daddy groans and says, "Luanne, that's hardly appropriate. We haven't even had the sex talk with her."

I plug my ears and am muttering, "I can't hear you," when Mutt walks in, smiling at what he's stumbled upon.

"Morning, Mr. Callaway," he nods. "Mrs. Callaway, breakfast smells awesome. What are we having?"

"Morning, Emmett. You grab yourself some juice and coffee and have a seat. I'll whip you up a stack of pancakes and some sausage. There's fruit salad on the table, as well."

I get up and head over to the coffee maker and grab my mug. Emmett looks at it, then quirks his eyebrow at me after reading what's written on the cup. "Do you really love dorks?"

"Well, you're one of the biggest dorks I know, so yes. Yes, I do love dorks."

His laughter is contagious. I don't remember the last time I was this happy. I give him a hug and say, "I'm glad you're here Mutt. I've missed you."

Sparing a quick glance at my father, who gives him a nod of assent, he kisses my forehead and says, "I've missed you, too, Lola." Then he spots the locket and the bracelet. "You still wear those?"

"Almost every day," I beam. "I had to replace the chain on the locket and get a couple of links added to the bracelet, though. They were getting too small."

His smile in response is brighter than the sun. He kisses me on the forehead again and heads back to the kitchen table to sit. I follow after I add sugar and cream to my coffee.

We have a lighthearted chat at breakfast, and then Mutt and I wander around town before we go to meet Kevin and Deedee for lunch. When we walk by a jewelry store, he makes me wait outside while he goes in. A few minutes later, he comes out, takes my hand, and walks me to the elementary school. He sits me down on the exact swing I was on when I met him and then sits on the swing next to me.

"This is where it all started," he says. "The scene of the crime."

"What crime?" I ask.

"You stole my heart, Lola. I know I've been far away, and my commitment and communication have been sketchy, at best, but I want you to know that not a day goes by where I don't think about you or dream about you. You're always here," he says, pointing to where his heart beats under his ribs.

I can feel the tears welling up in my eyes. He grabs my left hand and slides something on my ring finger. When I look down, I lose whatever control I had over my tears. He bought me a thin gold band with a heart formed in it.

"Lola, you have my heart. You always have, and you always will," he manages before I hear him choke back a sob.

I get up and go to stand before him. He is still sitting on the swing, and he grabs my hips and pulls me in between his thighs. I cup his face in my hands and lean down to kiss him. He smiles against my lips, and I can see the twinkle in his eyes and his dimples coming out to say hello. I smile back.

"I love you, Mutt," I breathe.

"I love you more."

"Oh. My. God. I'm going to barf!"

"Bite me, Butler," I yell over my shoulder.

Kevin and Deedee chuckle. Mutt gets up from the swing, grabs my hand, and leads me over to them on the sidewalk. "Let's go get lunch. I'm starving."

"You're always starving," I laugh.

"I'm a growing boy!"

As always, when the four of us are together, the laughter gets out of control. Today is no exception. Luckily, Deedee's parents own the country club, so we're asked to move to one of the smaller banquet rooms instead of getting kicked out. When I see it's 4:00 o'clock, I tell Mutt that we should head home. His dad is coming over for dinner.

When we get back, Mom's got a roast with potatoes and carrots in the oven, so there isn't much for us to do. We head into the backyard and go to our tree. Mutt smiles as he runs his fingers over our names. The carving is no longer fresh, a hint of moss growing from the grooves.

He sits on one of the tree swings and pulls me into his lap. I lean back against him as he gently rocks us back and forth with his feet. I'm pretty sure he's thinking the same thing as me: that the weekend has gone by too fast. We sit in silence for a while before he kisses the top of my head and lets out a humorless chuckle.

"What?"

"I was just thinking about how the last time we hung out at the tree, the same thought was running through my head," he says sadly.

"What thought is that?" I inquire, turning my head to look at his beautiful face.

He kisses me briefly and says, "That I just want to run away with you, Lola. I just want to be with you. I don't care where. Run away with me, okay?"

"You tell me when and where, Mutt," I whisper, tears spilling from my eyes.

He kisses me gently, one hand sifting through my hair, the other wiping tears away from my cheeks. Just as he starts to deepen the kiss, Mama calls us to dinner.

"Cockblock Callaway strikes again," he mutters.

I laugh, grabbing his hand to lead him inside. Coach Davis has finally arrived, and he greets me with a hug and a big smile. For Emmett, he has a sad smile and a handshake. I know that there's tension, but I want to see them both happy again. Some of my fondest memories are watching Sunday games with the Davis men, being rowdy, and loving every minute of it. They were so close then. It pains me to see the distance between them, and it appears to get greater with every minute that passes by.

Daddy comes out of the den with a glass of scotch for himself and one for Coach Davis. He points in the direction of the dining room and says, "Let's get settled. Vi, can you and Emmett help your mother bring out supper?"

"Of course, Daddy."

When we come into the dining room through the swinging doors, arms full of pot roast, potatoes, carrots, green bean casserole, biscuits, and gravy, Daddy and Coach Davis immediately stop talking and stare into their glasses of scotch.

We have a perfect dinner. Mama made her strawberry shortcake for dessert, Emmett's favorite. After cleaning up and having coffee and chatting, Coach Davis decides to head back to the hotel for the night.

He thanks my folks for a wonderful night and then turns to me. "You be strong, Vi. You push yourself to be everything you can be, do you hear me?"

"Yes, Coach," I manage through the lump that suddenly forms in my throat. "Please don't be a stranger."

He hugs me so fiercely, he almost takes the wind from me. "I'll miss you, sweetie. Do you remember what I said to you the last time we said goodbye?"

I nod.

"Good. Just keep that in mind. All right?"

"Yes, sir," I sob. I hug him to me a little longer and then let go.

He turns toward Emmett. "Son, I've told Jack that I'll drive you to the airport in the morning. I'm glad you've had all this time with Viola, but I'd like to chat with you before you go back to Albany. I'll be here at 7:30 a.m."

"Yes, sir," he says, tilting his head to the side in confusion.

Coach says goodbye to my folks one last time and then heads out the door.

My parents look a little uncomfortable. My father clears his throat and says,"Well, kids, it's 9:00 p.m. and it's a school night for Vi, so please don't stay up past midnight. And, um, no closed doors if you're both in the room. All right?"

"Yes, Daddy," I placate. "But is it all right if we go walk through the pecan groves and hang out in our tree?"

"Of course, baby girl. Just make sure you dress warmly, it's chilly out there," Daddy says, smiling sadly at me. He knows that a good portion of our childhood memories happened out on our property.

Emmett and I go upstairs and throw on some sweaters and meet in the hall. He pauses for a moment, and then grabs a couple of blankets from the linen closet before we head outside.

We walk past our tree and into the groves. When he doesn't stop, I know exactly where he's heading: the fishing hole. There's a little creek running through our property that has a great big weeping willow next to it. Emmett and I used to spend hours there lying in the sun, fishing poles stuck into the grassy bank, fishing idly. When we get there, Emmett unfolds one of the blankets and covers a patch of ground for us to lie on. Once we're settled, he puts another blanket over us.

He pulls me tight to him and kisses me. It doesn't take very long for our kisses to become heated, urgent. He runs his hand up underneath my t-shirt and sweater, gently massaging my breast when he arrives there. I arch my back, pushing my breast further into his hand. He rolls me underneath him, holding himself up on his elbows and forearms.

"I want you so badly, Lola. I want to be your first. Your last. But now isn't the right time. I want to be able to have you whenever I want. I can't just have a taste and then deny myself. But I want to be close to you. I want to feel your skin on mine. Will you...will you let me see you?"

I nod, unable to form the words in my throat. He sits me up and pulls my sweater off slowly. My t-shirt comes off with it, and I'm now sitting in my bra and jeans. He just looks at me, taking in my hair, my face, and my torso. For some reason, I'm not nervous even though this will be the first time I'll be naked in front of him.

"Your turn," I manage to squeak, as I lift his sweater over his head. He's got a long-sleeved, button-down shirt on underneath. I take my time with each button, watching his reaction. He licks his lips, and his breathing picks up. When I finally reach the last button, I put my hands on his chest and slowly slide his shirt over his shoulders, loving the feel of his muscles beneath my fingers.

He leans me down again. I run my hands over his pecs, down to his washboard abs. I can feel the heat and moisture building in my panties. I push him over on his back and straddle him. He grins and folds his hands behind his head. I pinch his nipples making him laugh, the action lifting me up and down as his body shakes.

I'm so overcome by the beauty of his body, I can't stop myself from leaning down to circle one of his nipples with my tongue and the laughter immediately stops. He takes in a sharp breath. I smile and do the same thing to the other nipple before slowly licking and kissing my way down his abs. I've never done anything like this before, but I'm guessing by his ragged breathing I'm doing just fine. When I get down to the little line of hair that trails into his jeans, he gently grabs my hands and helps me sit up. He sits up as well, and then covers his lips with mine.

Our tongues tangle, our breath mingles, and there is no denying the chemistry between us. His hands run down from my hair to where my bra hooks. He pulls back, asking me for permission with his eyes. I nod, and when he manages the clasp, I help him pull it down my arms.

"You are so perfect, Lola," he breathes, before lowering his head to nuzzle my breasts. He runs his tongue around my nipple and then surprises me by pulling it into his mouth and gently sucking. I can't even describe how good it feels. We moan in unison. He uses his other hand to massage my other breast and I'm thankful he didn't want it to feel left out. I grab his hair in my hands and pull him closer and say, "More."

His chuckle vibrates through me, and I shiver. He moves his mouth over to the other breast and pays homage to it. I arch my back, silently begging him to do what felt so good on the other one. He sucks my nipple into his mouth and nips it gently with his teeth. The sensation zaps from my nipple directly into my panties.

"Oh, God, Mutt."

He deftly rolls us, so I'm on my back beneath him again. He continues his ministrations to my breast with his mouth and, with the hand that isn't holding him above me, he gently caresses my hip. I buck underneath him, wanting him to touch me in the place no one ever has. He once again seeks permission with his eyes. I nod again. His head immediately bends back to my breasts and his hand slides slowly from my hip over to the button closure of my jeans.

I don't know how I'm managing to get oxygen right now, my breathing is so shallow and fast. This goes way beyond anything I have ever really imagined. And yet feels so natural, like he was meant to be my first, my only. I want this so badly. He unbuttons the top button and the world seems to stop spinning as he pulls down the zipper. There's just him and me, the sound of our breathing, and my zipper, mixing with the usual night noise. There's a half moon shining above us and the stars seem to twinkle happily at our union.

And then I lose all rational thought as his hand dips into my underwear. Thank goodness Deedee started making me get bikini waxes when we started getting hair down there. He slides his hand lower and sucks in a harsh breath when he feels how wet I am.

"God, Lola. So wet, so warm... just for me. I want to see you," he says as he pulls his hand out of my panties and maneuvers to a position to pull my jeans and underwear down.

I pout at the loss of his hand, which soon turns to a smile of delight as he starts to kiss my stomach and hip bones while working the rest of my clothes off. I slip my flats off when he's close to my feet. And then I'm completely naked, bare to him.

He sits up, and I see his eyes roaming, taking it all in. He closes his eyes for a moment as if taking a mental picture. And then he lies back down next to me. I run my hand down his torso and then unbutton his jeans. He kicks off his sneakers and helps me get his jeans down where I'm met by the sizable erection straining to be freed from his boxer briefs. This is Mutt so—with my newfound bravery—I slide my hand under his waistband and gently grab his length. The strangled cry that comes from his throat is almost my undoing.

"Not too hard, Lola. Just gently run your hand up and down, like this," he says as he puts his hand over mine and shows me how he likes it.

I continue the motion, loving how soft and silky, yet strong and hard he feels in my hand. His hips lift gently every time I slide from the top to the bottom. I see a bead of moisture at his tip. For some reason I want to lick it, so I bend over and do just that.

"Sweet fucking Christ, Lola. That feels so good," he groans. His response emboldens me. I flatten my tongue and run it along his length, from base to tip. When I take his tip in my mouth, he stops breathing.

"Lola. God, Lola. I can't be held responsible for what happens if you don't stop doing that right now. As bad as I want it, you'd better stop using your mouth, baby," he gets out between pants.

I definitely don't want this to end before it starts and I think that is what he's trying to tell me. So I kiss my way back up his torso, to his mouth and continue rubbing him as I go. He groans during our kiss and then says, "I want to explore you too."

He thrusts his tongue into my mouth as his hand runs down my stomach to between my thighs. When he hits my wetness, I moan. He softly rubs his hand from front to back, parting my lower lips as he does, his fingers sliding easily. He gently probes a finger into me. My breathing hitches for a moment, and I tense.

"Are you scared?" he asks.

"No, I... um... I'm not going to lose my virginity, am I?"

"No, baby. Don't worry. I may do all kinds of naughty things to you tonight, but you won't lose your virginity. I promise," he says, his accompanying grin is deliciously wicked.

"Okay," I whisper.

He pushes in a little further and then withdraws his finger. It feels really good.

"Again," I moan.

He chuckles and does as I command. On the third thrust, he adds another finger. It fills me up more and increases the pleasure I feel.

"Oh God. That feels so good," I draw out the last of the sentence with a long moan.

He leans over and kisses me, mimicking what he's doing below my waist with his tongue. I whimper and then buck as his thumb grazes the bundle of nerves at my apex.

"Mutt!"

"Relax, baby. I'm going to take care of you," he murmurs. And then he starts circling my clit with his thumb, steadily maintaining the thrust and retreat of his two fingers. My breathing gets faster and faster, and I feel a delicious warmth building low in my belly.

"Don't stop, Mutt. Oh God—please don't stop," I gasp.

"Grip me a little harder, baby. That's it. Faster. I want to come with you."

I do my best to comply, my brain in a dense fog. And then, it feels like fireworks are going off in my core. I shout out his name over and over again. I feel him start to shake underneath me and then I feel the wetness shooting from his tip.

"Fuck, I love you Lola!"

*Oh. My. God. I cannot believe that just happened! I*

*mean, I know it happened, but it all seems like a dream. A very delicious, naughty dream.*

When Mutt said he was coming home, I had imagined some kissing and handholding, maybe second base. But this? This was amazing. My first real kiss, my first real sexual experience, all with the boy— the man—I have loved since I was five years old. It feels so natural because it is Mutt, because of our history. They say absence makes the heart grow fonder. From where I'm sitting, that's an understatement.

We lie there, naked and panting, until our limbs once again feel solid enough to put shirts and underwear on and pull the blanket up over us. We stare into each other's eyes, smiling. He runs his fingers through my hair, I run mine over his cheekbones, his brow, down his nose, along his strong jaw, and finally, across his lips. He kisses the pads of my fingers and smiles, showing me those irresistible dimples. I lean forward and kiss each one, dipping my tongue in, making him laugh. When I pull back, he brings my hand back to his lips and kisses the ring he gave me.

"I love you, Lola. Forever and always. I'll come back for you," he says, suddenly serious.

"I know, Mutt. I love you, too."

He kisses me again, slowly and tenderly. I don't want this moment to end, but it must. We dress, shake out the blankets, and head back to the house, hand in hand in silence.

When we get upstairs, he pins me to the wall

beside my bedroom door, hands above my head. "Promise me you'll wait, Lola. Promise me you're mine."

"I promise, Mutt. You're the only one for me," I whisper, serious as a heart attack. He kisses me so hard our teeth clash. It's not entirely unpleasant, but it conveys the depth of his emotions.

When he finally stops kissing me, he spends a moment memorizing every detail of my face, as I do the same. He releases my hands and cups my face tenderly. "Forever mine, Lola," he murmurs and gives me one last gentle kiss.

"Forever yours," I whisper back.

He steps back and stays still, not wanting the moment to end. But it's past 1:00 a.m. and we all have to get up early in the morning, so I break the spell and say goodnight and head into my room.

As I close the door, I hear him whisper, "Mine."

# Chapter 11

## Emmett

I am floating on cloud nine as I head back to the guest room. I can still feel a tingle where her lips have touched my skin, still smell her all over me. She is—by far—the most amazing girl I've ever met. I don't think I can love anyone else. It's just not possible. There isn't a single thing about her that I don't love. And the way she responded to me this weekend, my God I'm going to have wet dreams about it until I die.

And then the honesty hits. I know that I'm going to hurt her. I'm so far away, I'm 17... She must know I'm not a frigging monk. How can I ask her to be faithful to me? I know she wants to, but I'd be a hypocritical sack of shit if I didn't practice what I preach. Can I honestly hold out until we can be together again? I'm hoping she can come to college with me, wherever I land. But that's still a year or two away. And there's no way that Dad's going to pay for plane tickets back and forth. Even the money I make from the job Coop's dad gave me isn't going to be enough to fly back here as much as I want to.

I run my hands through my hair as I sit on the edge of the bed. I lie down and try to think of ways to make this work. I look at the clock; it's 4:00 a.m. and I'm not tired anymore, so I throw on my running shoes, sweats, and a hoodie and head out for a run around town.

When I get back, the sun is just starting to make its appearance. I take a shower, get dressed, and then pack my bag. I'm just zipping it shut when I hear a soft knock on the open door.

"Hey," she says, shyly. She looks adorable with her wild hair and floor-length white linen nightie. I can see her hot pink underwear underneath and am just starting to raise my eyes up her body when I hear a throat clear behind her.

"Vi, time to get ready for school. Go have a shower and get dressed. I'll help Emmett get his things downstairs," Mr. Callaway says gruffly.

"Yes, sir," Lola acquiesces, her eyes downcast. She turns and heads back to her room to gather her clothes and a moment later, I hear the bathroom door shut.

"Emmett," Mr. Callaway starts, "I know that you and Viola are very close. I know you love her. But I also know you're a young man. And, having been one of those myself, back when dinosaurs roamed the earth, I know what runs through that head of yours. Please, just... try not to hurt her. We love you like a son and hope that one day we can call you son-in-law. But until that day happens, you're on my watchlist. Do you feel me?"

Mr. Callaway has been nothing but kind and nurturing to me. Seeing this side of him scares the crap out of me.

"Yes, sir. For the record, I love her more than anything, sir. And one day, I do hope to marry her."

He pats me on the shoulder and says, "Great. Until then, just try and behave yourself. And, for the love of God, keep it in your pants."

I can't contain the surprised laugh that bubbles out of me. "Yes, sir."

Mrs. Callaway is cooking up enough scrambled eggs, bacon, toast, and fresh-squeezed orange juice to feed a small army. Which is good because I'm starving. We eat a quiet breakfast, only the sounds of forks and knives scraping plates, and spoons stirring coffee mugs breaking the silence. When we're done, I help Lola clear the table. At 7:30 a.m. on the dot, Dad rings the doorbell, and we all head out to the front porch.

Lola stops, not going further than the edge of the porch. "I can't, Mutt. I can't do it again," she says as the tears come.

I run back up the front steps and pull her to me, hugging her as tightly as I can while my tears fall. She grips the front of my sweatshirt so tightly, I see her knuckles turning white.

"Don't leave me. I'm begging you, don't leave me. Please," she sobs.

I can't get words out I am so choked up. So I do the only thing I can to try and calm her. I put my finger under her chin, lift her face to mine and kiss her. It's chaste compared to every other kiss we've shared this weekend, but I pour every emotion I'm feeling into it. Sadness, love, yearning, but, most of all, promise; the promise that she'll be mine one day. Because that's the only promise I can make right now.

When we part, I lean my forehead to hers. "Forever mine, Lola."

"Forever yours," she whispers back.

I pull away from her giving her hand one last squeeze before I turn and head down the stairs to say goodbye to her folks. Mrs. Callaway is crying, hugging me tight, telling me to take care, work hard, and come back soon. Mr. Callaway shakes my hand hard, telling me with his eyes what he said with his mouth earlier.

Dad starts the car as I turn around to take one last look at my lovely Lola. Her hair is pulled over one shoulder, flowing down her chest. She's wearing a cute patchwork baby-doll dress with cowboy boots. She smiles but I know the moment I get in the car, she'll break down again, and it makes me die a little inside. I blow her a kiss that she catches and puts on her lips. When I've memorized every last detail about her, I get into the car. I know deep down that I won't see her again for a few years.

Dad turns on the radio; the sports station, of course. We're silent until we get out of town and onto the highway, headed toward Atlanta.

"I know you think I don't love you, son. But I

want you to know here and now that I do. It's been really hard for me, coping with the loss of your Mom and then you choosing hockey over football, and over me. And even though we don't talk much, Coach Smith gives me updates on what's going on. Keep your head in the game and your eyes on the prize, son. You're my boy. I might not have raised you as a hockey player, but I did raise you as a dedicated athlete and scholar. I know you'll succeed," he rushes out.

I am stunned at this admission. "Dad, I—" he cuts me off quickly.

"And when you're done making something of yourself, I want you to go back to Washington and marry that girl. She loves you more than a man deserves. You go and do right by her. If you don't mean those things you promise her, then you tell her right now. Don't lead her on."

"Dad, I have every intention of marrying her one day. I decided that in second grade. No matter what happens, after college, I'm going to marry her. You have my word."

"Good. I hope you were able to contain yourself around her this weekend. She's turned into a beautiful young woman," he says.

"Don't I know it. It wasn't easy, Dad, but I resisted temptation."

"Good. There's time enough for you to give me a football team of grandbabies," he quips.

I smile. This is the first time since we left Georgia that the two of us haven't been fighting or silent.

When he claps me on the shoulder, I grab his hand and squeeze. He looks at me, smiling. He knows it's a big moment.

When he drops me off at the airport, he hands me a large roll of money.

"I know you've been working at the auto dealership in your spare time, and I know you've been working hard at school and training. I want you to have this to fall back on. Don't jeopardize your future because you need cash. Ever. All you need to do is call, son."

And with that, he pulls me into the longest hug I think he's ever given me. I squeeze him back, relishing the moment. When he eases up, I pull away and see him wiping tears from his eyes. I bend down and grab my duffle bag.

"I love you, Dad," I tell him.

"Back at ya, kid," he says, with a weak smile.

I turn and head into the terminal, check in, get through security, and head to my gate. The flight is a little late, so I sit down, hang my head, and silently let the tears roll down my face.

# Chapter 12

*Viola*

I can't believe I'm going to be graduating from high school in a few months. It almost seems surreal. I've been studying really hard and have all kinds of extracurricular activities to pad my university applications: student council, yearbook, homecoming committee. Everything but sports and cheerleading. I just can't be bothered and I'm popular enough without it. I could have run track. After Emmett left the last time, all I did was run. Every day I'd come home after school, throw on some leggings and a t-shirt and my running shoes, put on my headphones, and just run until the hurt in my legs and lungs eased the hurt in my heart. The hurt in the legs and lungs always went away. The hurt in my heart, not so much.

He got better at the perfunctory communications over the past few years—always a card and a small gift for Valentine's Day, always a card, a phone call, and a big bouquet of flowers for my birthday and the bouquets were anything *but* roses, smart boy; a call to the family at Thanksgiving and Christmas. And a phone call in the morning every New Year's Day to tell me to have a wonderful year, that he loves me, and that we were one year closer to the end game. Pathetic as it was, I lived for these special occasions.

It hurt even worse when I asked him if he'd be my date to homecoming and prom. He said that college was harder than high school and it would be difficult to break away and visit, even though he was just over in North Carolina. When I asked if I could come and visit him, he said it wasn't possible for him to have guests at his dorm. I'm guessing he doesn't miss me as much as I miss him.

I'm not dating anyone. There just aren't boys around who even remotely compare to him. But I don't want to go stag to homecoming and prom, especially since I'm in the running for homecoming queen. I dial the only other person I'd want to share that with.

"Hello. May I speak to Chase, please?"

"Vi?"

"Yeah. Hi! How are you?" I ask.

"I'm great now," he laughs. "How's school going? Kev told me you're up for homecoming queen in a few weeks. Are you nervous? Excited? Tell me all about it."

"I'm more nervous about all the arrangements leading up to homecoming. There's so much to do. But I'm pretty sure I'll land in homecoming court, so I'm not nervous about that. Mama and I are actually heading into Atlanta next weekend to shop for my dresses and have a girls' weekend. I was wondering if maybe we can go for lunch or a movie or something. Are you up for that?"

"Absolutely! I can work around whatever time you can spare for me. Having my dad for a boss has its perks. It'd be great to see you."

"Good," I chuckle. "Hey. Um, I know you've got all kinds of stuff going on at your own school, but I was wondering if you might want to be my date for homecoming and prom?"

The silence seems to stretch on forever.

"Vi, I'm—I'd be honored. I was actually going to ask if you'd be my prom date here, if the dates don't collide."

"Chase, it'd be my pleasure." I'm grinning from ear to ear, which I hope he can hear through the telephone line.

"Listen, I've got to get to work. Call me at my dad's house when you get into town and, if I'm not here, leave me a message with your hotel name, number and room number. Oh, and figure out with your mom what day and time would work out best. I'll shuffle things around to spend time with you."

"Sounds good. I can't wait to see you!"

And it's true. I can't. Even though it's been a few years, and he's been too busy to come for more than a day or two to visit Kevin and his family, Chase and I have become pretty close. We talk on the phone every other week and not a day goes by where he doesn't email or message me.

"I can't wait to see you, too. I'm so glad you called, Vi. See you next weekend," he says before he hangs up.

The week drags on so slowly, I think it's never going to end. But when the bell rings on Friday afternoon, I race out the front doors of my school and hop into Mama's Jeep Cherokee and, after a brief pit stop for gas, sodas, and licorice, we are making our way to Atlanta.

"Carlyle called this morning. We're going to need to do some more shopping this weekend because he finally proposed to Christine. They're getting married next year."

"Well, good for him. He's definitely the winner in the relationship. She could do better, though," I say.

"I've never understood why you and Carlyle don't get along, especially now that you're older and haven't been living under the same roof. You should try and bond with him, you know. He's turned into a nice guy," Mama chides.

I shrug. "He was never there for me as a kid. He's never there for me now. He's got his life and I have mine. And never the twain shall meet."

"Well, I think the twain will be meeting a lot over the coming year, so I expect you to start making an effort. Why don't you ask Chase to come for lunch with Carlyle, Christine, and us tomorrow. I'll spend the afternoon with Carlyle and Christine going over wedding stuff and you and Chase can shop or go to a movie or to the arcade or whatever. Does that sound reasonable?"

"Yes, ma'am," I answer, smiling over at her.

I'm surprised when we pull into the valet loop at the Ritz Carlton. I practically gape as the door gets opened for me. "Mama," I whisper. "Does Daddy know we're staying here?"

She giggles. "Who do you think suggested it? Daddy had a good year with the plantation and his Civil War book is finally starting to gain attention and sell well. He wanted his girls to spend the weekend in the lap of luxury and shop until the credit cards melt."

I grin up at her. "If you say so, Mama! Let's get checked in so I can call Chase and then let's go out for dinner. Okay?"

"Sounds like heaven, baby girl."

When we get up to our suite, I call Chase.

"Hey, I didn't think you'd be home!"

"I wasn't expecting to, but I've been putting in so many hours, Dad let me have the weekend off. I can spend as much or as little time with you as you want. And when I'm not with you, I can work on homework or code or something."

"You're a big nerd. You know this, right?"

His laugh booms through the phone. "Yup. Biggest nerd you'll ever meet, right here! But it'll be worth it in the end when I'm loaded, driving around in my Porsche with a supermodel on my arm."

"Ha! You wish. But for now, you'll just have to settle for your Honda Civic and me on your arm."

"It's certainly not settling, Vi," he answers, voice deep and quiet.

Oh! That gets a blush out of me. "Well, um, we're

at the Ritz Carlton in room 514. Mama and I are going to have dinner and do some shopping tonight and tomorrow morning. Why don't you meet us at the room at 1 o'clock tomorrow? We'll have lunch with Carlyle and his girlfriend, sorry, fiancée, and my mom, and then I'm all yours until 7 o'clock."

"That sounds perfect. I can't wait to see you, Vi. Have fun with your mom tonight."

"Bye, Chase. I can't wait to see you, either."

Mama and I do some shoe shopping and then go for dinner on Peachtree in Atlanta. We have a lot of fun on our walk back to the hotel and I am utterly exhausted when we finally make it back to the room. I put on my jammies and read until I pass out.

The next morning, Mama and I go look for a homecoming dress. I find a lot of them that I like, but I haven't found 'the one' yet. So we head back to the hotel to meet Chase, Carlyle, and Christine.

I'm fixing my lip gloss when I hear a knock on the door. "I'll get it," I yell at Mama as I throw open the door. I'm disappointed when it's Carlyle and Christine.

"Oh. Hey," I mutter to Carlyle.

"Expecting someone else, were we?" He seems amused.

"Hi Christine! I'm so happy you're going to be my sister-in-law. I have to question your taste in men, though," I quip, sticking my tongue out at my brother.

She laughs, "To each their own, Vi. And I'm excited to be part of your family, too! I'm hoping I might invite myself to shop with you and your mom tomorrow, if that's all right."

"Yes, please! I can use all the help I can get to find the right dress. It's impossible!"

"I think I know a few places outside of downtown where we can go. Don't you worry, we'll find the one," she assures me.

I may dislike my brother, but I'm starting to adore Christine.

"Awesome!"

I jump when there's another knock at the door. I shout, "We don't want any," before I open the door. And when the door is fully open, I gape at what's standing before me.

Chase Butler is no longer a chubby-faced, nerdy looking kid. He's tall—about 6 foot 4. He's muscular but lean, like a swimmer. His black hair is longer in the front and sticks up in waves I just want to run my hands through. His chubby cheeks are gone; in their place are high cheekbones that most models would envy and a jawline that looks like it was chiseled out of granite. His blue eyes shine behind dark wire-rimmed glasses. He's wearing a white button-down shirt untucked over dark jeans, and motorcycle boots on his feet. He's got his hands in his pockets and is starting to look a little uncomfortable as he is taking me in in return.

"Chase, I... Um... Wow, you look great! Come on in," I say finally.

"Vi, you look... you're stunning," he says, stepping over the threshold.

I hold out my arms for a hug. After a moment to

think about it, he steps in and puts his arms around me, resting his chin on the top of my head. He engulfs me, in a good way. And I've got to admit, it's comfortable.

"I'm so happy to see you," I whisper.

"Me, too," he whispers back. "Why are we whispering?"

"Because if we don't, all of Washington is going to know how this went down."

His laughter rumbles through my bones. He kisses the top of my head and pulls away, moving toward my family.

"Hey, Carlyle. Long time no see," he says, holding out his hand to my brother.

"Hey, Chase. Good to see you. I want you to meet my fiancée, Christine Porter."

Chase shakes both of their hands and then goes over to give my mom a hug.

"Chase, you have grown up so much since the last time I saw you! Your aunt says you have almost every college in the country courting you right now. Your folks must be so proud! Are you leaning toward one campus in particular?"

"They're definitely happy about my prospects, Mrs. Callaway." He looks at me when he says, "I haven't made a decision about where I'll end up just yet. There's still some time to figure it out."

*Did I? Yup, I just blushed again.*

"Well, let's all have lunch and then you young'uns can have fun while we talk boring wedding details," Mama says, rubbing her hands together.

Lunch isn't as awkward as I assumed it would be. As a matter of fact, Carlyle is downright human when he starts asking about school and Kevin and Deedee and some of the other kids he knew. When he asks about Emmett, I purse my lips and shake my head. He leans across the table, grabs my hand and says, "Can we talk about him later?"

"Okay," I mutter, pushing around the croutons in my salad.

Chase didn't hear that last little conversation but it doesn't take a genius to know my mood just went from jovial to morose. He takes my hand, squeezes it, and looks to me for a smile. I give him a weak one.

"Mrs. Callaway, is it all right if I take Vi out for some fun?" he asks.

"Of course, Chase. Just make sure she's back by 7 o'clock—we're meeting Christine's parents for dinner at 8 o'clock and that will give Vi time to freshen up."

"Yes, ma'am. It was great to see you again. You, too, Carlyle. Pleasure to meet you, Christine."

We stop at the hostess desk on the way out. Chase asks for the bill for our table. He pulls out his wallet and pays the hefty tab before we leave.

"Chase! Thank you for doing that, but you really didn't need to!"

He stops and turns me to face him. "Vi, between my family money and what I've earned, I can afford it. I wanted to pay for lunch, it was my pleasure. So please, don't fuss about it."

I know that his dad is a CEO for a big software company, so that doesn't surprise me. But learning that he's making a lot of money at his job really does.

"Well, thank you again. You're going to score some major points with Mama and Daddy for doing that," I say, grabbing his hand and leading him down the sidewalk.

We decide to see a movie, and, after a long walk showing me around downtown Atlanta, he steers me into a little coffee shop. We each grab a giant mug of coffee and a snack and settle down on one of the most comfortable sofas I have ever sat on.

"So, I noticed you haven't mentioned Emmett at all. Is everything all right?"

"He's away at college," I say, shrugging. "He's too busy for me."

"Oh," he says, looking deeply into his mug; for what, I'm not sure. "Vi, I know that you're promised to him, but if ever a day comes when you're not, I want to be next in line."

"Chase, I'm deeply flattered. I'm not quite there yet. But when I am? You'll be the first person I'll call," I say, leaning forward and giving him a kiss on the cheek. I don't pull back immediately. His eyes are closed and I see his Adam's apple bob as he swallows. He really has turned into something beautiful, inside and out.

To show him I really mean it, I swipe my lips across his. His eyes snap open in surprise.

"It's not for sure, Chase. But it's a definite maybe," I murmur against his lips.

He smiles. "I'll take it."

He walks me back to the hotel and we say

goodbye in the lobby. If Mama wasn't back yet, she'd tan my hide for bringing him up to the room without an escort. I snuggle into the comfort of his hug.

"I'll see you in a few weeks, right?" I ask.

I feel him nodding, his chin touching the top of my head. He smells really nice, like soap and ocean. I take another quick, quiet sniff and pull away, holding his hands in mine.

"I can't wait for it, Vi," he says, smiling.

"Me either. Thanks for today, Chase. It was wonderful."

I go up onto the balls of my feet and give him another little kiss on the mouth. It goes on a little longer than I intended, but his lips are so soft and he smells so good I kind of get distracted.

"Bye," I whisper.

He looks like he's off in la-la land as I walk away.

Mama and I get ready and Carlyle comes to drive us out to Christine's house. Her parents are really nice and I think our families will get along famously. After dinner, Carlyle comes back into the hotel with us. Mama leaves to have a bath and Carlyle sits with me.

"Look, I know I can't make up for all those lost years, Vi. But being with Christine has made me realize how important family is. And I want us to be friends. I want to be the best big brother I can be. Do you think we can make that happen?"

I eye him suspiciously. "I don't know. Are you going to blow up all my Barbie dolls with firecrackers again?"

The belly laugh I get out of him makes me beam.

"I don't think so. I'm not much into firecrackers these days. Are you still into Barbies?"

"Hell no! I'd rather shop and have fun with my friends," I laugh.

We chuckle for a few more minutes before he gets serious.

"Tell me what's going on with Emmett. Did he hurt you?"

"Carlyle, you don't need to get all protective brother and kick his ass, if that's what you're inferring. I'm still a virgin for crying out loud."

He sticks his fingers in his ears and shouts, "I don't need to know this. I just found out you don't play with Barbies anymore!"

I pull his fingers from his ears and say, "Well, I didn't have any more Barbies to play with after you blew them up, now did I?"

"Vi, did he hurt you?" he asks again, his face so serious it hits me like a semi that he truly does love me, contrary to what I've thought my entire life.

"Not actively, no. He's just busy. He does what he has to in order to stay in my good graces, but he just doesn't have time for me. He promised he'd come back for me but he never promised to be faithful. And I shouldn't have been naive enough to think he would be. But I had hoped. He won't admit it, but I know. And, I think... I think I've finally realized that I need to move on."

"I'm sorry, Vi," he says, reaching out to hug me as the tears start to well up.

"I just—do you think he's going to come back for

me, Carlyle?"

"Only time will tell, Vi," he says, kissing the top of my head.

# Chapter 13

## Chase

When Vi called me to tell me she wanted to see me when she came to Atlanta for the weekend, I thought I had died and gone to heaven. When she asked me to be her date to homecoming and prom? I knew I was already there.

I haven't spent much time out in Washington over the past couple of years. Between work and school, there just hasn't been a lot of time. Even though I am young, my father's Chief Technology Officer has said I am one of their best software developers. I am actually a team lead on a project right now, working with guys almost twice my age. I had assumed that would be an issue, but none of them have given me any attitude. I respect the hell out of these men, I value their hard work, their ideas and input. And I think that makes all the difference.

But the past few days since Vi called, I am off in

my own little world. My dad called me out on it. While we are close, I haven't really discussed girls and the like with him; he just thought I wasn't interested, that I was more focused on work and school.

When I told him about Vi, he shook his head with a huge smile on his face, "Viola Callaway is a beautiful young woman, Chase. She's also bright and comes from a good family. If I could handpick someone for you, it would be her. But we all know her heart lies elsewhere. I just don't want you getting your hopes up, son."

I nod, knowing history has proven him right. But he doesn't know how close Vi and I have become the past couple of years. Even if we don't see each other a lot, we talk and email all the time. And I know deep down that this weekend is a game changer.

It's Saturday morning and I'm nervous as hell. My hands are shaking so badly that I dropped my coffee mug. And forget about getting any work done; my head is nowhere near on straight enough. I try playing video games to calm down, I try reading... Nothing is working. I just want to get in my car and drive to that hotel and see her.

I end up lying in bed and thinking about Vi. As if it has a mind of its own, my hand goes into my boxers and starts to stroke the erection I get in response any time I think of her. I close my eyes and use my memories to add to the experience: her beautiful green eyes, how soft her hair is, how she smells of vanilla, her amazing smile. Before I know it, I cry out, coming all over my abs.

I clean up my mess and head to the shower. Jerking off took the edge off just enough for me to be able to function a bit. I do it again in the shower for good measure.

It takes me forever to pick out clothes—I end up going dressed up casual, not knowing where we are headed for lunch. My hair doesn't seem to want to do anything today, so I leave it standing up. It is what it is.

I drive to the hotel, leave my car with the valet, and head up to the 5th floor. I spend a few moments at the other end of the hallway, looking out the window at downtown Atlanta, calming my nerves and willing my erection to go away. When I am finally ready, I head down the hall and lift my hand, taking another deep, calming breath before I rap my knuckles on the door and then shove my hands in my pockets.

"We don't want any!" Vi shouts and I can't control the smile that lights my face.

When she opens the door, the smile drops. Not in disappointment, she is just so beautiful she takes my breath away and the smile turns into awe, as it always does.

"Chase, I... Um... Wow, you look great! Come on in," she says.

"Vi you look... you're stunning," I tell her.

And she really does. She's wearing a floral baby-doll dress that fits snug across her chest and comes down to mid-thigh. She is wearing platform sandals that make her legs look so long and sleek.

I realize I have stared too long and step into the

room. Vi opens her arms out to me. Remembering that embarrassing moment from so many years ago, I hesitate a moment before I go and give her a hug. She wraps her arms around me and everything is right in the world. I hug her tight and rest my chin on top of her head, closing my eyes and taking in all the goodness that is Viola Anne Callaway.

"I'm so happy to see you," she whispers.

"Me, too," I whisper back. "Why are we whispering?"

"Because if we don't, all of Washington is going to know how this went down."

I laugh, knowing exactly how right she is. I'm willing to venture a guess that the entire town will know about this the day after they get back from Atlanta.

I don't want to, but I let her go to say hello to her brother, his fiancée, and her mom, then we all head out for lunch

Lunch is nice. I have always gotten along well with her family and Carlyle's bride-to-be seems like she will fit right in. I spend most of my time chatting with Mrs. Callaway and Christine while Vi catches up with her brother.

I know the instant her mood changes. I can see her body go rigid and the light in her eyes dim in my periphery. When she and Carlyle go silent, I turn my head and look at her. She looks so upset and I know why she looks that way: Emmett Davis.

It just empowers me. I reach over and take her hand and give it a squeeze. She gives me a sad smile, but I give her a big one to show her how happy I am she's here.

I ask her mom if it's all right if we head out now, wanting to get her mind off of Emmett and onto me. After a round of goodbyes, I head to the hostess station and pay for lunch. Vi objects, but I let her know in no uncertain terms that I have the means and am happy to do it.

And I continue to do so the rest of the afternoon, paying for the movie and treats, then coffee and a snack. I want her to know that when she is with me, she will be treated like a princess. Doors are held open, I rest my hand on her lower back to usher her to seats at the theater and the coffee house. I want her to know I'd give her the world if she would give me the opportunity. She has no idea that, aside from enjoying what I do as a job, I also do it for her. I want to marry her, have a life with her, and I want to do that comfortably.

We get settled on a comfy couch with our drinks, she sits with her legs tucked under her, facing me. I bite the bullet and inquire after Emmett. She informs me that he's too busy for her. Deep down, I am jumping for joy. But I don't let it show. I let her know that I am interested. She surprises me when she tells me that she's considering it. My heart starts beating out of my chest, and my mind is going a million miles a minute imagining my dream coming true: Vi in my arms, kissing me, my hands fisted in that soft hair, opening those beautiful eyes so I can gaze into their green depths and see nothing but love staring back.

Then she leans over and kisses me on the cheek. Her lips are so soft and I close my eyes, wanting to capture the moment. A few seconds later, those soft lips gently brush across mine. I am so shocked I open my eyes and stare into hers and I know without a doubt she will be mine.

I return her to her hotel a little before when she needs to be back. Knowing it would be improper to take her up to the room if her mom isn't there, I say goodbye to her in the lobby. I give her another hug, savoring the feel of her body against mine, her smell... just her.

She pulls back, rolls up onto the balls of her feet and kisses me. This is my first actual kiss from Vi Callaway. I don't want to push my luck by trying to take it further, so I let her take the lead. She is so gentle, her lips so soft that I am mesmerized. She looks a little dazed when she separates from me and turns to go up to her room.

It takes me a few minutes to shake myself from the trance her kiss put me in. I vow to spend as much time as possible kissing her in the future and then head home, a big grin on my face the entire way.

# Chapter 14

## Emmett

"Oh God, Emmett! Yes! Harder! HARDER!"

Whitney's screaming is just ridiculous. I don't know who she thinks is listening, but it's certainly not for my benefit. To me, she's just a means to an end. As I drive into her from behind, I picture Lola that night underneath the weeping willow tree. I'm getting there when I hear a knock on the door.

"Davis! Dude, Lola is on the phone for you."

I pull out of Whitney and roll off the condom. "But I didn't come yet," she whines.

"Well, the entire frat house thinks you did. Get dressed and go, Whitney."

"You didn't finish either," she purrs, running her claws down my back.

"I thought I told you to get of here, Whitney," I say as I pull on some sweats and a t-shirt.

I walk out the door. I don't give a shit if she

trashes my room.

I jog downstairs to the office where the phone is.

"Lola, baby. I was just thinking of you." I wince. Technically I was thinking of her—while I was fucking another girl. I'm so totally going to hell.

"That's nice, Em. How are things going?"

Uh oh. She's cordial. This can't be good.

"Busy, but good. I'm starting this season, so I've got to train all the time. But it's been great. Did you get the early birthday present I sent?"

"Yeah, your UNC jersey. It's great. Thanks!" She sounds a little more chipper.

"How are homecoming preparations going? Did you find a dress yet?"

"Mama and I just spent the weekend in Atlanta shopping. I found a beautiful dress and matching shoes," she gushes.

"Tell me what color it is. What does it look like? I want to picture you in it," I rasp out.

My hard on is creating a giant tent in my sweats right now, imagining her all dressed up, her hair down, looking sexy as fuck. That sexy little smile curving her lips, green eyes blazing.

I get up and lock the door to the office and start to stroke myself. Hey, don't judge me. I've got needs. And it certainly wouldn't be the first time a guy jacked off in here.

"It's black lace. It's got a sweetheart neckline; you know, sort of goes up and around the boobs. It's fitted and then there's a slit that goes down the left side from mid-thigh to the ground," she rambles off.

I'm picturing it and it's totally working for me. "Mmm, sounds beautiful. Tell me how you're going to do your hair."

"What are you doing? Are you masturbating?" she whispers the last word.

"Yes. Does that bother you?"

She giggles. "Well, it's a little weird, but I kinda like it."

"Good," I say. "Go on about your hairdo."

And she does. But her voice takes on a different quality. Like she's doing something naughty and she knows it. It pushes me over the edge.

"Oh God, Lola!" I spurt all over my stomach, then grab some tissues from the box on the desk—yeah, don't want to know why that's so conveniently placed—and clean myself up, tossing the tissues into the waste bin after, and walk over to unlock the door.

"Are you, um, finished now?" I can practically hear her blushing.

"Yes, baby. I'm done. I can't wait to see pictures. You're going to the most beautiful homecoming queen Washington-Wilkes High School has ever seen. I wish I could be there."

"Yeah, um. That's why I'm calling. Mutt, I'm taking Chase Butler to homecoming. And prom."

My gut just dropped. "What? Are you seeing him, Lola? What's going on? Explain everything to me."

There's a moment of silence before she unleashes her fury on me.

"Emmett, don't you dare give me shit! Do you honestly think I'm stupid enough to think you're not fooling around with other girls? You're probably even *fucking* them," she spits out. "You don't get to have your cake and eat it, too. Chase is a nice guy. And even though he lives in Atlanta, he makes time to come and see me. He treats me like a lady! He treats me with respect! He always has," her voice trails off.

I can hear her starting to break down. I'm close to it myself, feeling like shit for her completely hitting the nail on the head. I'm a fucking bastard for expecting her to be faithful to me.

"Lola," I whisper. "Just... just tell me if you've slept with him. Please, just put me out of misery. I know I don't deserve it, but please—have you?"

"No," she whispers. "I haven't even really kissed him, Mutt. But I'm starting to want to. And I think it'd be good for me to date him."

I nod. I know she can't see me, but it's involuntary. "Lola, I know I promised I'd be back for you. And that's a promise I will keep. But I never said I'd be a monk."

"I know. And I shouldn't have been naive enough to believe you would be. I knew you'd been getting in some... practice, especially after all the things you did to me when you were here last time."

The line goes silent. I'm pretty sure we're both picturing what happened. Vividly. Which is making me hard again.

"Lola," I choke out. "I love you. You are the only girl I'll ever want. I'll come for you as soon as I make something of myself. I promise. Just have faith. Okay?"

She sobs a few times and then manages, "I'll try. But I'm not going to sit around and not date while you're doing whatever to whomever, Em. It's not fair."

"I know, baby. I don't like it, but I understand." I pause, taking a deep breath and letting it out. "Are we okay?"

"For the time being? Yeah, I think so. Listen, Mama's calling me for dinner so I have to let you go. You take care, Em. Please don't fall out of my life again. I don't think I can take it."

"I'll try, Lola," I promise. She hangs up just as I say, "I love you."

Fuck.

When I get back up to my room, Whitney's still there, dressed, and pissed as all get out. She's looking at what my frat brothers refer to as 'the wall of Lola'.

"You're an asshole. You know that, right?"

"Whitney, I'm not getting into this again. You and I fuck. That's it. That's all it ever was, that's all it ever will be. I don't have the time to date. You're not my girlfriend, you never will be. Either you accept that and we continue to hook up or you don't and you can go find another victim. Either way, I'm not your guy."

"She's pretty and all but I don't see what makes her so damn special," she spits.

"You wouldn't. You don't have a soul," I say, with a chuckle.

"How come you never say my name when we make love?"

"Good question, Whitney. First of all, we don't

make love. We fuck. Second of all, saying your name would imply a level of intimacy that we don't have. And last, but not least, I'm not thinking of you when I fuck you."

"Fuck you, Emmett Davis!" she shouts as she storms out of my room.

"You just did, sweetheart!" I shout after her, hearing my frat brothers' laughter ringing after her.

# Chapter 15

*Viola*

Deedee and I are back at the beauty salon, getting all dolled up for prom. I can't believe it's finally here! We're getting manicures and pedicures and our hair put up and even getting our makeup done. Mr. and Mrs. Butler are having a little pre-party for our families and have hired a photographer to come and take professional photos.

Chase drove in from Atlanta last night. He comes out once a month to visit now. We're not officially dating, per se. But we're not *not* dating either. We're just taking things slow and getting to know each other in a new way. Although, every time he leaves it's getting harder and harder to say goodbye.

"So," Deedee draws the word out longer than necessary then continues, "Is tonight going to be the big night for Chase and Vi?"

"Hardly," I scoff. "Just because you plan on losing

your virginity to Kevin tonight—real original by the way—doesn't mean that I'm going to follow suit. Besides, Chase and I haven't done more than kiss, which you already know." After I think about it, I ask, "Why? Did he say something to Kevin?"

"God no! I just assumed that's what'd happen since Emmett's no longer in the picture."

"Way to ruin my mood, Dee. Thanks so much. And besides, he's not necessarily out of the picture, he's just a dark horse in the running."

"Please tell me you're not buying the whole 'I'll be back for you' crap, Vi. You're not twelve anymore."

I sigh. "I know, Dee. And that's why I'm moving on with Chase. But, part of me believes that one day he will come for me. He just may be too late."

"Well, let's not dwell on it. Let's think about how epic tonight is going to be! We're going to have so much fun! And remember: regardless of who wins prom queen, we won't be catty. Right?"

"I told you, me winning homecoming queen was a fluke, Dee. You and Kevin own prom king and queen. I don't give a shit. Really. Honest and for true."

She looks at me from narrowed eyes. "You're sure about that?"

"Hey, I wasn't the one who had a hissy fit at homecoming! I can't believe you couldn't let me have that one crown, you bitch! You're the one who does pageants and has a room full of crowns!" I can't contain the laughter anymore.

I see Julia making the 'come here' gesture, so I get up and duck walk over to her chair, careful not to ruin the fresh polish on my fingers and toes. When I'm seated she says, "So, describe your gown to me."

I point to my purse and say, "I can do better than that; there's a picture in there."

Julia pulls the picture out and does a catcall whistle. "Vi, this is beautiful. And I'm pretty sure I know what I want to do. So just you sit back and fantasize about your hot date tonight and let me work my magic, all right? I'm going to spin you away from the mirror so you can't see until your hair and makeup are done."

I nod and stare at the magazine page in my hands. Mama and I made another journey into Atlanta for this dress. We got it at the same store we bought my homecoming dress. This dress is elegant, sophisticated, and sexy all at the same time. It's an emerald green color and falls to the floor. There is a thick band under the boobs, an empire waist. There is a silver choker that goes around my neck from which is suspended the rest of the top of the dress. It didn't look that great on the hanger. But when I came out with it on, Mama and Christine both started to cry.

I told Chase that my dress was emerald green and that's all. He said he'd do his best to match his bow tie and cummerbund.

I get lost in thought while Julia works her magic. I hardly hear her when she starts waving her hand in front of my face. "Earth to Viola! Are you ready to see the finished product?"

"Yes," I cry, clapping my hands and bouncing up and down like a child.

She laughs and then spins the chair around. I hardly know what to say. I look like a Greek goddess. She's taken a few sections of hair at the front and braided them over my head so they keep the rest out of the way like a headband with the exception of a few tendrils. She's found some silver ribbon to weave into the braids to match the silver choker on the dress. The rest of my hair falls down in bouncy curls. My makeup is stunning. She's done my eyes in a smoky eye using shades of purple. Between that and my thick black lashes, my green eyes are hard to miss. She's done a naturally blushed cheek and has used my MAC Twig lipstick on my lips.

The salon is silent. I expect to hear crickets. Instead, I hear Dee say, "Vi, I don't normally go for girls, but even I want to jump your bones right now."

"You're all class, DeeDee Walker," I mutter.

Even though Deedee lives right next to Kevin, we go over to his house to get dressed. His mom herds the boys up to Kevin's room to get dressed when we knock on the door so that we can keep up the mystery until everyone's ready. When Mrs. Butler opens the door, she squeals excitedly. Mama and Mrs. Walker join us in the front hall from the kitchen.

"Girls, you both look so beautiful," Mrs. Butler cries.

Mrs. Walker is hugging Deedee, while Mama's fanning tears from her eyes.

"I don't want to mess anything up but you are stunning, Vi. Why don't you and Deedee go upstairs and put your gowns on? I know the boys are dying to see you."

We take our overnight bags and dresses upstairs. I help Deedee get into her light blue gown that has one shoulder, leaving the other bare. Then she helps me into mine.

"Going with the granny panties, I see. Sexy," Deedee laughs.

"Hey, at least I'm not flossing my butt crack!"

I open up my overnight bag and pull out the black lace panties that match the demi-bra I'm going to wear later, when we head out to the after party at the lake. I whirl them around my index finger. "Sexy enough for you?"

"Put them on now. It'll help you feel sexier," Dee goads.

"Fine," I huff. I pull down my plain cotton panties and pull on the sexy ones underneath my gown. I turn and look at myself in the full-length mirror in Mr. and Mrs. Butler's room.

Well, I'll be dipped in oatmeal; I *do* feel sexier.

Right after I slip into my gown, Daddy knocks on the door. "Are you girls ready? The boys are downstairs waiting and the photographer's up here to take a few shots of you girls getting ready.

"You can come in, we're both dressed!"

We take a few shots, touching up lipstick, putting on earrings, etc. And then the photographer races downstairs while we wait upstairs for his go ahead. Deedee and her dad go around the corner first, as the photographer takes pictures of the look on Kevin's face when he sees Dee. Then the photographer takes pictures of Dee and her Dad coming down the stairs, then of Kevin taking Dee's hand. Cheesy, but we only do prom once, so if our folks want these photos, then that's what they'll get.

I'm getting antsy. Daddy pats my hand that's linked through his arm. "You look beautiful tonight, baby girl. I'm so proud of you."

"Stop it, Daddy! I don't want to ruin my eye makeup!"

"Viola, we're ready for you!"

"Well, here goes nothing," I mumble. Dad chuckles as he leads me over to the top of the stairs.

I take a deep breath and close my eyes. I can't help but feel a bit disappointed that Mutt isn't standing at the bottom of the stairs waiting for me, all handsome in a tuxedo, that lopsided grin on his face. The thought makes me choke out a sob, my heart hurting. I feel like he betrayed me, not being here for this big moment in my life. Ever since we were little, we talked about him being my date to prom. And now... well, now things have changed.

Chase is... He is amazing. Handsome, intelligent, thoughtful, and funny. Every day I find my mind on Chase instead of Emmett. Am I making the best of a difficult situation or am I finally moving on?

With these thoughts in my head, I take another deep breath to calm myself and open my eyes.

When I finally look down the stairs, my heart stops beating for a moment. Chase looks like a model in his tuxedo. His hair has been expertly gelled so that the waves are in control, but still looks like he just ran his hands through them. He's got on some new frames I haven't seen before. He's looking very sexy, like Clark Kent. I almost want to run down and rip his shirt open to see if he's got a Superman suit on underneath.

But what really makes my heart stop beating is the way he's looking up at me. It's reverent, like he's seeing a goddess in the flesh. It takes my breath away. Daddy nudges me to head downstairs. I blush, knowing that he's probably been trying to get my attention for a few seconds.

I hear the shutter clicking and I know that the photographer's there, but I've got tunnel vision. The only thing I see is Chase. When we get to the bottom of the stairs, he holds out the box with my wrist corsage in it: magnolias. I smile. He's still nervous, but he's able to do it in one try this time, unlike our first formal together a couple of years ago. Mama hands me the magnolia boutonniere I picked out for him. I pin it on him and then run my hands over his lapels. The smile he gives me makes me giddy.

The next thirty minutes is all photos and I swear we're all blind by the time the photographer is done. When he leaves, Mr. Butler pops the cork on a bottle of champagne and we're treated to a glass. It's the sweet kind, the bubbles tickling my throat and nose. None of us are driving anywhere; a limo is waiting outside for us, our overnight bags in the trunk. The boys drove up to the lake earlier today to get our tents set up. They left Kevin's Jeep up there with the coolers and other supplies locked inside.

We finally get into the limo and are on our way

to prom. Kevin and Deedee are already making out. If I wasn't so used to it, I'd probably be disgusted. But I've learned to tune it out over the years.

Chase takes my hand and squeezes it. I turn to him and smile.

"Thanks so much for taking me to prom, Chase. I'm sorry our proms overlapped."

"Vi, I'm just glad I have the honor of taking you to yours. You look... heavenly, tonight," he adds.

"You look even more handsome than the last time I saw you. I love the new glasses."

"You think I'm handsome, huh?" he grins.

I lean over and whisper in his ear, "Very."

Feeling overly sexy thanks to the lace panties, I pull his earlobe into my mouth and suck on it before grazing it with my teeth.

The word that best describes the noise he makes is 'purr'. I chuckle softly as I turn his face to mine and look into his eyes as I run my tongue along his bottom lip. He grabs my tongue between his lips and pulls it into his mouth. I gasp. This is the first truly bold move he's made since we've started seeing each other.

He smiles a wicked little smile. "Didn't think I had it in me, did you?"

"You better not have been practicing without me," I warn.

"Nope, just been dreaming about it every night since my summer here."

"Chase and Viola sitting in a tree K-I-S-S-"

"Shut it, Kevin!" we shout in unison, cutting him off.

We're all laughing as we pull up to the entry of the country club. Our prom theme is 'Hollywood Premiere', so there's a red carpet, complete with paparazzi. When we get inside, Deedee and I lead the boys to our table at the front. Being on the prom committee has its privileges.

After dinner and a bit of dancing, the principal gets up on stage to name prom court and king and queen. When I hear my name called for prom court, I turn around to find Chase beaming.

"Get on up there, gorgeous!"

He smacks me on the butt as I walk away. I grin the entire way up to the stage. I grin even wider when Kevin and Deedee are announced King and Queen.

We stay for about another hour before we decide to head out to the lake. There are already a number of others out there, setting up camp, lighting bonfires, and starting the party by the time we arrive. Dee and I head into one tent to change into more comfortable clothes, the boys into the other.

We pile out of our tents at the same time, laughing, and head to the car to get our drinks, having learned our lesson at that party so long ago. Deedee and I mix ourselves Jack and cokes, the boys grab beer, and we head over to the nearest bonfire to chat with our friends.

Around 2:00 a.m., I'm seriously buzzed and starting to yawn. Most other people have already passed out or paired off. I'm pretty sure there are a lot of cherries getting popped in the tents surrounding us. I snicker at the thought. Thankfully, I packed my iPod and speakers so we can listen to music instead of the noises made by a lot of drunk, hormonal teenagers.

Chase goes into the tent first to change into pajamas. He opens the flap when he's all done, telling me he's off to brush his teeth 'and stuff'. I head into the tent and pull out the tank top and capri length sweats with WWHS on the butt. I leave on the black lace bra and underwear set. Even if I don't plan on losing my virginity tonight, there will inevitably be some naughty business going on. I've got my hair brushed out and my makeup wiped off by the time he gets back. I head out with a bottle of water and my toothbrush and toothpaste and give my teeth a quick scrub. I check my breath in my hand, and, after deeming it acceptable with a shrug, I head back into the tent.

Chase has put on a playlist he mixed for me— mostly ballads—and he's managed to turn our twin sleeping bags into a double. He must have grabbed some more pillows from the car, because in the low light of the lantern, it looks like something out of Arabian Nights. He pats the spot next to him. I don't hesitate to go and lie down.

He pulls me close and starts raining kisses on my face; my brow, my closed eyes, my nose, my cheeks, my chin, and finally my lips. By the time he gets there, I'm good and ready to make out. We spend a lot of time kissing. He's gotten really good at it after all the practice we do when we get time together. But tonight, he's kicked it up a notch, taking the kisses deeper. His hands have been in my hair or gripping my hip but finally, he gets the gumption to try something different. I feel his hand slip under the edge of my tank top and slide up my side. It tickles, but I am too engrossed in kissing him to giggle. When he reaches my breast, I feel his hand start to shake.

"It's okay," I pant. "I want you to touch me, Chase." I cover his hand in mine and show him what feels good to me. When I pull my hand away, he's gently massaging and squeezing like a pro. I tilt my head back and he begins kissing his way down my neck, toward where my breasts are heaving above the top of my demi-bra. He looks up at me, asking for permission.

"Yes," I breathe. He uses a finger to pull one of the cups down and then gently kisses my nipple. I put my arm around my back and unhook my bra. I slide one arm out of the strap under my tank top, then the other. He bows his head back down to my breasts and kisses, nips, and licks my nipples through my tank top. I grab the back of his shirt and start to pull it over his head. He pulls away from me long enough to get it over his head, and then gets back to exploring each breast with his lips, his tongue, and his fingers.

This is the first time I have seen Chase with his shirt off since we were kids. He's got a smattering of fine, dark hair covering his well-defined pectorals. It's very sexy. I run my hands over his pecs, gently grazing his nipples. He moans, but doesn't stop what he's doing. I run my hands around to his back, which is surprisingly muscular. His broad shoulders get my attention next, and then I run my hands into his hair, gripping tightly as he bites one of my nipples.

"Chase, help me take my top off," I whisper.

"Are you sure? I don't want to push you too far, Vi. I want you to be sure of everything we do."

I kiss his forehead. "Thank you for being so wonderful. I know I'm not ready for... that, just yet. But I want to do more with you. Is that okay?"

"I'm not going to complain, Vi," he says as he helps me lift my tank top over my head. He spends a few moments taking in the view.

"God, you're so beautiful. I can't believe you're with me."

I gently push him onto his back and straddle his hips. His hands find my hips and I take them in mine, running them up my stomach to my breasts. His erection is hard and massive under his pajama bottoms and when he starts to fondle my breasts on his own, I put my arms behind me on his thighs and start to move against him.

I've almost got myself worked up to an orgasm when he sits up and grabs my hips, stopping me. I gasp, staring into his big blue eyes.

"I want to look into your eyes when it happens, Vi."

I nod and we start moving together. Our noses are touching, our breath hot on each other's lips, and it's more intimate than anything I've experienced before. I drop my head back, bordering on ecstasy.

"Eyes, Vi. Let me see your eyes," he rasps.

God, that voice is sexy. I bring my head back up

to where it was before.

With three more swivels of my hips, we're both there. I cry out gibberish, he cries out my name. The entire time we're staring into each other's eyes. I need to have my lips on his. I close the tiny distance that separates our lips and kiss him like he is the air I need to breathe to survive. He lies down, taking me with him, and then rolls us over so I'm on my back. We kiss until my lips feel like they're bruised.

And then we kiss and explore each other some more. The sun is up when we finally fall asleep in each other's arms.

# Chapter 16

## Emmett

Last night was Lola's prom. I tried calling her a bunch of times during the day and night, leaving messages every time. The last few calls, I'm pretty sure I was really drunk and belligerent. Whitney found me sitting at the local sports bar, talking into my bourbon. She took me back to the frat house and gave her all trying to get my dick hard. But it just wasn't happening. She gave up in disgust and walked out. Like I care.

It's poignant that what should have been the best night of my life was also my worst.

I know their plans were to go to prom and then head out to the lake for an after-party and camp out. I know what that means: she's sharing a tent with Chase. I have been up all night wondering if he took her virginity. If he made her moan the way I did. If he made her come as hard as I did. Most of all, though, I wonder if he makes her happy.

I'm finally falling asleep when I hear someone bang on the door. "Call for you, Davis!"

I get up and stumble downstairs. I'm still pretty fucked up. When I get to the office, I pick up the phone. "Hello?"

"Emmett? Are you all right?" It's the voice of an angel, my angel.

"Lola, I miss you. I've been thinking about you all night."

She snorts, "Yeah, I got that from the 20 messages on my voicemail. By the way, you might want to think twice before you drink and dial."

"Lola, I want you. Come out here and visit me. I want you in my bed with me. I want to make love to you. Let me. Please? Let me love you." I'm beyond caring about how drunk and desperate I sound, I just want her so badly.

"Get some rest, Mutt. We'll talk about this when you're sober, all right?"

"No," I snap. "It's not all right. Did you let him inside you, Lola? Did he fuck you last night?"

"Emmett, for the sake of our friendship, I'm going to give you the opportunity to hang up the phone right now before you say something you won't remember to regret and I won't bother to explain because I won't speak to you ever again!"

"Lola, I love you. Don't leave me."

"Goodbye, Emmett."

One of my frat brothers finds me passed out in a puddle of my own vomit about 2 hours later. Not my finest moment.

When I wake up, I realize I've got a week off before training camp starts, so I pack up a duffel bag and hop in my Audi and drive to Georgia. I know I'm playing with fire, but I don't care. I need to see her. When I drive up her driveway, I see a shiny red Porsche parked next to Lola's Volvo sedan. I'm really hoping that is her dad's mid-life crisis car.

But when Lola opens the door and I see *him* behind her, I know I'm shit out of luck.

"Emmett, what are you doing here?"

"I had some time off so I decided to come and see you."

"Um, come on in. I'm pretty sure you guys met a long, long time ago, but Emmett, this is Chase Butler. Chase, this is Emmett Davis."

I take his proffered hand and squeeze it while I shake it. Hard. He's stronger than he looks, not even wincing.

"Good to see you, man. I've heard a lot about you from Kevin, Deedee, and Vi."

"Good to see you, too," I manage to get out without sounding too bitter.

"Vi, I'm going to go and help your dad set up the new equipment in his office, okay?"

"Thanks, Chase," she says, smiling at him. She used to smile at me like that.

Once he's in the office, she grabs my ear and drags me into the front parlor and closes the door.

"What. The. Fuck. Emmett! Give me one good reason why I shouldn't have my Daddy drag your ass out of this house right now!"

"Lola, I... I miss you. I just wanted to see you."

"Not good enough. Tell me why you're really here, Emmett."

I sit down and put my head in my hands. "I've lost you haven't I?"

She sits down next to me and sighs. "Emmett, you haven't *had* me to lose for a long time. You've been off doing your own thing, or having it done for you."

"That's low," I admonish.

"I know, I'm sorry. I just... I can't deal with the roller coaster ride, Mutt. I need the straight and narrow."

"I'm hoping I can offer that to you soon, Lola. I got drafted by the Atlanta Confederates the day before yesterday. I start training camp in a week. I wanted to spend some time with you before I go because it's going to be awhile before I can do that again."

"That's fantastic news, Mutt! I'm so proud of you!"

She scoots over on the sofa and throws her arms around me in a loose hug. I hug her tighter to me and take in her scent. She tenses for a moment, but then relaxes. I pull her head to my shoulder so I can smell her hair. It smells like vanilla; it smells like home. I hear her sigh and then she pulls her head up to look at me.

"What about school, though? Don't you have another year left in your business degree?"

"I do. The team can arrange for me to finish up

remotely or I'll go back and finish later. I'll complete my degree, Lola. I'll make you proud."

"You already make me proud, Mutt."

I smile. "Say you'll spend some time with me. I can only stay for a couple of days, then I have to go back to North Carolina to pack up my stuff and go to the apartment the team rented for me for the summer."

She thinks for a minute and then lets out a long breath. "All right, Emmett. But there's not going to be any making out. I can't do that to Chase. Or to myself. We hang out as friends."

I rub my face. "Okay, I can do that."

"All right," she says, standing up. "Chase is heading back to Atlanta tomorrow morning. Why don't we meet up for lunch at the diner around noon."

"Sounds good," I say. I know I'm being dismissed. "I'll see you there."

She opens the front door and steps out onto the front porch, shading her eyes with her hand.

As I hit the bottom step, I hear her say behind me, "And, just for the record, I haven't lost my virtue yet. I decide who gets that honor. Not you. Not him."

I smile and head over to my car.

# Chapter 17

*Viola*

The following day, it's graduation. Unfortunately, Chase's school is holding their graduation ceremony today, too. We're both pretty bummed that we can't be there to see each other get our diplomas, or for me to watch him give his valedictorian speech, but that's just how things happened. We get up and have breakfast with Mama and Daddy. He's really grown on them over the last few months.

He says goodbye to my folks and then we take his bags out to the car. I lean against his shiny new candy apple red Porsche—his graduation present to himself—as he throws the bags in the trunk. Then he comes over and puts his hands on my hips and leans until our foreheads are touching.

"I made my decision about where I'm going to school," he says.

I swallow, knowing that he can literally go

anywhere in the country on full scholarship, he's that smart. "I hope it's somewhere near Atlanta."

"It is. In fact," he pauses for effect, "I'm going to be rooming with Kevin."

"Ohmigod, Chase! You're going to Georgia Tech, too?" I can't contain my excitement—and relief. But then, I can't contain the guilt.

"What about Stanford, MIT? Chase, I don't want you to get an inferior degree just because you want to be close to me."

"Don't worry, I'm not. Georgia Tech is a great school for computer science. I'm not compromising. Besides, I've already proven myself as a software engineer without a degree while working for my Dad. I've even got a venture capital firm willing to back any project I want to do at any point in time. All I need to do is tell them what I need and they'll provide the funding."

I kiss him. "Well, then I'm glad. I don't think I'd ever forgive myself if you didn't go to a good school just because of me."

"It's not just because of you, Vi, although you played a role in my decision. But so did Kevin. And Dad. And, well, I just felt a lot more comfortable being close to home."

"I'm glad. So when do I get to see you again?"

He rubs the stubble on his chin. I watch the motion with my eyes, wanting to follow along with my tongue. He smiles at me, knowing I'm thinking something naughty.

"I don't know, Vi. How long is he going to be

here?"

"Jealous isn't a good look for you, Chase," I state. "But I love the fact that you are. I don't know. He said he only has a couple of days to hang out before he has to go back to pack up and move. But don't worry, I'm not about to jeopardize this," I point between the two of us, "to get my heart broken by him again. I can't and I won't. He's clear on the fact that we can hang out as friends, nothing more."

"Well, I hope so," he sighs. "If it came down to me and him duking it out for you, I'm pretty sure he'd win. My hand still hurts from when he squeezed the blood out of it yesterday."

I throw my head back and laugh. He chuckles along with me. "Oh, I think you're doing all right in the muscles department."

He smirks. "Yeah?"

I nod, licking my lips. "Mmhmmm. And you know what else?"

He leans in closer. "What?"

"I think," I pause. "I want to make things official."

"That's the best news I've ever heard, Vi." He grabs the back of my neck and pulls me in for a long kiss.

Daddy clears his voice behind us. "It's almost 9:00, Chase. You should probably be getting on the road soon."

"Yes, sir, Mr. Callaway. Just saying goodbye to my girlfriend," he says proudly.

"Drive safely, son," Daddy says, with one eyebrow quirked up.

I see Chase off and then go inside to shower and dress. Christine sent me a beautiful dress to wear for graduation. It's a tea-length strapless dress in a white cotton eyelet fabric with a big black satin sash. I pair it with a pair of black wedge sandals and leave my hair down, but tie a black satin ribbon into a bow at my crown. After I put on some sunscreen and makeup, I head downstairs to grab my purse and my cap and gown.

"Mama, I'm going to go meet Emmett for lunch at the diner and then I'll see you at the school, all right?"

"Are you going to invite him?" she asks, a hint of unease in her voice.

"Mama, we may be going through some struggles right now, but he's been an important part of my life since kindergarten, and we're still friends. If he's here, I'm going to invite him."

She comes over to give me a hug. "You're right, sweetheart. I just don't want you to get hurt by him again."

"Mama, most of that was me being young and foolish. I've grown up a lot in the past couple of years, in case you didn't notice."

She pulls back and plays with one of my curls. "Yes you have, love. But you'll always be my baby."

I put my sunglasses on and grab my keys from my purse. "I'll see you later, Mama. Love you!"

"Love you, too, baby girl," she shouts after me.

I pull up to the diner and park my car. I'm not surprised when I walk in and see a couple of my female classmates all over Emmett. They've seen me with Chase, they know Emmett's available. He smiles and flirts and laughs. And then his eyes meet mine and I hear him say, "Sorry, ladies, but you'll have to excuse me. My best girl is waiting for me."

I shake my head and walk over and give him a hug and a kiss. We sit across from each other in the booth. When the waitress comes over, her attention is solely focused on Emmett. I'm trying to order, but she's just all kinds of flustered. It's understandable. He *is* sex on a stick. He sees I'm getting nowhere, so he orders for both of us.

"Can I please have a large coke, four chicken salad sandwiches on wheat bread, a side salad, and an order of fries? And the gorgeous girl across from me will have a large diet coke, a glass of water, and a club sandwich on wheat bread—no mayo—with fries."

I mouth thank you as the waitress gushes and then turns to walk away.

"So, you look particularly delectable today. Special occasion? Or is that for me?"

I give him a withering stare to answer the last question. And then I say, "It's graduation today. You wouldn't happen to want to come and watch me get my diploma, would you?"

"Lola, I can't imagine anything else I'd rather do today. Did you make valedictorian?"

The waitress returns with our drinks.

I take a quick sip of my water and shake my head. "No, Kevin beat me out by half a percent. But I'm proud to be salutatorian to him after all he's had to overcome to get there."

"You've always been so gracious. You're pretty amazing, you know."

I shrug.

"So, the girls were telling me you got a full ride to Georgia Tech for architecture. That's a huge deal. I'm proud of you," he says, reaching across the table to hold my hand. "We'll be living in the same city in a few months."

"I know," I say, gently pulling my hand back.

But he doesn't let go. "Lola, I'm not going to ask you to stop seeing Chase. I know I'm going to be busy and traveling with the team and that's not fair to you. But... just..."

"Mutt. I told you the other day, I get to make that decision. I really like Chase. He's a good guy. He's really smart and he's going places. And he's kind of intimidated by you," I say, throwing him a scowl.

"Good," he snorts. "He should be."

"No, he shouldn't," I say, ripping my hand from his. "Until you can prove to me that you're ready and serious, you don't get to be all possessive of me, Emmett. I don't belong to you."

"But you do, Lola. You've always been my girl."

I see him searching for the locket, the bracelet, and the ring. Then I see his face fall.

"Mutt, I haven't worn them since I woke up and realized you were messing around. I couldn't."

His head drops down to his chest and I see him heave a big sigh. "I deserve that. Do you still have them, though?"

"Hey, look at me," I insist. When he looks up, I

continue. "I have every single thing that you ever gave me. You are one of the most important people in my life, Mutt. I have a chest at home that has all the cards, all the flowers dried and pressed, every gift, every letter, every postcard, every movie stub... Everything. No matter what happens in our lives, you will always have a big chunk of my heart. I love you."

"I love you, too, Lola. I hope... I hope that I can be the man you need before it's too late."

Our food arrives, interrupting the moment. We eat in silence. I'm wiping my mouth with my napkin after polishing off my club sandwich when he raises his eyebrows and asks, "A single strawberry milkshake with two straws? For old times' sake?"

I shake my head and laugh. "You are a sentimental fool, you know that?"

"A guy's gotta try, right?"

"All right, Mutt," I say, still laughing.

He drives over to the school with me. I find my folks in the crowd and bring Emmett over. They welcome him as they normally would, which makes me relieved. I take off to the gymnasium to line up with my class.

Dee runs over and accosts me. "Holy shit, Vi! Is it true that Emmett came back for you? I heard that you were all over each other at the diner today."

I can always count on Dee to lay it out there for me. The girl has no filter. At all. I look over at the group of girls shooting daggers in my direction and then turn back to Dee.

"Emmett did come to visit, yes. He and I did go

out for lunch, yes. We were not all over each other. We've always been friends first and foremost. We've always hugged and held hands and shared milkshakes. Those gossipmongers would do anything to get either Emmett or Chase."

"Sorry, I should know better. You've been my best friend since we were toddlers. I was just shocked. I thought for sure, after getting drafted, this was it."

"Dee, he showed up at my house yesterday. We had a brief chat but I didn't think it was fair to Chase for me to have Emmett there, so I sent him away after telling him I only wanted to be friends. I told Chase this morning before he left that I wanted to be his girlfriend."

I plug my ears so I don't go deaf from all of Dee's shrieking.

Kevin rushes over, shoving his index cards into his pocket. "Are you all right, baby? What's the matter?"

"Chase and Vi are officially a couple! Can you believe it? College is going to be awesome now!"

Kevin turns to me. "Is it true? I thought for sure with Emmet showing up..." he trails off.

"Kev, I'm done putting myself through that shit. I adore Chase. I think I might be falling in love with him, even," I say and immediately cover my mouth. "Holy crap! Did I say that out loud? Please, please, please don't tell him I said that! I want to wait until I know for sure."

"Vi, I know for a fact that he's been in love with you for years. And I'm happy you've finally come around," he says, giving me a big hug and a kiss on the cheek. "You're like family and he is family. It's the best thing that's happened since the day Deedee was born."

"You big softie," I say, pushing him away and wiping tears from my eyes.

"All right, folks, time to get this show on the road," the principal shouts. Kevin and I take our places with the faculty and watch as the rest of the class files out to the folding chairs lining the football field. I give my salutation, my voice quivering with emotion. Kevin's speech is magnificent, and there's not a dry eye in the house when he's done. I can see him being a politician, like his dad. But I can see him going all the way: Senate, maybe Congress.

It's finally time to receive our diplomas. When I hear my name called, I stand up and look for my folks in the crowd. They're sitting with the Butlers and the Walkers and Emmett, all of whom are standing, clapping and cheering. Emmett looks so proud of me that I get tears in my eyes. I accept my diploma from the principal, shake hands, and then move my tassel over to the other side of my cap. I stop for pictures and then head back to my seat.

When I look back up in the stands, Mutt's still smiling like a proud papa. I smile back and shake my head.

After the ceremony, I return my gown and cap, take pictures with a few friends, and then head over to my folks and Emmett, who are chatting with the Walkers and the Butlers. I see a bunch of girls trying to get Emmett's attention, but he's ignoring them, talking to Deedee and Kevin. I finally make it to the group. My parents both come over and hug me until I can't breathe. When they're done, Emmett taps me on the shoulder and says, "My turn."

I turn to hug him. He pulls me in and rests his head on top of mine, squeezing without need or possession.

"Lola, I'm so proud of you," he whispers. "I know you're going to succeed because you're a fighter. You know, I always thought when we argued you were fighting against me, but I've realized today that you were fighting for me. I'm so sorry I messed up so badly."

I can't control the sob that escapes me. He turns us away from my family and friends and cups my face in both his hands.

"Hey, I didn't mean that to make you sad. I just... after what you said at lunch today, after talking to your folks while we were watching you down there, it just finally sank in. No matter what, you will always be my best friend. You're also my best girl. No one will ever compare to you. And I hope that, someday, I can marry you and spend the rest of my life with you. But what's more important than that is that you're happy. And if it's Chase that makes you happy, then I'll back off. But I won't ever stop loving you. Never."

I look up at him through my tears. "What does this mean?"

"It means that I'm not going to be a selfish bastard anymore. I'm going to hope, but I'm not going to push. I love you too much to completely lose you,

Lola. So if it has to be friends, then that's what we'll be."

"Mutt," I choke. I know that I should feel good about this, but for some reason it feels like I've lost him entirely.

# Chapter 18

## Emmett

After all these years, I think I've finally grown up. It hurts like a son of a bitch, but I realize that I need her in my life, no matter what. I might love her, but I might not be the better man. So, until I get my shit together, I'm going to back off and let her be happy.

"Are you coming to dinner with us?"

"No, I think I'm going to head back to UNC tonight," I say.

She looks at me like she's going to start crying again. I hug her to me and say, "I think this is what needed to happen, Lola. It's what's best for both of us—for now. And if I stay any longer, I'm going to second guess my epiphany."

She chuckles at that. "I love you, Mutt," she says with a sniffle.

"I love you, too," I whisper back. I kiss her on the head and let her go.

I head over to Kevin and Deedee and say goodbye, then say goodbye to all the parents.

"Do you want me to drive you back to your car?" she asks.

"Nah, I think the walk will do me good. Take care, Lola."

"You, too, Mutt," she says softly.

I turn to head toward the diner. I can't look back. If I do, I'm going to take back everything I just said, pull her to me, kiss her, and make her mine right here on the football field in front of God and everyone. So I just put one foot in front of the other.

I check out of the hotel and get in my car and head back to the frat house. By the time I get back, it's really late. Or really early, depending on how you look at it. But it's a frat house, there's always something going on. And the party tonight is no exception. Whitney jumps on me the second I get through the door. Fucking her isn't going to magically make me forget my pain, but it'll help rid me of some of my pent up frustration.

I wrap her legs around my waist and head upstairs. I don't kiss her; I never do. When we get into my room, I kick the door shut with my foot and throw her on the bed. She lays on her back, trying to look seductive. I spin her over onto her front, hike her skirt up, and pull her panties down.

"Emmett, I..."

"Shut up, Whitney," I interrupt. "Don't say anything. At all. I hear even a whimper, I stop. You got me?"

She nods.

"Good. Up on your knees. I'm not going to be gentle," I say as I grab a condom from my stash in my nightstand.

I kick her out when I'm done. She's used to it. She's the town bike, everyone's had a ride. I just happen to ride her more frequently than anyone else.

I grab my emergency bottle of bourbon, twist off the cap, and chug directly from the bottle. I may have pulled up my big boy pants and done the right thing today, but I don't have to like it. I drink until I can't feel anymore, lie back on my bed, and stare at the wall of Lola before I pass out.

In the morning, I pack up my room. Thankfully it's not much; just clothes, hockey equipment, my laptop, a few books, and my Lola memorabilia. I say goodbye to my frat brothers and get on the road. I don't even bother to tell Whitney I'm going. I'd rather make a clean getaway.

The next couple of weeks go by in a blur. The apartment in Atlanta is being shared by a couple of other rookies. We get along well enough but most of the time we're there, we're sleeping. And when we're not, we're playing xBox. Training camp is way more intense than high school or college. I'm thankful that

I grew up under my Dad's influence, otherwise I'd crack and quit or get scratched. We're almost at the end of training camp and three guys have already tapped out under the pressure.

I get up, go train, practice, come home, have a shower, have some supper, play some xBox with the bros, and then crash. I hardly have time to think about Lola, and the last time I got my wick dipped was that time with Whitney.

Lola called to tell me she'd be in town after next week. I gave her insight into what my training schedule was like and then what life would be like once the season started. She understood and told me to just call when I might have time because she'd love to see me. And honestly, now that we're in the same city, I am going to make an effort to do that. She is, above all, my best friend.

# Chapter 19

## Viola

I think I really like college! The classes are challenging but I love a good challenge. I hate being away from Mama and Daddy, but I've got Chase, Deedee and Kevin, Carlyle and Christine, and Emmett nearby.

Deedee and I share a dorm room and it's been a lot of fun. Kevin and Chase share a dorm room, too, so we can always figure out some privacy if we're not all hanging out together, which is good because Kevin and Deedee have sex. A lot. It's actually kind of disturbing how much sex they have.

I have been spending an afternoon every weekend hanging out with Carlyle and Christine. I never knew my brother could be such a good guy. He was always such a jerk to me when we were kids. But seeing the way he is with Christine makes me smile. And the way we get along now totally blows my mind. He's become my sounding board, my buddy. We even hug. Who'd have guessed?

Things with Chase are amazing. If he's not in class, we're together, even if I'm studying and he's working away on his computer. He's working on a private project which, if all goes well, will net him seven figures. He's the perfect gentleman; always opens doors for me, always pulls out my chair for me. If his hand isn't on my thigh or my lower back, it's around my shoulder or grasping my hand. He kisses me on the forehead for no reason at all and kisses me elsewhere for lots of good reasons. I've become addicted to him. Which is why I'm going to try and tempt him to stop coding right now.

He's working on his laptop at my desk in my room while I study one of my textbooks on my bed. I sit up and put my arms up, arching my back. I see his eyes immediately zero in on my chest. *Atta boy!* I lean forward and crawl down to the end of my bed.

I rest my head on his shoulder. "Whatcha doing?"

I hear him hum at our contact. "Just got to finish up a bit of code. Are you done studying?"

I shrug. "For now. You know what I want to do?"

I see his lips rise in a grin. "I can't imagine. Why don't you come here and tell me," he says as he rolls the chair back from the desk and pats his lap.

I hop off the bed and straddle his lap, resting my forearms on his shoulders, plunging my hands into his hair.

"I was thinking," I pause and lick my lips. His eyes are riveted to the tip of my tongue, watching it slowly cross from one side to the other. "Maybe we should stay in tonight and put the do not disturb sign on the door."

His breath hitches a little. "And why would we do that instead of going to Little Five Points with Deedee and Kevin?"

"Well, I was thinking I want to spend some quality time with you." I lean over and lick his ear. "Naked."

He was erect before I sat on his lap, but that just got him so hard he could probably ram a railroad spike through a brick wall.

"Don't write checks you can't cash, Petal."

"Why don't you see if I'm good for it," I tease.

He stands up and guides my legs to wrap around his waist. When we're good to go, he strides over and picks up the sign Dee and I made to make it not so obvious to others that there's going to be some R-rated activity going on inside. He opens the door, hangs the sign on the knob, and then shuts the door behind us with his butt. I lock it and immediately put my lips on his.

He walks us over to the bed and sits down on the edge. His hands cup my bottom as he begins to grind me against his rigid length. I let a moan escape me. He knows exactly what to do to me to get me all kinds of hot and bothered. I break away from his mouth and pull his shirt over his head.

He returns the favor and then gives me a smirk before he dives into my cleavage. I'm surprised when he manages to get the front closure of my bra open with his teeth and tongue. That? Was hot. And I show him just how hot it was by going to the spot on his neck that makes him shudder when I kiss it.

With a growl, he lies down and rolls us over. He sits up and starts to pull down my shorts and panties.

"Time to pay up, Petal. Are you ready for me?"

I nod. I love it when he takes charge. It's seriously sexy. When he's got me naked, he picks up one leg and starts kissing his way up from my ankle, past my knee. He nips just above my knee and then licks the rest of the way up, just shy of where I want him to be. I can't stop the whimper I make. I buck my hips up.

"Please, Chase," I cry.

"We wouldn't want your other leg to feel left out, now would we," he purrs, raising his eyebrow.

I squirm under his gaze. God, he is so insanely beautiful. "No," I whisper. "We can't have that."

He repeats the process and, when he gets to my apex, he grabs me by the hips and pulls me to the edge of the bed. He steps off, kneels on the floor before me, throws my legs over his shoulders, and leans down.

Just at the point I'm about to use my legs to urge him forward, he plants a gentle kiss against my lower lips. And then his tongue darts in between them. I throw my head back and moan. I feel him smile against me. Then the torture starts. He flattens his tongue and licks from bottom to top and then teases my clit.

"You taste so good, Petal. I could eat you for breakfast, lunch and dinner and possibly in-between meal snacks, as well," he murmurs while he starts to fuck me with his fingers.

"Oh God, Chase. More," I cry.

He clamps his lips around that little bundle of nerves and sucks. I put my hand on his head, urging him to continue. His rhythm gradually gets faster until I feel my orgasm building. When he feels my walls gripping his fingers, he gently bites me, sending me over the precipice. He continues to slowly move his fingers in and out, while lapping up my juices.

I am still trying to catch my breath, remnants of my orgasm shaking down my thighs, when he kisses my pubic bone and rests his chin on it.

"Are you happy, Petal?"

"Deliriously so, Champ," I answer, smiling as I ruffle his hair.

He chuckles, "I'm never going to live that down, am I?"

"What? You mean the time you tried to wake me up by coming up under the covers from the foot of my bed, scaring me so badly I kicked you in the face, giving you a shiner? Nah, probably not."

His belly laugh makes me grin like an idiot. When he finally gets his laughter under control, he heaves himself up onto the bed and rolls onto his side next to me. I put my hand on his cheek and he grips me by my hip and pulls me into him. I can feel every hard inch of him against me.

I slide my hand down his body and then run my fingers underneath the waistband on his athletic shorts. His eyes are full of lust as I reach under his boxer-briefs and gently pull him out. I keep my eyes on his as I start to glide my hand up and down his shaft, his breath starting to grow ragged. I slink down, slide his shorts and underwear down, and lick his tip, satisfied with the growl I receive in response. I take him in my mouth and love the hiss that comes out of him. I'm heady with the power I have over him right now. I slide my tongue from base to tip, following with my hand. When I reach the tip, I gently nip, watching his stomach muscles clench at the sensation.

"That feels so good," he says as he looks lovingly down at me, pulling away the curtain of my hair with one hand. He grips my hair in a ponytail so he can see me. I keep my eyes on his as I continue to lick, suck, and rub him to his orgasm.

He closes his eyes and drops his head back, gasping for breath as I fondle his testicles with my other hand. I feel them tighten up and take him to the back of my throat as he releases into my mouth, moaning, "Fuck!"

I lick the last of his essence off him and then slide back up his body, coming to rest my head on his chest. His breathing is still heavy, so my head rides up and down on his ribcage. He kisses the top of my head and lazily runs his finger up and down my arm.

"I love you, Petal," he whispers.

"I love you, too, Champ."

"Marry me, Vi," he asks. Again.

I push back so I can see his face. "Chase, why do you want to rush this? We just finished our second semester. Don't you think it's a little too soon?"

He rolls to his side and positions me so we can

talk face to face.

"Vi, I know what I want. I want you to be my wife. I know you think it's weird for a guy to want to get married in his first year of college, but I've wanted you since we were ten years old, before that, if I'm being completely honest. I have more than enough money to cover living expenses for us for the rest of college so we can just focus on school. I can buy us a house in Druid Hills. Or we can buy a condo in town. Whatever you want, I will give it to you. I just want to make you happy, Petal. For the rest of our lives."

I sigh. He's not going to give up on this until I say yes.

"Chase, I don't remember ever being this happy. You bring out the best in me. And I love you with all my heart. I just... give me some more time, okay? I'm not saying no, I'm just saying not yet. All right?"

He searches my eyes for something. Whatever he finds there, he nods. "All right, Petal. I've waited this long for you to be mine. I can wait a little longer."

# Chapter 20

## Emmett

I seriously cannot believe this is my life. All my hard work has paid off. I'm a forward for the Atlanta Confederates. The media has labeled me the"bull in the china shop" because I barrel through the defense like they are nothing. And I've got to tell you, I love the limelight and the limelight loves me.

I get laid in every different city I'm in. I don't even work for it, women just throw themselves at me. Except back in Atlanta. Whitney managed to find me and sink her talons into me again. Her folks are ridiculously wealthy and just throw money at her to keep her out of their lives, so I wasn't completely surprised when she showed up after one of our home games and told me she dropped out of school and moved to Atlanta.

She shows up everywhere, trying to stake her claim on me. Frankly, it's annoying. There's so much pussy to be had. But, at least I know she doesn't expect anything in return. At least, I didn't until now.

We're two games from the playoffs when she drops the bomb on me. I've just finished pulling out of her, pulling the condom off, and tying it in a knot. I head over to the bathroom to toss it in the trash.

"Emmett, I'm pregnant," she says softly.

"What? How? Why? How?" I shout, "I thought you were on the pill? How is it possible when you're on the pill and I'm using condoms?"

She sits up, crosses her arms over her large, fake breasts and huffs, "Neither method is 100% foolproof, Emmett. Didn't you take sex ed?"

I run my hands over my face. "Are you sure you're pregnant?"

"I've got a bunch of positive tests in my purse. I'm pretty sure, yeah," she snaps.

"Okay. Um..." I don't even know what to say here. "Do you want to have this baby?"

Her voice is like nails on a chalkboard when she shrieks, "You aren't seriously asking me to have an abortion, are you? I am going to have your child, Emmett. End of story."

Fuck. I need to think. I run my hands through my hair then lace my hands together behind my neck, taking in a deep breath, holding it, and then exhaling so I am as calm as I can be, given the circumstances.

"Whitney, I need some time to digest this bit of news. Do you mind going back to your place? I promise I'll call when I can actually think about this clearly," I say.

"Fine, Emmett. I'm tired anyway," she says, slipping her shirt over her head. "Just call me when you're ready to talk, all right?"

"Sure, Whitney."

There's one person whose opinion I value the most but I can't talk to her about this. No way in hell am I going to tell Lola until I know for sure what's going on. So I call number two on my speed dial: my Dad.

"Hey, Dad. Do you have some time to chat? I need some guidance here," I say.

"Sure thing, son. I was just sitting down to watch the news. What's going on?"

"Well, I'm in a bit of a pickle," I start. And then I tell him what's going on. The line is silent when I finish.

"Son, I can't say I'm surprised about this. That girl has been trying to make herself a permanent fixture in your life since freshman year of college. You know what your mother would expect."

I groan. "Dad, that's a low blow. Fuck! I really don't need this right now."

Dad barks, "Need it or not, you've gotten yourself into this situation so you need to man up and take responsibility. Now, go call your uncle and get Whitney in to see him. If I'm going to have a grandchild, your uncle is the only doctor I trust to bring it into this world."

"Yes, sir," I say meekly. "Dad... I've messed up, haven't I?"

"Royally," he grunts before he hangs up.

The next call I make is to my mom's brother. He's one of Atlanta's top OB/GYNs. "Hey, Uncle Pete. How are you?"

"Emmett, my boy! I was just watching clips of you on ESPN. Couldn't be more proud of you!"

"Thanks," I mutter. "Uncle Pete, I'm, um, in need of your services."

"Very well, then. I'll have my nurse call you first thing in the morning, I'll squeeze Viola in."

"Uncle Pete, it's not Viola."

"Oh." He clears his throat. "I just assumed you were together. You looked like quite the happy couple when I bumped into you the other weekend."

"She's my best friend and she's got a boyfriend who makes her happy. I'm not about to go and mess that up for her," I tell him.

"Well, it's a shame, son. You two look good together. I can tell she cares about you a lot."

I take a deep breath and blow it out. "I know. And I love her more than anything. But now I've got to face facts: I'm about to go and propose to a woman I don't love and become a father."

"Give me the information I need and the nurse will call you with an appointment time tomorrow morning, Emmett," he says sadly.

I take a long shower, get dressed, and head to the nearest jewelry store. I pick out a nice 2-carat solitaire ring and then, as an afterthought, buy a dozen roses and head over to Whitney's condo. I let myself in and find her asleep in her bed. I kneel down beside her and take a good long look at my fucked up future before I gently nudge her awake and ask her to marry me.

The next morning, the nurse calls early to tell us Whitney has an appointment at 10 o'clock. We arrive and are immediately ushered into one of the patient rooms. Whitney gets undressed and puts on the gown. They take some blood and ask her for a urine sample. And then my uncle comes in. I can see the smile doesn't reach his eyes when I introduce him to Whitney, my fiancée. She gushes over finally being introduced to a family member.

Uncle Pete asks her to lie down and put her feet in the stirrups. He rolls a condom down over the probe of the ultrasound (it's seriously disturbing watching my uncle put a condom on anything) and then he puts the probe into Whitney. I watch the screen, turning my head this way and that, trying to figure out what I'm looking at.

"There we are," Uncle Pete says, pointing to a small smudge. "It looks like you're about 10 weeks along. Let's crank up the volume and see what the heartbeat's doing."

I hear a rhythmic swishing noise and then I hear a frantic thumping. "Uncle Pete, the heartbeat is so fast. Is that normal?"

"Calm down, boy. A baby's heartbeat is always fast. And from the number of beats per minute, I'd say the little peanut is doing just fine. Not to worry. I'll take great care of Whitney and my great niece or nephew."

Well, fuck me running. I'm going to be a dad.

# Chapter 21

*Viola*

I don't think I've looked at anything else but the front page of the sports section for the past two hours. The headline blares "Bull in the China Shop Picking out China Patterns" while underneath is a photo of a somber looking Emmett and the infamous Whitney.

At their wedding. She's smiling like she just won the lottery.

"Tell me what's going on in that head of yours, Vi. I can see the hamster running full out on the wheel," Dee says.

I purse my lips before I respond. "I'm shocked. I knew he was having sex with her on the regular. I just didn't think he was that into her, to be honest. Why didn't he tell me? I just saw him! That fucker knew he was getting married and he didn't bother telling me, his best friend. What the fuck?" I shout.

"Hey, hey. If I wanted to do dinner theater, I'd

have majored in drama not literature. Dial it down a few notches and talk to me," Dee soothes, while looking around in embarrassment.

"Why, Dee? Why didn't he feel like he could talk to me about this?" I sniffle, tears on the way.

"Do you want my honest opinion?"

"No, Dee, lie to me," I spit.

She raises her eyebrow at me before I mutter, "Sorry, please continue."

She sips her latte and then enlightens me. "She's knocked up, Vi. There's no way he'd actually marry someone who's not you unless he had to."

I nod my head. It makes sense. "But why didn't he tell me, Dee?"

"Because he didn't want to look you in the face when he broke his promise to you," she whispers.

I snap my head up and look at her. She's completely right. And then it hits me: he's not ever going to come for me. I excuse myself from our table and go to the bathroom. The tears start to form before I can stop them. Until recently, I had always pictured me standing in a big princess dress next to Emmett at the altar. Tears roll down my cheeks as it dawns on me that it was never meant to happen. When I think of who I have been envisioning in that scenario lately, I finally stop crying. I splash cold water on my face and pat myself dry with some paper towels.

When I look up, I see with absolute clarity the path that lies before me. It's not the one I dreamed of since I was a little girl, but it is not one that I haven't wanted to take.

I told him that it would be my choice. He took his hat out of the ring. There is no other choice for me, and I am content in finally realizing it. It makes me shake my head at the thought that I have wasted so much time waiting for Emmett Allan Davis.

Chase's dad is taking his latest conquest to Bermuda for a few days, so we head out to the house in Druid Hills, stopping on the way for groceries. When we get in and settled, I excuse myself to go to the restroom. I change into the pink lace camisole and underwear set Dee helped me pick out for this very occasion a few months back.

"You need to be prepared," she'd said.

When I've checked my breath and my makeup and hair, I look at myself in the mirror and say, "This is it, Vi."

I go back downstairs and find Chase in the kitchen chopping up vegetables. He looks up and smiles broadly.

"I like your outfit. A lot," he tells me with a wink.

I walk over and give him a thorough kissing. When I'm done, he lifts me onto the countertop on the island and passes me a glass of wine that he poured for me. I thank him and take a sip.

"Are you hungry? I was going to whip up some chicken Marsala and a salad," he says, getting back to his chopping.

"Sounds good. But I'm not starving or anything. Are you?"

He shrugs. "I'm always hungry, but I can wait until you're hungry. The prep work has been done, it won't take long to finish."

"Good," I chirp. "Then get over here."

He puts the salad bowl into the fridge, rinses off his hands, wipes them on a dishtowel and then comes over to stand between my thighs. His hands run from my knees up to my thighs while he leans in to give me a kiss. I kiss him back with everything I've got, making him growl and grab my hips, pulling me into his erection.

"Chase," I pant. "I'm ready."

"I know you are, baby. I can feel how warm and wet you are," he murmurs.

"No, Chase. I'm ready," I enunciate.

He looks deeply in my eyes. I can see the passion swirling in his dark blue depths. "Are you absolutely certain about this, Petal?"

"More certain than I've ever been about anything else in my life, Champ. Make love to me."

He doesn't need any further validation. He picks me up and carries me upstairs to his bed, laying me down gently and then kneeling on the bed beside me, opening his nightstand to get condoms. I look at him in surprise.

"Petal, you're my first. I've had these in here for a few months, hoping that one of these weekends, I'd have need of them." He clears his throat. "I'm really nervous."

My voice quivers when I ask, "Do you not want to do this?"

"I've wanted to this for a long, long time. I've been waiting for you to decide you're ready. I'm not sure what made you make up your mind, but I want you more than anything."

He leans over and kisses me. I can feel the years of yearning, the lust, the love. I know in my heart that this is right, that he is the right one for me.

I sit up, not breaking our kiss, and get onto my knees so we're chest to chest. He takes my head in his hands and tilts it so he can have the access he wants and then he sneaks past my lips with his tongue. He runs his tongue over my top lip, over my bottom lip, and then teases my tongue out to tangle with his. The things this man does with his tongue amaze me.

His hands leave my face and slide down to my shoulders.

"Perfection," he murmurs before using his hands to slide my camisole straps slowly down my arms, baring my breasts to him. My nipples are already hard with want and he takes one into his mouth, nipping it with his teeth and then kissing away the sting.

I unbutton his shirt and slide it off his shoulders, down his arms. His mouth doesn't break contact with my breast. I run my hands up his torso, loving the feeling of the rippling muscles under my palm. I gently pinch his nipples, loving the jerk his cock gives in response.

He dips his hand into my panties, feeling my wet core. He gently rubs back and forth, my hips rocking involuntarily. I unbutton his jeans and slide them and his boxer-briefs down over his firm ass. I reach down and tease the tip of his cock with my fingertips.

"Petal," he groans, before he puts both of his thumbs into the waistband of my panties and slides them slowly over my hips. He helps me onto my back and then removes them entirely. He spreads my legs and lies in between them. Today, there will be no teasing, no torture. He grabs my hips with his strong hands and leans down to pleasure me.

I writhe underneath him, loving what he does to me with his mouth. My back arches off the bed when he thrusts his tongue inside me, gently rubbing my clit with the pad of his thumb. He licks and teases and thrusts until I'm on the edge of climax. His hum puts me over the edge. Wave after wave of pleasure rolls over me, as I moan his name, clutching his hair.

He keeps kissing and licking gently until my orgasm is over. When his head pops up, I motion for him to come kiss me. He licks up my stomach, stopping to give each of my breasts thorough attention and then finally holds himself above me on his forearms, nuzzling my nose with his.

"Make me yours, Chase," I say, hardly recognizing my own husky voice.

He grabs a condom from beside us and sits up to put it on. I stop his hands and then lean over to take him in my mouth, moaning at how hard he is.

He shivers and says, "Vi, I don't think I'll last long if you keep that up."

I finish my trip from bottom to top and then kiss the tip before I take the condom from him. Having seen the videos in health class, I open the wrapper and pinch the tip before placing it over his shaft. I use my fingertips to gently roll the condom down his considerable length, watching him watch me, chest heaving.

When it's on, I lie back and take his hand. He lies on his side and says, "I don't want to hurt you. I don't know the best way to do this without hurting you."

I throw my leg on top of his, hooking my knee behind his thigh and try to bring him on top of me.

"I just want you inside me, Chase."

He positions himself above me and then uses one hand to direct his cock to my opening. He slides the head through my wet folds a few times and then gently eases into me, stopping when my walls won't let him pass any further.

The difference in girth between fingers and his dick is overwhelming. "God, Vi. I don't know how long I'm going to last, it feels too good."

When I feel myself relaxing a bit, I shift my hips. He looks down at me, "Petal. Are you absolutely certain?"

"Yes," I murmur.

He pushes himself a little deeper. I can feel him hit the barrier and I wince.

He stops again, voice and eyes full of concern when he asks, "Are you okay? Do you want me to stop?"

I shake my head no. He takes a deep breath, pulls himself out a bit and then forcefully thrusts forward, stopping after we both feel the barrier break. He rains kisses down on my face.

"Oh, God, I'm so sorry. Please say something."

The pain is incredibly intense, but it eases after a minute. Now I just feel full and warm.

"Love me," I whisper as I raise my hips in invitation.

He pulls out slowly and glides back in just as slow. I wrap my legs around his waist and use them to help set the pace. Every stroke feels so much better than the one before it. I don't want it to stop. I'm starting to feel the telltale signs of my pending orgasm, but I need a bit more friction. I pull myself to him when he thrusts, grinding our hips together when I'm full.

"I'm going to come soon. Oh God, that feels so good," he moans. He picks up the pace a little more, grinding at the end of each thrust. Before I know it, stars are exploding and I'm chanting his name while he roars his release.

Chase collapses on top of me, kissing each cheek and my nose before placing the most tender kiss on my lips.

"I love you, Vi," he whispers.

"I love you, too, Chase," I whisper back, taking a moment before I say, "Ask me again."

He sits up, a look of surprise on his face. Then he says, "Give me a minute."

He gets up and heads to the bathroom to dispose of the condom. When he gets back, he throws on a pair of boxers and digs in his weekend bag. He comes over to the bed, gets down on both knees in front of me, opens a box from Tiffany and Company revealing a gorgeous two carat pink diamond solitaire ring, and with a gulp, asks, "Viola Ann Callaway, will you be my wife?"

I lean over and kiss his nose. "Yes."

# Chapter 22

## Emmett

I guess it's my turn to look at the paper in utter shock. It's right there in black and white:

*Luanne and Jack Callaway are pleased to announce*
*the engagement of their daughter*
*Viola Ann Callaway*
*to*
*Chase Everett Butler*
*Son of Evelyn Butler and John Butler*

She looks radiant in the accompanying picture. He looks like the cat that ate the canary, grinning down at her.

As much as I hate to admit it, I do like the guy. I've spent enough time around him now to know that he's good to her, that he's good for her. I'm just some asshole who made her promises I couldn't keep.

I hear Whitney throwing up again. I want to feel bad for her, but I can't.

We got married four weeks after I proposed. Her mother hired a planner and honestly, I was amazed at the size and scope of the wedding they threw together in such a short amount of time. But if anything, her folks aim to impress, even if it is for all the wrong reasons. They sent us off to St. Lucia for a two-week honeymoon. When we got back, the news was all over the place. The wedding, the pregnancy—it was all out there, thanks to her folks blabbing to the media.

I had decided before we left Atlanta that I'd try to make an effort, since this was my lot in life. I went to grab some condoms to pack up for the wedding and honeymoon when I realized the damage was done. I picked one up and held it up to my face.

"Traitorous little fucker," I snarled. And then I saw it. It wasn't blatantly obvious, the tiniest little damage to the packaging.

I held it up to the light. And sure enough, I could see a pinhole of light shining right through. So I threw it down and grabbed another. And another. And another. Until all four boxes in the nightstand were scattered on the floor around me.

When Whitney came home that night, I was *livid.*

"When did you go off the pill?"

"Emmett, I went off after I found out—"

"Don't. Lie," I interrupt, shouting. "When?"

"When I moved to Atlanta," she whispers.

I slammed my fists on the table so hard I knocked over the bottle of bourbon and the tumbler that were there to keep me occupied while I waited.

"God dammit, Whitney! What. The. Fuck," I scream.

"I love you, Emmett," she sobs. "You're the only one who stuck around, even if you treated me like shit."

"Whitney, I treated you like shit because I didn't give a shit. Why would you think I'd ever want any part of... of.... this," I spit, pointing back and forth between us. "I can't even look at you right now. I can't be in the same room with you. I need to go."

I had already called Lola and asked her to meet me for a drink at the pub around the corner. I picked up my keys and wallet and was heading out the door when I heard her ask, "What's going to happen, Emmett?"

I spun around and said, "I'm still going to marry you, Whitney. But it's only because you're carrying my child. I. Will. Never. Love. You." I slammed the door behind me.

Lola was sitting in a booth, reading a textbook when I walked in the door of the pub. I stopped and watched her for a few moments, trying to calm myself. I had every intention of telling her. Honestly, I did. But when I actually saw her, I couldn't do it. I couldn't bear to look her in the eye and tell her.

The smile when she looked up and saw me was electric. Her big green eyes were shining with happiness at seeing me again. I walked over and sat down at the booth and grabbed the hand she held out across the table.

She tilted her head to the side. "What's wrong, Mutt?"

I smiled. "Nothing, Lola. Why would you ask that?"

"I've known you almost my whole life. Your smile isn't reaching your eyes. What's going on?"

"I'm just pissed about fucking up in the playoffs, that's all."

She narrowed her eyes at me, calling me out on my shit. "Emmett, getting slammed and put on the injured list isn't your fault."

"I know. So tell me what you've got going on this summer. Put a real smile on my face and tell me you'll run away with me," I said, not even remotely joking.

"You're hilarious," she snorted, rolling her eyes. "Carlyle's wedding stuff is going to keep me here a good chunk of the time since I'm in the wedding party. There have already been all kinds of showers and mixers and parties and I'm seriously exhausted thinking about doing any more. Her family's lovely, though. It's just she's got this obnoxious cousin who is all over me, even when Chase is around."

"Do I need to go and kick some ass? I've got some pent up frustration to get out," I quipped.

"It's all right. Chase is ready to deck him the next time he ogles me and I've already prepared Christine and her folks for that actuality."

We spent the next three hours getting caught up. My time with her calmed me down enough to go home to the mother of my child and then go and get married, sealing my fate.

And that leads me to this moment, sitting at my kitchen table, staring at the paper, my coffee and breakfast gone cold.

"Emmett, we've got to get going to Uncle Pete's office for the ultrasound," Whitney whines.

"Go get your purse and get ready. I'll be there in a sec," I say, giving the paper one last look before I crush it into a ball and throw it into the trashcan.

Uncle Pete is gabbing on about the wedding while squirting gel on Whitney's stomach. She's finally started to show, making my situation even more real. Uncle Pete puts the ultrasound probe on her belly and shifts it around, smearing the gel until he finally gets a picture. This is our third ultrasound and it just doesn't ever get old looking at my baby growing inside Whitney's belly.

"All right, we're going to do measurements first and then we'll reveal the gender," Uncle Pete says as he moves the probe around, clicking buttons on the machine here and there.

I stare in awe at my child in profile. The eyes, the button nose, the mouth. Then there's the arms and fingers, legs and toes, all squirming around, like it knows we're watching. I see the heart beating fast and furious. And I know without a doubt that I'm going to love this little being with all I've got, regardless of Whitney's deception.

"Are you guys ready?"

We both nod. Uncle Pete shifts the probe around.

We get a view that looks like we're standing underneath a sheet of glass, baby sitting on top.

"Congratulations! I'm getting a great niece!"

I immediately make a mental note to go out and buy a shotgun and a shovel.

# Chapter 23

*Viola*

"Vi? Vi, say something. You're scaring me," Dee says, poking me in the arm.

"It's just... so soon, Dee. I was expecting to have a bit more time to prepare," I say, swallowing.

The Walkers offered us the country club for the reception venue as our wedding present. The only weekend they had available for the next year and a half is only a few weeks away.

Not that I don't want to marry Chase. I do, more than anything. He's managed to sway me to his way of thinking; that we don't need to wait until we've graduated. We've known each other since we were little. We know we want to get married. Our school costs are covered. He's got more money at 20 than a lot of CEO's have in their 50's. We've already bought a home in Druid Hills close to his Dad. Why have a long engagement when we can do it now? I was just expecting to have a few more months.

"Mama, do you think we can pull it off?"

"Both of my babies married! I'm going to be a grandma before I know it," she squeals, off in her own little world. I guess she's good with it.

Christine rolls her eyes. Having just married my brother two weeks ago, she's in no rush to have kids.

I grab my cellphone. "Well, I'm going to call Chase and give him the good news."

The phone rings once before he picks up. "Are you having fun dress shopping?"

I snort, "Not really. I haven't found anything I like yet. But we just got to the bridal salon and had a glass of champagne. Mama's already buzzed."

His chuckle makes me smile. "Well, whatever you wear, I know you're going to be so beautiful."

"Stop it, I'm blushing," I joke. "What's on your calendar for September 24th?"

There's silence.

"Champ? Are you there? Is this thing on?" I tap my phone.

"I'm here," he laughs. "I was just smiling because you just made me the happiest man in the state of Georgia. I'm going to call my folks and then I'll shuffle a few things so I can take the rest of the week off to help figure things out. I'll call you later. Love you!"

"Love you, too. Before you go, though, I just want to make one thing perfectly clear," I say seriously.

"What's that?"

"There will be pink at this wedding. Lots and lots of pink."

I hold the phone away from my ear, listening to his laughter until it dies down. "I wouldn't expect anything else, Petal."

I head back into the bridal salon, rubbing my hands together. "Chase is on board. Let's find me a wedding gown!"

Deedee pulls one off the rack. It's the mullet of wedding gowns: short in the front, long in the back, with ruffles everywhere. "What about this one?"

"What about no."

She looks through a few more and holds up another monstrosity, looking at me with a hopeful expression on her face.

I groan. "Dee, did you just meet me?"

After four or five more attempts, I hold up my hands. "Deedee Walker, I love you. But your taste is all in your mouth. Step away from the gowns."

Mama hoots in laughter, Christine somehow manages to snort elegantly, while Dee sits down with a huff.

"I think I might be able to help," says a smooth voice from behind us. I turn around to see a dashingly handsome gentleman leaning against the doorframe, arms crossed.

He uncrosses his arms, crooks his finger at me and says, "Come with me."

I hand my champagne flute to Mama and follow him into a dressing room.

"You just sit tight. I'll be back in about five minutes with your gown, a veil, some accessories, and someone to help dress you, love," he coos. "By the way, my name is Daniel."

True to his word, there's a knock on the door five minutes later. I've stripped down to my strapless bra and underwear and have on one of the silky robes they had hanging in the room. Daniel comes in with a selection that's surprising. I look up at him and smile.

"Daniel, it's like you've known me my whole life."

The attendant helps me slip into the first gown, zips up the back, and calls for Daniel. He comes back in with a few hairpins and gets to work doing a mock hairstyle. He pins the veil into place, and helps me put on the gorgeous strappy heels. I turn around and hold my breath.

This gown is perfection. The strapless sweetheart crossover bodice is made from the palest pink silk dupioni. It ends at a sash and then there are layers and layers of pink and cream tulle. It makes me want to spin like a ballerina.

"We won't even need to alter it. It fits like a glove," Daniel says, nodding approvingly. "What do you think?"

"I think you are incredibly good at your job, Daniel. Let's go show the gals," I say, leading the way.

Mama bursts into tears when she sees me. "It's gorgeous!"

"It's perfect," Christine gushes.

Dee tilts her head and looks at me. "It's pink!"

"It's mine," I add. "Now, what about bridesmaid dresses? Daniel, do you have any ideas?"

"Of course! Follow me, my lovelies."

Christine and Deedee get up and head back to the dressing rooms.

In a couple of minutes, Daniel marches Dee out in an olive green dress that looks like she's going to a square dance. I spit out my champagne and start howling in laughter, trying not to get champagne all over my beautiful gown. Daniel snickers behind his hand.

Dee scowls at him. "You're just plain mean."

He gives her a hug and says, "I'm just teasing, love. The dress I have in mind is in your room now. Go and try it on."

Christine comes out a few minutes later and I'm nodding my head vigorously, clapping. When Deedee joins her, it seals the deal. Their dresses are floor-length strapless cream-colored lace with scalloped edges. Daniel ties pink silk sashes around their waists, to compliment my dress. I stand with Christine on one side and Deedee on the other. Mama digs into her purse for a tissue and her credit card.

"Wrap them up, Daniel!"

"Mrs. Callaway, aren't you going to feel scandalized to have your daughter get married in something other than white?" Dee asks, sticking her tongue out at me.

"I wore ivory to my wedding for a reason, dear," Mama says softly, taking a final sip of champagne.

That goes to the top of the list of things I never needed to know.

We decide to have a leisurely lunch, since we wrapped up most of what we had to do today in just over an hour. I open my planner and started going over the list out loud.

"Date? Check. Reception venue? Check. Wedding gown? Check. Bridesmaid dresses? Check. Now we just have to..." I trail off when I see who just walked in the door.

Mama gets up and runs over.

"Emmett, sweetie! How have you been?" She pulls him into a big hug. He's shocked to see her, but hugs her back lovingly.

"Congratulations on your wedding! And expecting, too! That's just wonderful. This must be your blushing bride. I'm Luanne Callaway. It's a pleasure to meet you."

Whitney looks at Mama's outstretched hand like it's dirty. Mama's smile drops. As does her hand.

Emmett looks at Whitney in horror. And then he looks back at Mama and spies me sitting in the booth. His face goes pale.

"Whitney, why don't you go and order, I'll be over in a few minutes."

"But I don't know what you want to eat," she whines, sounding like a petulant child.

"Just order for yourself then," Emmett grits out. She huffs and follows the hostess to their table.

Emmett puts his arm around Mama's shoulder and walks her back over to our table.

"I'm sorry for Whitney, Mrs. Callaway. She's... well, she's never understood my relationship with Viola," he apologizes looking directly at me.

"It's understandable, sweetie. You two do have a

strong bond," Mama says, patting his hand.

"Deedee, girl, how are you?" Emmett bends over and kisses her cheek.

"I'm great, Em," she responds, sounding strained. "Congratulations, by the way."

"Thanks. And you must be Christine. It's a pleasure to meet you. I'm Emmett Davis."

Christine shakes his outstretched hand and smiles. "Nice to meet you, too, Emmett. I've heard a lot about you."

He turns his attention to me. "Can I speak to you for a moment, Lola?"

"I don't think now's the best time, Emmett. Why don't you go and have lunch with Whitney and we'll talk another time?"

"Because you don't answer my phone calls or texts anymore. Please. Just give me five minutes," he begs.

I look at Mama and she nods, Deedee's giving me the no-go, Christine bites her thumbnail in thought, looking like she could go either way. I go with Mama's call and get up and follow him outside.

"What do you want, Emmett?" I sigh heavily and then continue. "Do you want me to tell you I'm happy? Do you want me to tell you it's okay?"

"No, Lola. I want you to be angry. I broke my promise. I just didn't think..." He blows out a big breath, running his hands through his brown curls, hazel eyes sad as he continues, "I didn't think you'd marry him so quickly."

"Well, I didn't think you'd marry Whitney *at all.*

You want me to be angry? You got it. But I'm not angry that you got married or that you're having a baby. It's your life, Emmett. I'm angry because you didn't have the balls to tell me to my face. How do you think I felt finding out from ESPN?"

"Probably the same way I felt for finding out about your engagement to Chase in the paper! Dammit, Lola!"

"Don't you dare, Emmett! Above all, we're friends. At least, I thought we were," I say, turning away to hide the tears in my eyes. "I love him, Emmett. Even before I found out the news, he was going to be my choice."

Whitney picks this exact moment to come outside with a sneer on her lips.

"Well, well, well. I am in the presence of the infamous Lola Callaway. Whitney Davis," she says with a snarl, holding out a bony hand with long, red talons. "Emmett's wife and the mother of his child."

It's my turn to refuse a handshake. "I'd say it's nice to meet you, but my Mama raised me not to lie. Emmett, I've got to get back to my table. It's been... eye opening."

I spin on my heel to go back into the restaurant when a hand grabs my wrist and spins me back.

"Just for the record, you may have his heart, but I have him in my bed. And now I'm his wife."

I don't hesitate at all when I plaster a smile on my face and say, "Just for the record, you may be his wife, but I'll always be his girl. He'll never love you the way he loves me."

Emmett comes over to break it up between us. Whitney seriously looks like she's going to come at me like a spider monkey. I rip my arm from her grip and look at Emmett.

"Congratulations, Emmett. She's quite the catch."

And with that, I walk back into the restaurant, hail the waiter over to our table and order a double bourbon on the rocks.

# Chapter 24

## Emmett

"God dammit, Whitney! What the fuck did you have to go and do that for?"

We're driving home and I am beyond furious with her.

She pouts and then finally turns to face me and says, "Why is it always her? Why does she always win? You're married to me, not her. I'm carrying your child!"

"Yes, Whitney. You are carrying my child because you're a deceitful little bitch. I married you because I want to do right by my daughter, not by you. I will love my daughter, I will dote on her, I will give her everything she ever wants and more. But I will never, ever love you because you don't even know what it means to love someone."

"I love *you*, Emmett," she yells.

"No, you don't, Whitney. You think you do, but

the truth is that you don't know the meaning of the word. Hell, you don't even love yourself! If you did, you wouldn't have slept with anything with a pulse. Why do you think I chose to fuck you? Because you were easy. I didn't have the time or patience to impress. I needed an outlet. And because you don't love yourself, you kept coming back every single time I called."

The tears streaming down her face tell me that I've just taught her more in two minutes than a lifetime of therapy would have.

"I'm not sorry about what I just said. You need to hear it, Whitney. I want our daughter to grow up in a house with parents who think the sun rises and sets on her. And if you can't be that parent, then let's divorce now and you can give me custody of our daughter. But hear me on this: you better figure your shit out before she gets here."

I drop her off at the condo and head to the gym, needing to blow off some steam. I'd much rather go out and get drunk and fuck some random groupie, but I can't do that anymore. I've got my daughter to think about.

I bump into Kevin and Chase coming out of the gym.

Kev gives me a bro-hug. "Hey, man. Congrats on the nuptials. Kinda pissed you didn't invite us, but whatever."

"Yeah, sorry, dude. Whit's parents really didn't leave a lot of room on the guest list for my side. Only my Dad, my aunt and uncle, and my buddy and his family from Albany made the cut."

"Well, I hope you'll be able to make it out for our wedding in a few weeks," Chase says.

"Yeah, congratulations by the way. But I don't think I'll make the guest list, man. Lola's pretty pissed at me."

He looks at me and nods. "She's just upset that you felt like you couldn't tell her. You're one of her best friends and even though you guys have... history, she figured you could still tell her anything. She'll come around, Emmett. Just give her time."

That? Right there? That's why this guy deserves her. I feel like an even bigger asshole right now.

"Well, regardless of whether or not I'm invited to the wedding, congratulations. You take good care of her, Chase. She's the most precious thing on God's green earth."

He shakes my hand. "I know it, man."

I go into the gym and run on the treadmill until I feel like I'm going to throw up and then I go do circuit training until I actually do. My body can't take anymore, so I go hit the showers and head home.

Whitney's sleeping when I get back. I'm starting to feel a little sheepish about what I said to her this afternoon, but she needs to know that my daughter will not grow up in the kind of environment she did. My daughter will know only love, adoration, and devotion. I'm not kidding when I told her I'd divorce her and get custody of the baby. If she can't offer the kind of upbringing my little angel deserves, then I'll do what I have to to make sure it happens, even if it means hanging up my skates. Coop's starting up a real estate business here in Atlanta, I can always go and work with him.

I grab a beer from the fridge and sit down in my easy chair. I twist off the cap and take a sip, flipping the cap in between my fingers. *My little girl.* I love the way that sounds. I can't believe how crazy in love I am with her already. My marriage may be a sham, but my little girl will be worth putting up with Whitney's crazy shit. I'll do anything for my angel.

I just wish there was a way for me to let Lola know that, to get her to understand why I did what I did. I know how damn stubborn she is. This isn't going to blow over quickly.

I drift off in my easy chair, dreaming of my little girl and the woman who should have been her mother.

# Chapter 25

## *Viola*

I sit and stare at my reflection. Julia just finished my hair and makeup. My hair is pulled straight back from my forehead to the top of my head and held back by my headband of pale pink flowers and Swarovski crystals. The rest falls down my back in gentle waves. Chase is going to go nuts when he sees it. He loves it when my hair is down.

Julia's just pinning my veil behind my headband when Mama and Daddy walk in. I'm in my underthings and my robe, waiting for Dee and Christine to come and help me into my gown. I look up and see tears in both of their eyes.

"Don't you even start, either of you!"

"I used waterproof mascara, Vi. It's not going to be so bad. But keep a tissue handy and blot the tears at the corner of your eye if you can so that they don't mess up the rest of your makeup," Julia says. And then she squeezes me so hard I'm gasping for breath.

"Sugar, I'm so happy for you. You enjoy yourself. And if you need a touch up, just come and find me."

"Thank you, Julia. For everything," I say, smiling back at her.

When Julia walks out of the room, Daddy hands Mama a bag of goodies.

"What's that?"

"This," Mama says, "is your bag of traditions."

She pulls out a delicate handkerchief that has the letter C embroidered in blue. "This handkerchief has been held at every Callaway wedding for the last 120 years. I carried it at mine, Nana Callaway before me, and so on. This is going to do double duty as your old and your borrowed."

She digs down into the bag and then comes up with something frilly. "This garter is your something blue." Daddy rolls his eyes when Mama whirls it around her finger. Mama giggles.

"There are two parts to the new. One is from us, one is from Chase," she says, bringing out a small box from Neil Lane. When she opens it, I gasp. Inside are the most gorgeous earrings I have ever seen. They are two giant pear-shaped diamonds set inside concentric diamond-studded pear-shaped bands. They are beautiful.

"Can you please hand me a tissue?" I choke out. Daddy passes me the box and I dab gently at the corner of my eye, as Julia told me to.

Mama starts to take them out of the box. "Your Daddy and I love you so much, baby girl. We are so proud of you for all you've achieved so far and the promise you have in the future. We were a little surprised when Chase came to ask your father's permission last Christmas, but we knew early on that he is everything we could ever want for you as a husband."

Mama starts to cry in earnest, so Daddy picks up the remaining item in the bag and brings it over to me.

"We went with Chase to find these gifts for you. We wanted you to have something you'd be able to remember the day by, not just a dress hanging in the closet or pictures on the mantle. He's a good man and loves you fiercely, Viola. You done good," Daddy says as he opens up the box.

The necklace is platinum and studded with diamonds. From it hangs a four-carat pear-shaped diamond. I cannot manage words, just squeaks. I am overwhelmed.

Daddy lifts it from the box and I hold up my hair while he puts the necklace on me. He moves in front of me and holds my hands, squeezing tightly. I can see the tears welling up in his eyes before he says, "You're so beautiful, baby girl. I love you, so much." He chokes off the last word before pulling me into a hug and sobbing. I can't help but lose it myself. Mama comes over and we all have a moment together.

Dee and Christine poke their heads in and ask if it's a good time to come and help me get dressed. Daddy nods, wiping his eyes, and excuses himself.

The photographer comes in and takes pictures of my room, of my gifts, of the gown, of me trying to control my tears. Then he turns his back while I step out of the robe and into my gown. He takes pictures of Dee zipping up my gown and tying the sash, of Christine helping me put on the shoes. Then we head out into the yard to take pictures with Mama and Daddy and Carlyle. The photographer wants to take pictures of me on the swing hanging from the oak tree.

"No," I say harshly, looking at the carving on it. "Not there. Anywhere but there."

Looking a tad stunned, the photographer clears his throat and then suggests doing some fun pictures in the grove.

A little while later, a loud honk lets us know the limos have arrived. Two white vintage Rolls Royce Phantoms wait to take us to the church. We head to the front drive. Carlyle heads into the first limo with Mama and Daddy because he needs to get back to the church to stand up with Chase. The girls and I take more photos with the Rolls Royce and then we're off.

When we get to the church, it hits me, "Holy shit, I'm getting married right now!"

Dee laughs. "Did you just figure that out?"

Christine chuckles and says, "Wait until it's your big day, Dee. When you pull up in front of the church, shit gets real."

Daddy is waiting for us on the front steps. He herds the girls in and then holds his arm out to me. We walk through the front door and then Mama hands me my bouquet of pink and cream colored peonies tied with pale pink tulle and pearl strands.

Carlyle comes to escort Mama down the aisle, after giving me a big hug and a kiss on the forehead, the sap. Dee and Christine both give me big hugs and then get themselves ready to go. And then the music starts. Daddy pulls the blusher down on my veil, after giving me a kiss on the cheek.

"Are you nervous?"

I don't even need to think about it. Without hesitation, I shake my head no. Daddy pats my hand and says, "Then let's do this thing."

I giggle and smile as Daddy leads me through the doors. Everyone stands up and turns to the back of the church. I see the motion in my periphery, but I can't take my eyes off what's waiting for me at the end of the aisle.

Chase looks magnificent in his tuxedo. And the look on his face is joy mixed with awe. I see him wipe tears from under his glasses, which makes me drop a few myself. When we reach him, Daddy lifts my blusher, kisses me on the cheek, and then hands me over to Chase, giving him a clap on the back. He laughs and then turns back to me.

"I can't even come up with words to tell you how beautiful you look, Petal," Chase whispers.

I know I'm blushing as I beam back at him. "I can't believe you're mine, Champ," I whisper back.

He squeezes my hand and whispers, "Let's get married," as the minister clears his throat.

The ceremony is long but lovely. If someone were to have counted tears of joy, it would probably have been a toss-up between Chase and me. But it finally comes down to the part I've been waiting for.

"I now pronounce you man and wife. You may kiss the bride," the minister says.

"It's about time," Chase mumbles loudly, earning a laugh from our guests.

He cups my face in his hands and then kisses me gently, but with such a passion it takes my breath away. When we part, we can't stop grinning. And then we hear, "Ladies and gentleman, please say hello to Mr. and Mrs. Chase Butler."

We take photos at the church and then we finally get into the limo and head to the country club. The second the door closes, he pulls me to him and kisses me like he'll die if he doesn't.

"God, Petal. You look so amazing," he murmurs between kisses down my throat. "This dress is... I never would have imagined it, but now that I've seen it, I couldn't picture anything else on you. It's just... you: blushing, elegant, sophisticated, and beautiful." When he makes his way to the pendant, he brushes it with his fingers. "Do you like it?"

"Chase, it's stunning. Thank you so much. You've already spoiled me enough with the engagement ring, the house, the new car.... This was over the top," I say, trying really hard not to succumb to the desire I feel coursing through my veins.

"I'll give you the world, Viola Ann Butler. Anything you want, all you need do is ask," he whispers.

"Then kiss me again."

He does, just as the car pulls up in front of the

country club. We take a moment to collect ourselves before the driver opens the door for us. We form a receiving line with Chase's folks and mine and the wedding party (Deedee, Christine, Carlyle, and Kevin) and greet all the guests and have photos taken with them.

I know he RSVP'd he'd attend, but I'm still surprised to see Coach Davis coming up to greet us.

"Vi, sweetheart. You look so beautiful," he gushes, giving me a hug and a peck on the cheek.

"Coach, it's fantastic to see you," I say.

"Then why are you looking at me like that? Do you think I'd miss the wedding of my favorite football buddy?"

I laugh, "No, sir. I guess not. Can I introduce you to my husband? Chase, this is Coach Emmett Davis. Coach, meet Chase Butler."

They shake hands while Chase says, "It's an honor to meet you, sir. Vi has told me so much about you and I know how the whole town feels about the fantastic job you did here. Thank you so much for coming today."

"You're a lucky man, Chase Butler," Coach says, giving me a sad wink.

The DJ announces that dinner is about to be served, so we all head to our tables. Deedee and Kevin have known us for a long time, so their speeches do not hold anything back. I think my folks are mad at me for a few things they never knew about. But I'm not their problem anymore. I belong to Chase. The thought makes me smile.

I don't get much to eat, but there's always a flute of champagne in my hand. I'm a little dizzy after all of the dances and am just heading to sit down when I hear Coach ask me for a spin.

"Of course," I say. "Just one sec." I grab a dinner roll and then take his outstretched hand, stuffing half the roll in my mouth.

He leads me to the dance floor, laughing. "They really don't let the bride and groom eat at these things, do they?"

I shake my head no, still chewing.

After a moment of silent dancing, Coach finally says, "This isn't how I pictured this day, Vi. But I can see how happy you are. I hope that Chase treats you well. You deserve it. I just hope that, at some point in time, you can forgive Emmett. That's the only way he'll forgive himself."

I nod my head before I ask, "Is he happy?"

Coach smiles sadly and says, "I think he will be happy when his baby girl is born. But I know he won't truly ever be happy without you, Vi. You're his one and only."

I choke on a sob and nod my head again. I calm down enough just before the dance is over to say, "Tell him I'll always love him, Coach. I had faith in him. He just didn't have faith in himself."

I kiss Coach's cheek and then head to the bathroom to cry in solitude.

Julia finds me in there a few minutes later and helps me get the red out of my eyes and fixes me up so I look fresh as a daisy. "Vi," she says, putting another coat of lipstick on me, "Don't you shed one more tear on him."

I nod and hug her again, knowing exactly what she's saying. I head back out and find Chase leaning against the wall across from the bathroom, looking concerned.

"Are you all right, Petal? Someone told me you'd been in there for a while. Is everything okay?"

I smile up at him and grab his hands. "It is now. Take me home, Mr. Butler."

"Anything you wish, Mrs. Butler," he says, beaming.

We aren't going on a formal honeymoon until school break, so we're spending a long weekend at our new house. We say our goodbyes and pack up into the limo and head home.

We're both exhausted and fall asleep on the ride back to Druid Hills. The driver wakes us when we arrive and Chase helps me out of the limo. He picks me up and carries me over the threshold, even though I've been here a bazillion times since we bought it to help design and plan. He's nothing if not traditional. I play with the hair at the back of his neck and stare at him while he takes me upstairs. The corner of his mouth lifts up before he says, "Whatcha thinking, Mrs. Butler?"

"I'm thinking I'm the luckiest lady alive, Mr. Butler," I sigh. "How about you?"

"I'm thinking I can't wait to get my wife out of that gown and do all kinds of naughty things to her," he purrs.

"Well, then, you might want to pick up the pace!" I reach as far down his back as I can and swat him on the rear. He takes the stairs two at a time and then pushes the doors to our master suite open with his elbow.

I haven't been allowed at the house all week. And now I see why. Even though I picked out everything that went into this room, he wanted to make it absolutely perfect. I was inspired by our pending honeymoon and found a beautifully carved Balinese four-poster bed in dark wood. From it, white sheers hang, parting to show a mountain of downy soft pillows, the white cotton pin-tucked comforter is peeled back to reveal super soft white sheets underneath. There's a bench that spans the end of the bed in the same dark-stained wood, upholstered in white tufted raw silk. A carved armoire, dresser, nightstands and a comfortable chaise covered in the same white tufted raw silk as the bench complete the furniture set. We've hung pendant lights with rice paper covers over each nightstand. They are currently on the lowest setting, emitting a soft glow.

There are candles lit all over the place and magnolia petals litter the floor and the bed. Chase puts me down and says, "Don't worry, I had our housekeeper come and light all these about 15 minutes ago. I called her when we left Washington. She's getting a big tip."

"Chase, this place looks like a dream," I breathe.

"I think we need to get you out of this dress and get you into a nice, warm tub. What do you say?"

"I think that sounds perfect."

I close my eyes as he brushes my hair from my back over my right shoulder. I love feeling his breath warm my neck and shoulders. I feel him untie my sash, and then I hear him undo my zipper. He guides me to one of the bedposts to hold on while he helps me step out of my gown. I open my eyes and turn around when I don't feel him return from putting my gown aside.

In the soft glow of the candles and the bedside lights, he looks like sin itself staring at me with his dark eyes. He starts to slip off his bow tie. I walk over to help him out of his tuxedo jacket and lay it gently on the bench. He unbuttons his cuffs while I unbutton his shirtfront. He watches my hands as they slip inside and run along his abdomen while he peels his shirt off and tosses it on the floor.

He picks me up and takes me to the master bathroom, which is also lit with about a hundred candles. The gigantic dark stone tub is filled with steaming water and more magnolia petals. Chase sets me on the edge of the marble counter and then kneels down on the floor. He rests one of my feet onto his knee, unstraps my shoe, pulls it off slowly, and repeats the process with the other foot. He runs his hands from my ankles all the way up to my hips as he stands up and lines himself up between my thighs, licking his lips as he finally meets my eyes. He kisses me gently as he puts his arms behind me to unhook my strapless bra.

I undo his pants and help shift them down his

body. He kicks off his shoes and then steps out of his pants, bending down to take his socks off, then turns around and I cannot help but howl in laughter. He had "Property of Mrs. Butler" ironed on to the seat of his boxer briefs.

"You are too much, Champ," I finally manage after I get down to sparse chuckles instead of non-stop laughter. In the interim, he's come back over to me and is now cupping my face.

"I love it when you laugh, Petal. Now, let's get you out of these panties and into that tub over there," he says, helping me down from the countertop. He helps slide my undies down as I help him slide out of his. He takes my hand and leads me over to the tub. I climb up the marble steps and over the edge, knotting my hair up on top of my head. The water is perfect, hot but not scalding. I sink down as Chase gets in and settles in behind me.

He pulls me back into him, wraps his arms around my chest and squeezes me tightly, saying, "Mine."

I run my hands up and down his thighs, smiling at the twitching behind my back. He releases his grip on me and starts to massage my neck and shoulders. I lean my head to one side when I feel him lean forward to kiss my neck. One hand moves forward to fondle my breast, the other slides down my front to my apex, lazily stroking me. I slide a hand in between us and gently glide up and down his length, turning my head enough for him to kiss me. Our tongues tangle as we work ourselves up from gentle exploration to the point of no return.

I break away and turn around to straddle him kissing him as I slide myself over his length. He cups my bottom and guides himself into me.

"Mine," he says, as he thrusts into me.

I take control of the rhythm while he suckles and nips my breasts. My head lolls back as I let out a throaty hum. "Don't stop, Chase. Don't ever stop."

"I'd come back from the dead to do this to you, Petal. Fuck, I love it when you grind into me like that. Do it again."

I slide back down and swivel my hips, generating friction on my sweet spot.

"Mmmmm. So good."

I pick up the pace, grinding a little harder because I can feel the tingling and warmth spreading throughout my body.

"Just like that," Chase pants, moving his hands to my hips to help me get the leverage I need.

I shove his head back down to my breasts. He takes a nipple in his mouth and, with the sting of his teeth clamping down, I climax, shouting his name.

My clenching walls milk his release when he joins me in orgasm. I open my eyes and stare at my beautiful husband as he smiles up at me. I pull his face to mine and kiss him, hoping to convey all the love and contentment I feel at this precise moment.

When we finally part, he says, "I think we're going to have a bit of a mess to mop up."

I look over the edge of the tub and laugh.

"You'd be right about that. Let's get dried off and

I'll go grab some more towels from the linen closet."

We pat each other down and head into the bedroom. I'm about to put on the robe that's lying on the bed when I feel Chase's erection press up against my back.

"I think the cleanup is going to have to wait. We have other matters to attend to at the moment."

I smile before I spin around and we start round two.

# Chapter 26

## Emmett

Dad's in town to visit and take in a home game. He's helping me get the nursery ready. We've painted the bottom of each wall white and added decorative trim and a chair rail. The upper half of the walls are a pale pink. Dad's hanging a chandelier while I put together the four-poster wrought iron crib. There's a white antique armoire that's been retrofitted as a changing table. And then there's the plush, comfortable pink rocker and ottoman in the corner with a round table beside it. Nothing but the best for my princess.

Whitney's been on bed rest, having been diagnosed with pre-eclampsia. The morning sickness finally subsided. But now with the pre-eclampsia, it just seems like one thing after another with this pregnancy. She's under the care of my uncle and a dietician to help make sure she and the baby are getting the nutrients they need and are gaining weight. She doesn't have anyone but me out here, or anywhere, really, and I'm traveling all the time with the team, so I've hired a live-in nurse to watch over her. I've also hired a full-time housekeeper to cook, clean, and run errands.

Things between us have gotten better. Still strained, but she's been seeing a therapist twice a week. I've sat in on a session or two and I know how messed up I felt afterward. I can't even begin to understand what runs through her head with all these revelations. I don't think I'll ever love her, but we're figuring things out. She doesn't want to raise our daughter the way she was raised. She knows what it would do to our girl later on. She wants to do right by her and, for that I'm making an effort.

I finish with the crib and slide the mattress in. I'll put the linens on and hang the curtains up later.

"Come on, Dad. Let's get over to the arena. The guys are all looking forward to meeting you. Coach is, too. They don't usually let anyone else in the players box so this is kind of a big deal," I say.

He smiles at me, the first smile that's reached his eyes since he got here. "Well, now. How about that? Will I be on TV?"

I laugh, "It's very likely. Need to call anyone to tell them to watch for you?"

"Nah. If they aren't already watching my boy play hockey, then they aren't really my friend, now are they," he says, ruffling my hair.

We get into my Land Rover and head to the arena. When I get us through security and into the locker room, the guys are all over Dad. Dad coached the brother of one of the goalies in high school and he cannot stop telling stories about Dad. Dad even recognizes him and gives him a firm handshake and a pat on the back, asking, "How's Sammy doing?"

Coach comes over and I introduce them. He, too, is kind of in awe—and he coaches professional hockey.

The game is an easy one. The other team's defense is scared of me after I knocked a guy unconscious last game against them. They try to block me, but they don't get too close. I score a hat trick. Dad couldn't be more proud of me.

We head out to Ruth's Chris Steakhouse after the game for a celebratory dinner. We place our orders and are both sipping scotch when I finally ask him to tell me about the wedding.

"I was wondering when you were going to ask," he says, rubbing the back of his neck. "What do you want to know, son?"

"How'd she look?"

"Beautiful. Happy."

I take a gulp of my scotch. "Good. I actually like the guy, if you can believe it. He's a good egg."

Dad lets out a big sigh. "Yup, he is a good guy." There's a moment of silence before he asks, "How do you feel about all of this?"

"That's the million dollar question, Dad. The bigger question is, after how many times I fucked up, do I even get the right to 'feel' about this?"

"She still loves you, son. She always will. And, as

her lifelong friend, first and foremost, I think you do get the right to feel about it. So tell me."

"I couldn't man up and tell her face to face that I had gotten Whitney pregnant and was going to marry her. I saw her the night before we left for North Carolina for the wedding and I couldn't tell her. Then, I got back, and she was engaged... I knew that I lost her the second Whitney said 'I'm pregnant,' but it just felt... Set in stone after that. I kind of knew I had lost her to Chase but now, I've also lost my best friend," I say, wiping a tear out of my eye.

"Dad, I don't know what to do. She won't answer or return my calls, she won't answer texts or emails. She wants nothing to do with me. Tell me how to fix this."

"Emmett, after talking to her at the wedding, I know that she'll eventually forgive you. Just give her time. There's a lot of healing that needs to happen. And who knows, perhaps my granddaughter will help bridge the gap."

He's smiling. Full-on smiling.

I shake my head. "You're going to spoil her rotten, aren't you?"

"Damn straight I am," he says, lifting his scotch to his lips.

# Chapter 27

*Viola*

The first few months of married life have been absolute bliss. I love being married to Chase. He's so thoughtful and tender and... and dear Lord, but the man is sexy. It's a good thing we're in completely different classes, otherwise we'd be all over each other all day, every day. We have sex in the morning, we are sometimes naughty and find someplace on campus to have a quickie. Then there's before dinner sex and bed time sex. Will we ever stop wanting each other like this?

Our house is so comfortable. We picked it out together just after we got engaged. Since it was an all-cash deal, and the house was unoccupied, we were able to close and have the keys in hand in 72 hours. It needed updating, so Chase let me have at it with no budget. This is going to be the home we live in and raise children in, so he wanted it to meet my wants and needs. One of my architecture professors was willing to assist and advise, as well as oversee the renovations, so I was actually able to truly make it mine. With his guidance, I moved walls, moved plumbing and electrical work, plotted lighting, and redesigned the bathrooms and the kitchen. And I love the way everything turned out. So does Chase.

My favorite room is the master suite. But my next favorite is the kitchen. We opened the kitchen to the great room, using pillars and arches to support where load-bearing walls used to be. The space is gigantic but cozy all at the same time. On the far wall my Aga 4-oven cooker takes center stage with marble counter tops and white wood cabinetry and a pressed tin backsplash. On the far right side, our Sub-Zero fridge has been seamlessly hidden into the cabinetry and on the far left is the large pantry to balance things out.

Facing the great room is the two-tiered island that runs the length of the kitchen. The large dark stone farmhouse sink in the middle compliments the marble countertops. On the kitchen side of the island, white cabinetry hides our dishwashing drawers and prep items. On the other side, open shelves hold knick-knacks and cookbooks. The top tier of the island acts as an eating and serving surface as well as housing appliance garages—slow cooker, mixer, coffee maker, everything has a spot so I never have to duck under and lift them out.

I'm in the kitchen, chopping up veggies for a salad to go with the pot roast and potatoes I have in the oven when my cell phone rings.

Chase picks it up and looks at the display. "Private number. Do you want to take it?"

I shake my head. "No, just let it go to voicemail."

The ringing starts up again brief seconds after it stopped. Whoever this is, I guess it's urgent.

"This is Viola Butler," I answer.

"Lo...Vi... It's Cooper Forsythe."

"Cooper. Um, call me Vi, please. How'd you get my number? What's going on?"

"Vi, I know things are strained between you and Emmett, but do you think you can set that aside? I think he's going to need you right now. Something's happened."

My heart sinks into my stomach. "Oh God, is he all right?"

"No, Vi. It's... both Whitney and the baby are gone. Can you come meet me at the hospital? Emmett's on his way back from Dallas right now. I think it'll really help him if you're here."

I look at Chase, tears forming in my eyes. My voice breaks when I say, "I'll be there soon, Cooper."

I take the food out of the oven and put it in the fridge as Chase gathers our jackets, my purse, and his wallet and keys and ushers me into the Land Rover. "Can you talk about it?"

I nod, clearing a few sobs out of my throat and then tell him.

He's somber when he says, "I agree with Cooper, Petal. He's going to need you to get through this. He's going to need his best friend."

# Chapter 28

## Emmett

It's happening—my little girl is on the way! The nurse, Lisa, called to let me know she was taking Whit to the hospital for an emergency C-section after tonight's examination. We knew that this going to be the case. With everything that's gone wrong with this pregnancy, it would be easier on both Whit and my angel to not try to deliver the old-fashioned way.

I was just gearing up to go on the ice in Dallas when I got the call. I changed back into my street clothes, got claps on the back from most of the guys on the team, and then raced to the airport. One of the team assistants was able to get me a seat on a flight that left in an hour.

I call Coop on the way and ask him to meet me there. Since he's going to be her godfather and all, I want him around. Then I call Dad to let him know. I really want to call Lola, but I doubt she'd even take my call.

When we land, I call Coop. It goes straight to voicemail. I call Lisa. Straight to voicemail. I call the hospital and ask for my uncle. I'm told that he's in surgery. I don't know if that's a good thing or a bad thing. So I just ask the cab driver to hammer it and offer him $100 extra to break as many traffic laws as possible.

I run into the labor and delivery ward and can't contain my smile when I see Coop and Uncle Pete standing together talking. They separate and turn to look at me and I stop short when I see the third person in their party: Lola.

"What's going on? Coop? What's Lola doing here? Why are you all looking at me like that? What's going on?"

Uncle Pete walks over and takes my arm, leading me to sit in a chair nearby. "I don't want to sit, Uncle Pete. I want to see my little girl. Where is she?"

"Son, she—she didn't make it," Uncle Pete says, looking me in the eye.

"Whitney told Lisa something didn't feel right. When Lisa did an examination, she noticed there was some blood and then she felt the umbilical cord. It had been pushed through the cervix. It's something called a prolapsed umbilical cord. The baby wasn't positioned properly and the umbilical cord was trapped in between her and the cervix. Lisa got her here as quickly as possible, but the baby's oxygen supply was cut off. There was nothing we could do, Emmett. When that happens, there's not much time to do anything unless you're already at the hospital. And even then, the odds aren't great. I'm so sorry."

I don't think I hear half of what Uncle Pete just said after, "She didn't make it." I don't feel like I can breathe. I lean forward and put my head in my hands, trying to make sense of it. My little girl. She's gone.

I can't contain the yell that comes out of me before I burst into tears. I feel Lola's hand on my back, rubbing in small circles. I reach up and clutch it in mine, squeezing so hard I think I may have broken something. If I did, she doesn't say anything. She just looks at me through teary eyes and says, "I'm so sorry, Mutt." And then she hugs me. She doesn't stop hugging me for the next two hours while I cry and choke and try to get out my immediate grief.

When I've finally got some sort of control over myself, I look up. Coop and Uncle Pete are still there, and Chase has joined them. I finally manage to get out the words, "What about Whitney?"

Uncle Pete tells me that Whitney bled out during the C-section. The preeclampsia caused clotting problems and she didn't make it.

I nod. Whitney had had a few small seizures in the last couple of weeks. We knew she wasn't doing so well, but it wasn't putting the baby in jeopardy, so we continued with the pregnancy instead of having the baby early.

"Son, I did everything I could to save both of them. Both matters were completely out of my hands. They're both with God now."

I hug Uncle Pete. He's the best damn OB/GYN in

Georgia, possibly in the United States. If he couldn't save them, no one could have. And while I really want to blame him, I can't. I can't really blame anyone.

"There are things I need to see to for Whitney and the baby, but I'll be back in a bit. I've asked the nurses to close off this room to others so that you can have some privacy. I'll be back." He walks over and hugs Lola, whispering to her. She nods and sits back down next to me, putting her hand on my back again.

I see him shake hands with Chase and Cooper before he leaves.

Lola gently takes my hands and helps me turn to face her.

"Uncle Pete asked me to let you know that it's up to you if you want to see her. He will personally coordinate with whatever funeral home you choose. He's called Whitney's parents and they are coming to collect her body tomorrow to be buried in the family mausoleum. They figured you'd want to bury the baby where it means most to you."

I nod. "Will you come with me? I want to see my angel but I don't think I can do it alone."

"Of course, Mutt. Let me go and get one of the nurses and we'll see her, okay?"

Lola gives my hands a squeeze before she stands up and heads off to find a nurse.

Coop sits down beside me. "I'm so sorry, man. What can I do?"

"You got Lola to come. You've already done more than enough. Thank you, Coop," I say before I give him a big hug and start to cry again. He holds onto me until Lola comes back with a nurse.

"This way, Mr. Davis," the nurse says. I stand up and give Coop one last clap on the back before I turn to Lola.

She holds out her hand and I take it, needing the connection more than I realized.

"I'll wait here and then take you home when you're ready, Em," Chase says. "Vi is going to stay with you, all right?"

"Thanks, Chase. I appreciate that."

We head back through some security doors that the nurse opens with the swipe of a card from her hip. It seems like we're walking for hours before she leads us into an empty operating room. It's been cleaned recently, the strong antiseptic scent invading my nostrils. I didn't realize I had stopped in the doorway until Lola squeezes my hand and says, "We don't have to do this, Mutt. Some parents who suffer the loss of a child find it comforting, others don't. It's up to you. I'll be here for you, whatever you decide."

I close my eyes and try to think. Will I ever forgive myself if I don't hold her in my arms and say goodbye? Will I ever get over seeing her like this? It takes me about five minutes to determine that I need to say goodbye.

I clear my throat and say, "I need this."

The nurse ushers me to a chair they've brought in and then proceeds to bring a bundle over to me. I'm already sobbing before the nurse puts her in my arms. She gently lifts the blanket away from the baby's face, my beautiful little angel. I weep uncontrollably and clutch her to me, rocking back and forth. I hear Lola ask the nurse for a few moments and then I hear the door gently close.

I continue rocking my daughter back and forth while I cry. I cry tears for Whitney, who went through so much to have this little girl, only to lose her and her own life. I cry for the life my daughter won't get to live. I cry for not getting to watch my little girl grow up. And then, when I look up and see the tears rolling down Lola's beautiful face, I cry some more, because I see my pain mirrored in her eyes.

I'm not sure how much time passes before the nurse comes back into the room. "Mr. Davis, sir. We need to take her now."

I wipe away the tears from my face and give her one last kiss on her sweet, cold little forehead.

"Goodbye, darlin'. Daddy will always love you."

I adjust the blanket back over her beautiful face and hand her up to the nurse.

"Sir, is there a name you had picked out so we can add it to the paperwork?"

"Violet Grace Davis," I say, looking directly at Lola.

Uncle Pete meets us back at the waiting room we were in before. He and Chase are both sitting in somber silence. They both stand up when we come in.

"I've arranged for some sedatives for you for the next couple of days, Emmett. The psychiatrist I work closely with in situations like these is going to call on you tomorrow and check in every few days after that. He'll be there to help you work through your grief. I'll pick your Dad up from the airport tomorrow morning and bring him to the condo. Viola and Chase are going to take you home, and Viola's agreed to stay with you until I come tomorrow. If you need anything, son, please call me."

"Thanks, Uncle Pete," I say, hugging him tightly.

He says goodbye to Chase and Lola and then we head out to the parking lot. Lola gets in the back with me and pulls my head to her shoulder. I cry silently the entire drive home, Lola whispering, "It's okay, Mutt. Let it out."

When we get to my condo, Lola digs in my bag for the keys and lets us in. I lean on her heavily as I direct her to my bedroom. She helps me sit on the edge of the bed and then opens and closes drawers until she finds some pajama bottoms. She lays them next to me and tells me she's going to get me some water so I can take a sedative and then she'll be back.

I hear her say goodbye to Chase, promising to call him in the morning, and then I hear the door close. I undress and put on the pajama pants and am sliding under the covers when Lola comes in with a glass of water and the bottle of pills. She gets one out for me and hands it and the glass of water to me. I take the pill, swallow the water, and then lie down.

"Is it all right if I borrow some clothes to sleep in?"

"Of course," I say, my voice so rough it is unrecognizable to my own ears. "Grab whatever you need."

"Thank you," she says, grabbing a pair of my

boxers and a t-shirt. She goes into the bathroom and then comes out a few minutes later, turning out the lights and starting to close the door.

"Lola, I—do you mind staying with me until I fall asleep? I—" I start sobbing again.

A few seconds later, I feel her slip into the bed beside me and cradle me in her arms, kissing the top of my head and running her fingers through my hair.

That's the last thing I remember before my world goes numb.

# Chapter 29

*Viola*

I lie awake for a while after Emmett passes out. I don't let him go, though. I heard the desperation in his plea and felt the need as he clutched me as he cried. We may have been on the outs for the past few months, but he's still my best friend.

I start to cry, thinking back to the pain in his eyes as the nurse laid the cold, lifeless body of his daughter in his arms. Watching him cradle her and kiss her and tell her how much he loved her nearly broke me. I can't even begin to imagine the pain of losing a child. And then losing Whitney as well? He must be out of his mind with grief. I may have had my differences with him, but I love this man and I mourn his losses like they are my own.

I look down at this broken man in my arms. I forgot to draw the curtains closed, so the light spilling in from the French doors to the balcony allows me to view him in repose. His breathing is deep and even, thanks to the sedative. This is the first time I have been truly alone with him in a number of years and I take the opportunity to look at him. He is beautiful, there is no denying it. His hair is longer and curly, just like it was when I met him all those years ago. I run my fingers through it, smiling at the memory of that day. His jaw clenches in his sleep. He's grinding his teeth. I run a finger along his jawline and he immediately relaxes. Boldly, I run my finger along his lower lip. He sighs and says, "Lola," before rolling toward me and throwing his arm across my stomach, effectively pinning me.

Where did it all go wrong? I look at the ceiling, as if it will provide me with the answers I seek.

I love Chase. He is the man I was meant to marry. But I wonder if things had been different, would Emmett and I have ended up together? Would he have come for me? Should I have said to hell with it and driven to UNC and given myself to him, like I started to do more times than I can count? Would that have changed anything?

These are the thoughts that consume me as I drift off to sleep.

I wake up confused about my surroundings. When I see it's Emmett wrapped around me instead of Chase, I remember what happened. I gently extricate myself from his hold, and head to the bathroom. I decide to have a quick shower and get dressed. Emmett is still sleeping when I am done, so I head to the kitchen and am startled when I find an older woman scrambling eggs at the stove.

I think she's more startled at seeing me, as she screams and starts calling me some not so nice things. Emmett runs out of the bedroom, rubbing his eyes. "What's wrong, Mrs. Johnson?"

"Who is this lady? Where's Miss Whitney?"

I see his face fall when the realization hits him. I run over and help him to a chair to sit while he sobs.

"Mrs. Johnson, is it? My name is Viola Butler. I am an old friend of Emmett's. Miss Whitney and the baby both passed away last night. I stayed here to make sure he was all right. His father and uncle should be here within the hour," I babble, not knowing what else to say.

Mrs. Johnson bursts into tears. "I am so sorry, Mr. Davis! What can I do?"

"Thank you, Mrs. Johnson. If you don't mind getting the guest room ready for my Dad's arrival and making sure we have groceries for the next few days, maybe some meals we can just heat up, that would be a big help."

"Of course," she says, nodding. She wipes her eyes with the corner of her apron. "I am sorry for yelling at you, Miss Viola. You surprised me."

I put my hand on her arm, "It's okay, Mrs. Johnson. Excuse me a moment, please."

I walk back over to Emmett and crouch before him, putting my hands on his knees. "What can I get you? What can I do, Mutt?"

He puts a hand on one of mine, wiping tears away with the other, and says, "You are already doing it, Lola. You're here, even though I don't deserve it."

"Mutt, of course I am going to be here. You're my best friend and you need me. There's nowhere else I would be."

A knock at the door stops me from getting into things further. Mrs. Johnson answers the door and guides Uncle Pete and Coach into the room. Coach immediately drops his bag and runs over to Emmett. He drops down and hugs him, both men crying openly.

"I'm so sorry, son. I'm so sorry," Coach sobs.

I step away and head over to Pete. He gives me a hug. "Thank you for staying with him, Vi. I know it can't have been easy. The nurse told me that you went with him to see Violet. Thank you for that, as well. I think he needed to say goodbye."

"It's no trouble, Pete. He needed me. No matter how upset I am with him, I will always be there for him. But now that you and Coach are here, I'm going to call Chase and have him pick me up. I will keep my cell phone on and with me all the time. Just call if you need anything," I say, squeezing his arm.

I call Chase, who, bless him, is already on the way to get me.

Coach ushered Emmett back to bed and helped him with another sedative while I was on the phone. I go to say goodbye. His sobbing has stopped, but he still has tears in his eyes.

"I named her for the two most important women in my life: you and my mother. Whitney only ever knew you as Lola. When I suggested Viola as a first name, she said it sounded like an old lady," he says with a somber chuckle. "But she said she could live with Violet. Violet Grace Davis."

I can't stop the tears that flood my eyes. I kiss the top of his forehead as his eyes close.

"Thank you for that, Mutt. It is an honor. You get some rest and I will check in on you later. I love you."

"I love you, too, Lola. Thank you for being here for me."

I close the door to the bedroom and walk out to the main hall. Chase has arrived and is talking to Pete and Coach.

I go and hug Coach, not having been able to before. He begins to cry again, softly this time.

"Coach, I am so sorry," I whisper. He grips me tight and nods his head.

When he gains a bit of composure, he says, "If he hasn't told you, your being here means everything. Thank you, Vi. If you hadn't been here, I don't know what he would have done. That little girl meant the world to him."

"I know, Coach. I'm heading home. Please call if you need anything. I'll check in later, okay?"

He nods and smiles sadly. I grab Chase's hand and walk out the door. When we get into the car, I let out everything I had been holding in for the sake of Emmett and Coach. Chase leans over to hold me as best he can over the console. He kisses my hair, soothing me with gentle shushing noises and assertions that it'll all be okay. I finally calm down enough for him to drive home. When we get home, I change into pajamas and crawl into bed. He does the same and he holds me while I tell him about baby Violet.

# Chapter 30

## Emmett

I don't know how long it has been since the funeral. Days? Weeks? Definitely not months. I don't think my agent would let me skip out on that much of the season. The coach and the team have been really supportive, as have all of my friends. Lola, most of all; that woman truly is a saint.

The last time I felt immense pain over my loss was the day after Violet died. I didn't take a Seconal when I woke up and it hurt like a bitch when I remembered what happened. So I just keep taking Seconal. The psychiatrist my uncle referred me to stopped prescribing them but the team doc wasn't so stingy. And when the sedatives started losing their edge, I started drinking.

The last thing I really remember clearly is the funeral. Putting my little angel in the ground was the hardest thing I have ever had to do in my life. Dad,

Uncle Pete, Lola and Chase, Cooper, Kevin and Deedee, Mr. and Mrs. Callaway and even Alma came to be there with me when I placed her in the ground next to my Mom in Texas. I got her a beautiful headstone with angel wings carved into it. It reads:

*Violet Grace Davis*

*My little angel,*
*I held you in my arms for a moment.*
*I will hold you in my heart forever.*
*Love Always, Daddy*

Since we all got back to Atlanta, I've spent my time drowning my sorrows. Mrs. Johnson comes twice a week to clean and make sure I have food and clean laundry. But I think she's scared of me now. Cooper and Lola and Chase come on alternating days, letting themselves in. I have been giving Chase a lot of shit. He's a better man than me, letting his wife tend to her first love in his grief. I should be nicer to him.

The phone rings. It's my agent again. He's screaming at me, telling me that if I don't get my ass in uniform and onto the ice in the next week, the team may cut me. I don't think they'd actually do that to a man who just lost his wife and child, but I don't want to find out. Besides, I need something to keep me occupied.

I head into training the next day. The guys are all really sympathetic, telling me how sorry they are. I've been gone for 6 weeks and they were starting to get really worried. I'm not worried, though. I have my sedatives to get me through.

I take a week or so to train and get back some stamina and then I'm back on the ice. There is no stopping the 'Bull in the China Shop' now. Those fuckers come at me, I slash, I elbow, I don't give a shit about the penalties. Bastards should know better than to fuck with me when I've got the puck.

One suspension. I'm back on the ice for two games. Another suspension. I'm back again. I get my third suspension and coach tries to quietly pull me aside after the game, while interviews are being done in the locker room.

"Listen, son. I know you're going through a rough time right now. And I don't blame you for wanting to take out your anger at the world. But doing it to your opponents isn't the right way to go about it. Maybe you need to take break for the rest of the season. You're a great player, we aren't going to trade you. We just want to make sure you take enough time to heal emotionally."

"What? You no longer like The Bull? He's not good enough for you?" I goad, poking him in the chest.

"Son, we love The Bull. The Bull has been very good for our team. But your current mental state has us concerned," coach says, trying to put his hand on my shoulder.

"Fuck you!" I push him away. I guess I pushed harder than I thought because he flies back into the wall. There's a loud thunk and then I watch as Coach slides down the wall, a trail of blood in his wake. And then, all I see are the camera flashes.

Before I know it, I'm down on the ground with my hands zip-tied behind me. Things go black.

I wake up in a cell. My head hurts, my throat feels like the Sahara, and I am having a hard time trying to figure out why I am here. And then it all comes flooding back to me. What have I done? I call for someone.

"What can I do for you, slugger?" The cop looks like he lives at the donut shop, his belly straining the buttons on his shirt like a cartoon. I'd laugh if my head didn't hurt so damn much.

"Am I allowed a phone call?" I ask, unsure of what to do in this situation.

"Actually, your bail was just posted and you are free to go. Just don't leave the state. While your coach doesn't want to press charges, the league just might," he says, unlocking the door to my cell and escorting me out to the main section of the police station. I sign some documents, get my personal effects back, and head out to the entryway where Cooper, Lola, and Chase are waiting.

Lola runs over to me and hugs me tightly. After a few moments, she pulls back and starts her tirade, "What the fuck, Emmett? What were you thinking?"

"Evidently, I wasn't thinking, Lola," I shout, pushing her away from me.

"I'm sorry, Emmett. I've just never seen this side of you. Frankly, it scares me," she says, sheepishly.

"Well, then, perhaps you'd best just leave me alone," I spit out.

"Hey, man," Chase butts in. "No need to get upset with her. She's concerned about you, Emmett. We all are."

"Aww, isn't that sweet? You know what, Chase? I'm tired of watching the two of you judge me all the time. Please just take her home and keep her the hell away from me."

"Mutt, you don't mean that," she whispers. She looks like I just slapped her across the face. I suppose I just did the verbal equivalent. But I can't deal with her right now.

"Maybe I do. Just go home and live your perfect little life," I say, turning away.

Coop comes over and stands in front of me. "Look, man. I know you had a hard night. I don't blame you for lashing out. Obviously you should have taken more time. But don't push away the people who care about you."

"Coop," Lola says through her tears. "Don't bother. He's not going to listen. Chase and I will go home. When he's ready to have me back in his life, he can call." She walks over to me and stands on her tiptoes to kiss my cheek. "I love you, Mutt, no matter what. Just, please take time to heal. And know that I am always here for you. Okay?"

After I don't say anything in response, she turns to Chase and he leads her out, glaring back over his shoulder at me as they head out the door.

"Come on. I'll take you home and perhaps you can explain what went on last night," Coop says, putting a hand on my shoulder.

I don't talk to him the entire ride home. Honestly, I don't know what happened last night. When we get to my building, there is a media circus outside. I'm thankful for two things: the first being that Coop has super dark tint on the windows of his Maserati; the second that I have a key fob for the parking garage on my keychain. We head into the secure area and he drops me off. I don't thank him. I just get out of the car and head upstairs.

When I get upstairs, I immediately grab my bottle of Seconal and a bottle of vodka to take them with me. I don't feel anything the rest of the day.

Time heals all wounds, they say. Except in my case. It seems the more time I spend with only my thoughts as company, the worse I get. But I just don't have the energy to get showered and dressed and leave the condo. Besides, there are press out there 24/7, just waiting for a glimpse of me.

It's been four weeks since I shoved my coach in front of my whole team and, evidently, the whole world. Coach didn't press charges. In his press conference, he said that I needed more time to heal from the emotional trauma caused by the deaths of my wife and daughter. The league representatives took their cue from coach and decided to be lenient with me. Their press conference announced my expulsion from the league. My agent called to say "fuck you very much". My dad called to tell me he's worried about me. And, even though Lola calls each and every day, I don't answer. Mrs. Johnson quit. The condo is a mess and I've been living without clean clothes for a few days. Coop has come by with some necessities, but he's the only person I'll see.

I spend my days in a drunk and drug filled stupor. At night I can't sleep, so I spend hours in the condo building's gym, sweating out my frustrations. And then I crash, wake up, lather, rinse, repeat. I have no idea what day of the week it is or even what month.

The psychiatrist is knocking at the door again. I let him in.

"Emmett. I see you've actually started to shower again. That's progress. Are you eating well?"

I shrug. "Cooper signed me up for a meal delivery service and the fridge always has prepared fruit and vegetables and milk. I'm doing okay."

"I see that Cooper is also keeping you well stocked in alcohol. Do you think that's wise?"

I raise my eyebrows. Who does this fucker think he is?

"I'm not judging, but perhaps there is a better way to deal with your grief," he says.

"You're right," I say, picking up the vase from the table beside me. I throw it at the wall.

"Did that make you feel better?"

Seriously, who is this prick?

I pick up a lamp and throw it, too. Then I get up and throw the side table. About the time when I pick up the chair to hurl it at the psychiatrist, he heads out the door. I continue in my rage until every single thing in the living room is broken.

Does it feel better? No, it doesn't. But I can't stop myself from doing the same thing in the kitchen. And my bedroom. And the guest bedroom. When I hit Violet's room, I calm down. I've got a bottle of Whyte & Mackay Original in my hand, drinking it like I drink water during training. I sit in the rocking chair and start to cry. I just want the pain to go away. So I open the full bottle of Seconal.

# Chapter 31

*Viola*

"Vi? It's Coop. I got a call from the psychiatrist. He suggested I might want to check in on Emmett later today. I was wondering if you might want to join me? I think it's time we have a come to Jesus with him."

I sigh. That's the last thing I need during finals. But I suppose it is time. We've let him fester. He needs to move forward. "All right. What time were you thinking?"

"I can come and grab you in about an hour, if that works," he says.

"Yeah, that'll be fine. See you then," I say, ending the call.

Chase looks up at me over his glasses. God, I love it when he does that. He's magically delicious, this man of mine. "Heading out?"

"Cooper wants to check in on Emmett, have a come to Jesus discussion," I say, walking over and sitting myself in Chase's lap. I run my hands through his dark, wavy hair.

He pouts. "I thought I had you all to myself tonight. We've both been studying so hard lately, I feel like the only time I see you is in bed."

"Well, we do have an hour before Cooper gets here," I say coyly.

He grins and stands up, holding me in his arms. "I'm sure there's something we can do for an hour."

I'm just coming out of the bathroom after freshening up, a big old after sex glow on my cheeks when I hear the doorbell ring. Chase opens the door for Coop. They do a little bro-hug. Those two have developed a serious bromance since that horrible night.

"Thanks for coming with me, Vi. I know he's been a dick to you, but I don't think I can do this alone," Coop says.

I grab my purse and jacket and give Chase a kiss as he hands me my cellphone.

"I know, Coop. I wish he'd let me in so you wouldn't have to bear the entire burden. But he's my Mutt and I know that he will need me in due time. I'll see you later, Champ."

We get into Coop's Maserati and head downtown.

"He used to talk about you all the time, you know. If he wasn't talking about hockey, he was talking about you. Stories about when you guys were younger, how he was going to marry you one day. It killed him to marry Whitney, Vi. But he did it for Violet."

"I know, Coop," I say, staring out the passenger window, willing the tears to just go back where they came from.

"I just want you to know that he loves you, Vi. You were his whole world until Violet. And now that he doesn't have either of you, I don't think he knows how to handle things."

We're silent for the remainder of the ride. We park in the underground lot connected to Emmett's building and head up the elevator to his floor. Coop uses his key to let us in. When he flips on the lights, I gasp. The place looks like it was hit by category 5 tornado. Literally every piece of furniture is broken. Every dish, every plate, every accent piece is trashed.

Fear grips my heart like a vise. "Emmett! Emmett where are you?" I start to run through every room searching for him with Cooper right behind me.

I stop in my tracks in the doorway to the nursery. Emmett is face down in a pool of vomit and lord knows what else. There's an empty bottle of scotch and then I see the empty bottle of sedatives as well. I race over and shout to Coop, "Call 911! NOW, Cooper!"

I feel for his pulse. It's there, but barely. I hear Cooper talking to the emergency operator as I pull Mutt's head into my lap. I am hysterical.

"Don't leave me, Mutt. Please don't leave me again! I need you, Mutt. Please, just don't leave me," I sob, rocking over him and running my fingers through his hair.

What seems like hours later, we hear the paramedics burst through the front door. Coop guides them back and they check his vitals, clear his throat, and put an oxygen mask on him. They bundle him up on a gurney and ask which of us wants to ride to the hospital with him. I volunteer.

I've never been in the back of an ambulance before. It's claustrophobic with the EMT, the gurney and me back there. I wish they had a window to roll down. All I smell is the vomit that is covering Emmett and me, and antiseptic. I don't know if I'll make it to the hospital before I lose my dinner.

Fortunately I am able to get a lot of fresh air when we get to the hospital. After they roll Emmett away and I answer some questions for the staff, I am told to wait until they assess him and come back for me. Coop joins me on the bench outside the ER to wait for Chase, who he called en route.

"I did not see that coming," Coop says, running his hand behind his neck.

"Me either," I squeak out before I see Chase running up to us. He's got some fresh clothes for me to change into. "Better save the hug and kiss for the clean clothes, Champ," I say, sadly.

After I freshen up, I head back out to the waiting room. Chase, being the wonderful man he is, has grabbed some coffee and snacks. I take my cup from the holder and take a sip. I hadn't realized how badly my hands were shaking until I end up spilling half of my coffee on the floor while putting it down.

"That's just fucking fantastic!" I shout, needing

to let out some of the stress that has been building inside me since we walked into Emmett's place.

Chase comes over to rub my shoulders and ease some of the tension. I squeeze his hand, silently thanking him for his support.

He looks at Coop. "You okay, man?"

Coop just shakes his head. And then he breaks down. "I don't know what else I could have done. I put up with the silent treatment, I just let myself in, even bringing bolt cutters to snap the chain lock when he put it across. I wasn't taking no for an answer. He pushed everyone else away but me. And I failed him."

I run over and put my arms around him, hugging his head to my shoulder. "Coop, you did more than anyone else. There was nothing more that you could have done. This is not your fault. He's going to get through this. We will make sure of it," I vow.

Coop wipes a tear or two from his eyes with the back of his hand and then looks up at me. "The more time I spend with you, the more I understand his love for you. You're truly amazing, Vi," he says as he kisses me on the cheek.

"Hey now, Coop, that's my wife you're smoochin'," Chase chastises him in jest, breaking the tension a bit.

We wait in silence for another half an hour or so before the doctor comes out to tell us he's okay. He was lucky to have thrown up so much, as it helped get the sedatives and booze out of his system. But they still pumped his stomach for good measure. He's stable and awake if we want to see him before they put him on a mandatory 72-hour psychiatric hold.

Coop gets up and turns back to me. I shake my head no. He pleads with his eyes.

Chase rubs my back and says, "You should go, Vi. Even if he doesn't want you there, he needs to know you care."

I get up, take a deep breath, and head back to the private room they have him in. It's not far from the waiting area where we were seated. When Coop opens the door, Emmett looks up. I don't know what I was expecting, but anger certainly wasn't it.

"Get the fuck out of here," he shouts, pointing directly at me.

"What did she do to you, Emmett? She's been nothing but patient, putting up with your shit. You're lucky she's even here after what an asshole you've been to her. She loves you, for Christ's sake. Don't push her away."

"If she loved me, she would have waited for me," he screams.

I turn around and grab the door handle to exit when he says, "Go ahead. Walk out the door, Lola. Go back to your husband and forget about me."

I don't turn around to look at him when I open my mouth and say, "Do you really want me out of your life, Mutt? Is this what you need to make you happy?"

"Yes. I can't even look at you anymore," he spits.

I take a moment to gain a small amount of composure.

"Then, I'll go, Mutt. But before I do, I just want

you to know I'll always love you. Always. Please, just take care of yourself. Find whatever you need to make you happy."

I open the door and walk out, not looking back. I can't. It will end me.

I don't say a word to Chase, he just gets up, takes my hand, and leads me to the car. I am silent the entire ride home. Chase knows not to push, that I'll open up when I am good and ready. But I don't think I can ever open up about this. Emmett Davis just ripped my heart from my chest and crushed it with his bare hands. He's done some shitty stuff before, but this? I don't think I can get over this.

I meant what I said. I will always love him. And I do hope that he can somehow find happiness. I know that he's not himself right now. But he just cut me to the core. And no matter how understanding Chase is, I don't think he'll truly get why I am so heartbroken over this.

When we get home, Chase runs a hot bath for me and brings me a big glass of wine after I'm settled. He sits on the edge of the tub and starts to massage my shoulders. I ask him to put the wine glass on the counter and join me.

When he settles in behind me, I lean back against him and sigh.

"Are you ready to tell me?"

I think about it for a moment before I say, "I don't think we'll be seeing Emmett Davis for a long, long time. If ever."

I feel him kiss the top of my head. "I'm sorry,

Petal. He's pretty messed up right now. He's directing his anger at you."

"I know. I just... I don't know if this is something I can get past, if he even does. It cut too deep," I say, picking up his hand and kissing the back of it.

I feel him stiffen. "What did he say to you, Vi?"

"It doesn't matter anymore, Chase. I'm done," I tell him, hoping I've managed to convey the conviction I don't feel in my tone.

"I love you, Petal," he whispers before he starts kissing down my neck.

"I love you back," I murmur.

He stands up and holds his hand out to me, stepping out of the tub. I step out and he grabs a towel and pats me down, then himself, before leading me to our bed. He stops me at the edge, turning me around to face him. He sits down and I straddle his lap, wrapping my arms around his neck.

"Let me show you how much I love you, Petal. Right now. I want you to know how much I love you," he rasps.

I nod, leaning forward to kiss him. The way he kisses me, I know without a doubt that I am his whole world. I kiss him back with everything I have, hoping to show him he is my everything. He lies back, taking me with him. I feel his hands move down my sides. He rolls me over and props himself up on his arms.

He pushes my hair back out of my face and breathes, "You're so beautiful. I remember the first time I saw you. We were 8. You and Emmett came over to play the day after Thanksgiving. You were wearing a green dress and you had your hair down, held back in a black ribbon. Even though Emmett was holding your hand, showing me that you were his, I couldn't help but stare at you. You were so beautiful, even then. I know I must have seemed like a complete dork, following you around, but I couldn't help myself."

He bends down and kisses the tip of my nose. "I still can't help myself around you, Petal." He kisses me again and then guides himself into me.

Tonight isn't about passion. It's about love, pure and simple. He kisses me gently as he slowly makes love to me. Every kiss tells me how much he loves me, every plunge into me emphasizing the point. When he knows I'm close, he stares into my eyes and tells me he loves me over and over as I tip over the edge.

I know now, more than ever, that he was the right choice.

# Chapter 32

## Emmett

I cannot believe it's been a year since I got out of rehab. Cooper and my Dad managed to convince me to go to Pine Grove Treatment Center in Missouri. They both drove there with me and saw me settled.

I was admitted to a dual diagnosis treatment program. They helped me through the grieving process, as well as the detox process. It shed a lot of light on some things, in particular, how badly I mistreated Lola. I wouldn't blame her if she never talked to me again. But I'm hoping that she will. I need her forgiveness to move on.

Dad got the condo cleaned up and sold in my absence. I bought a new condo downtown. I needed a fresh start. When I got back, Coop hired me on as his Chief Operating Officer. He made a lot of progress with his real estate empire in the short months of my treatment, having already made a name for himself beforehand. He needed me to back him up and start overseeing the contracts and negotiations, as there was just too much going on for him to do it all. It's given me something to get up for every day. And surprisingly, I am enjoying it.

I wake up every day at 5:30 in the morning, I throw together a protein shake and drink it while I head to the gym. I do cardio for an hour and then spend another 30 minutes lifting weights. I shower, get dressed, and I'm in the office by 8:00, having stopped to grab a protein-heavy breakfast at the diner around the corner. I eat breakfast and have my coffee at my desk while I check emails and then I get to my phone calls, contract reviews, and meetings.

Every night, Cooper and I head out, rubbing elbows, making business contacts, and all that. Don't worry, drinking is not even a temptation for me. I know that my excessive drinking was to deal with my grief. Now that I've dealt with it, I don't need to drink anymore. I may have the occasional beer or scotch to celebrate a big win for Forsythe, Inc., but most of the time, I just sip water or club soda.

I also meet women. Lots of women. They throw themselves at me; they all want to tame the bad boy in me. That's the funny thing. I don't need to be tamed because I already am. Unless the woman in front of me is Viola Anne Callaway, I don't want to be tied down to her. If it means I never marry again, so be it.

That was another big revelation that came out of rehab: that I couldn't have a serious relationship because in my own twisted way, I was saving myself for Lola. I'm not about to go and break up her marriage, although I have thought about it. A lot.

Today, though—today is a big day. It's the first time I'll see her since the night I told her to walk away from me. Cooper and Chase have become pretty tight over the past two years since my world went sideways. I asked Cooper to talk to Chase about me arranging some time to talk to Lola so I can make my amends. She finally agreed to it.

I am really nervous right now, sitting in my car in front of their house. I close my eyes, take ten deep, cleansing breaths, and then get out of the car with a bouquet of peonies in hand. Chase opens the door before I even have a chance to knock.

"Emmett. How are you, man?" His voice isn't harsh, but it's not exactly friendly.

"Better, Chase. Much better, thanks. I want to apologize. I was a real prick to you when all you were trying to do was help. You are nothing but a good guy and I shat all over you. I am incredibly sorry," I say, rubbing my hand behind my neck.

He nods for a moment and then says, "I know you were going through a rough time, Em. And I have already forgiven you for how you treated me. But I can't forgive you for how you treated Vi. If she forgives you, then I'll let it go. But hear me on this: you ever hurt her again, so help me, I will straight up murder your ass."

"Understood," I respond.

"She's out back on the patio," he says, turning to head into his office.

I make my way through their home. I am beyond astounded at how beautiful it is. I haven't seen it since they purchased it. The difference is like night versus day. Lola did such an amazing job. She really is talented. It doesn't surprise me that she's been courting offers from all the major architecture firms in the city. What does surprise me is that she's decided to open up her own office, focusing on restoration projects.

I smile, thinking back to the day we met when she was telling me all about the antebellum homes along the way back to her place.

I stop at the French doors that lead to the patio from the great room. They are open and I can see Lola lying in a chaise. I can tell she's asleep, her book is resting on her lap and her mouth is open just slightly. I always loved watching her sleep. After a few moments, I head through the doors.

I sit next to her, put the peonies down, and decide to move the book. When I lift it up, she jolts awake and puts her hand on the book, pushing it down.

"Emmett! You scared me!"

"I'm sorry. I just wanted to make sure you didn't drop your book," I say, smiling.

She lifts the book up, showing me her slightly swollen belly. She must be just past the first trimester.

I look up at her. "Wow! Congratulations! How far along are you?"

"Sixteen weeks. Pete's taking good care of me," she says shyly.

"That's fantastic, Lola. I'm so happy for you. Are

you going to find out the gender?"

"You know me well enough to know how much of a planner I am. I need to know so I can decorate the room, and get all the registries together..." She trails off with a laugh and then looks down.

"Thanks for letting me come to see you. I'm sorry I haven't been sooner, but I needed to take care of all my smaller atonements before I could see you. I know I don't deserve your forgiveness. I was an asshole to you before I even started drinking and getting addicted to Seconal. But you are the most important person in my life, whether or not you believe me. You know more about me than my father, more than Cooper.

"You have always had my heart and you always will. You'll always be my best girl. I never should have said those things to you. I was horrible to you and I can only hope that one day I can earn your forgiveness and your trust. I will do whatever it takes, Lola. Anything," I say, choking up.

She's holding my hand, tears running down her cheeks.

"Emmett, I'm not going to lie. You hurt me more with your words than your actions ever did. You broke a part of me that day. And while I've had time to ponder and heal, I think—I know I need a bit more time. I want you to move past this, and for the purposes of your recovery, you have my forgiveness. I still love you. I always will. But my trust and friendship is going to have to be earned."

I nod. "I thank you for your forgiveness. And I

accept that I have to earn your trust and friendship again. I deserve that, Lola, and so much more. You are the most compassionate and wonderful human being I have ever met."

We hold hands for a few minutes. I can see she's fatigued, both emotionally and physically.

"Why don't I help you inside and I'll head home? I'll get Chase to help you upstairs for a nap," I say, helping her up.

"Thank you, Emmett."

Chase meets us at the doors to his office. "Is everything all right?" he asks, giving me a menacing look.

"It's fine, Champ. I'm just tired. Emmett's heading back to town and I'm going to go upstairs for a nap. I ended up falling asleep outside," Lola says, leaning on Chase.

He gives her a squeeze and then says, "I'll come up and get you settled after I see Emmett out."

"Goodbye, Lola. Thank you again."

She smiles and nods.

When he closes the front door behind us, Chase turns to me and holds out his hand.

"I hope that this helps your recovery. I know you're a good guy, Emmett, she wouldn't love you so much if you weren't. Just take it slow with her. Especially now. I don't want her upset more than she has to be. All right?"

I shake his hand and say, "Got it. Thank you for letting me visit today. And congratulations."

He grins. "She's going to be an amazing mother,

isn't she?"

"I can't think of anyone who is better for the job," I say, stepping down the stairs to my car.

I drive back to Atlanta. It's mid-afternoon on a Saturday. I call Coop. He's just finishing up a round of golf so we decide to meet up for a drink.

"Why didn't you tell me, man?" I ask.

He shrugs. "Wasn't my news to tell. Besides, no one knew the best way to tell you."

He lifts his glass of beer and empties half of it.

"How'd it go?"

"Well, she forgave me, so that was good. But I've got a lot of work ahead of me to win back her friendship," I say, swirling the lime in my soda water around the heavy cut-crystal glass with my straw.

"We knew this was going to be the case, right? But it's good. I think you need to earn it."

I smile. "Yup, that's something I do need to earn." I point to a brunette at the bar with giant fake breasts and say, "But that, I won't need to."

Coop bleats like a sheep. "You're horrible, man. Have fun." He claps me on the back, throws some cash on the table and stands up. "I've got to go and meet Tiffany at some art show in a bit. I'll see you Monday."

# Chapter 33

*Viola*

"Sweet fucking Christ, just give me the God damn epidural already!"

"Petal, Pete says we can't do it just yet. You still need to dilate a bit more," Chase murmers.

"Don't make me twist your nut sack, Chase Butler! I will do it, so help meeeeAAARGH!" Fucking contractions. I've been blessed with back labor. It's fucking fabulous.

"Why don't we try—"

"Pete, if you tell me to walk or squat or go doggie style again, I will tear off your testicles and feed them to you with a spoon!"

"Just one more centimeter, Petal. We don't want to slow down your labor," Chase says, wincing as I crush his hand with the inhuman strength I suddenly seem to possess.

"Actually," Pete says, sensing I'd make good on

my threat, "Let's take another peek, shall we?"

He settles my feet in the stirrups and takes a look.

When he stands up, taking off his gloves, he says, "We can call for the anesthesiologist now."

"Thank God," Chase says a little too loud.

I glare at him, willing him to burst into flames.

Thirty minutes later, I'm relatively comfortable, the contractions more of a nuisance than anything.

Six hours after that, I'm positively tuckered. This birthing thing? It's not easy. I have no idea how women do it in the middle of nowhere without epidurals or ice chips. I hear Pete shout, "One more push, Vi!" and so help me, I bear down with all I've got. I feel the baby slide out of me.

I see Chase crying as he cuts the umbilical cord. I haven't heard her cry. Oh dear Lord, please no! And then, I hear it. It's shrill in the confines of the room, but I hear my little darling cry and it's the most glorious sound in the world.

The nurses take her for her APGAR test and a little cleaning and then bring her over to me. I can't even describe how I feel when I hold little Ruby Ella Butler in my arms. She's stopped crying and is trying to open her eyes. When she finally does, I smile down at her and say, "Hi, sweetling! I'm your Mama. And that guy there? He's your Daddy. And we love you more than anything else in the whole wide world."

Chase snorts and says, "That's what you said to the anesthesiologist."

I smack his arm and say, "Hush, you. Just look at

your beautiful baby girl."

"Can I hold her?"

I nod and he gently lifts her from me.

I melt watching him with her. I watch him pout at her little yawn, lean in for a kiss and whisper, "I love you, Ruby." I see him pick up her little hand and hold it in his, kissing each finger, opening the blanket to count each and every toe.

"We should get her back to Mama for a feeding now, Chase. But don't you worry, you'll have lots of time for cuddles," Pete says, smiling and clapping him on the back.

"Watch it, Pete! Precious cargo here!"

Chase gently places her back on my chest as I open my gown to guide her to my breast. I rub my nipple against her lips, like the lactation consultant told me to and she opens her mouth and gets a grip on it. The lactation consultant pokes her head in really close and then nods. "You can hear her gulping. It looks like she's got a decent latch. She'll probably conk out pretty soon. Try on the other side when she wakes up. If you have any issues, have someone come and get me."

Pete smiles and then tells us he'll be back in a bit to check in. When we're alone in the room, Chase looks at me and smiles. "I love you so much, Petal. You did great today." He kisses me softly on the lips.

"I'm sorry for all the cussing and the broken fingers," I say sheepishly.

"I never knew you could curse like that. It was impressive," he laughs, looking at me totally differently than ever before. "Next time I need someone cussed out, I know who to call."

True to the consultant's words, little Ruby passes out. I snuggle with her for a bit, and then pass her over to her Daddy so I can get a bit of rest.

I wake up when they're moving me from the birthing room to my overnight room.

"Your folks are here. I'll go and get them after you and Ruby get settled," Chase says, rocking back and forth on his feet with Ruby against his chest. He kisses her on the head for what must be the millionth time. It makes me smile.

"Sounds great, Champ. You know what?"

"What's that, love?"

"Daddy is a sexy look on you."

"Careful. We're not allowed to do that for at least six weeks. Besides, that's how we got into this mess to begin with," he chuckles.

I'm feeding Ruby again when my folks come into the room. Mama's in tears and Daddy looks so proud. I finish up, give the little one a burping, and then pass her to her Grandma.

Mama and Daddy fuss over Ruby. She's the second grandchild, but you'd never know it. They're totally enthralled. Carlyle, Christine, and my nephew Connor join us soon after, but they don't stay too long; they know I'm exhausted. And that I'll need all the help I can get when we get home tomorrow.

They make plans with Chase to come by in the afternoon with food and supplies, and then they head out, leaving Chase and I with our darling daughter.

The first few weeks of motherhood have been a struggle. Breastfeeding is harder than it looks. But after several visits from the lactation consultant, we've finally got it down. It's one of my favorite parts of motherhood, this bonding time with her. Chase is a little jealous, so I've been pumping so that he can feed her and snuggle. She's a good little sleeper, going in 4-hour stretches at night with a feeding in between.

I didn't take on any new clients after the start of my third trimester. I knew I'd want some time with her. That's why I chose to hang out my own shingle. We knew we wanted to start our family. This way, I can take on as few or as many clients as I want. A well-planned pictorial of our home came out around my graduation and I had people pounding down the door the day I had my 'grand opening' in my home office.

Chase started a consulting company, also out of the house. It gives him the freedom to be his own boss, he gets to work on a number of different projects, and still work on his own projects for profit. He's currently working with one of the software titans out in Silicon Valley and has to travel back and forth every few weeks. When he's away it stinks, but it keeps him busy.

Daddy's been writing up a storm. He's being touted as 'the next Tom Clancy' and has been able to hire folks to look after the plantation so he can write full time. When my nephew Connor was born, he and Mama bought a house out here in Druid Hills to be close to all of us, but they go back and forth. Daddy says he does his best writing at the plantation. It's nice to have them close by when they are in town.

Today we're having some guests over to meet Ruby for the first time, Emmett among them. I am nervous because this may not be a good thing for him. I don't want to trigger anything. Cooper, Chase, and I discussed this a lot. We decided to give Emmett the option. He's been going to therapy twice a week since he left the treatment center. He discussed it at length with his therapist and the decision was that there was no way he could avoid babies forever and that, if he wanted to be part of my life, he was going to have to get used to Ruby.

While he seemed happy for me during my pregnancy, I could also see it pained him. I'm not sure if that was because I was pregnant with Chase's child or because of his own child lost.

We hired a caterer so no one would have to fuss. I just want everyone to relax and enjoy the afternoon. Mama, Christine, and I are sitting on the patio watching Connor on the play structure with Carlyle. Mama's clutching her granddaughter to her chest while she can, knowing she's going to have to give her up soon. Chase and both of our dads are over by the new outdoor kitchen, talking grills and other caveman stuff. Chase's mom and new husband haven't arrived yet.

I stand up when I see Coop and Emmett walk through the French doors. Both of them have boxes and bags piled high. I run over to help.

"Good lord, did you boys buy out Toys' R' Us?" I can't contain my laughter.

"Uncle Coop and Uncle Emmett have to make their presence in her life known," Emmett says with a huge smile on his face.

"Well, thank you! She's officially, truly good and spoiled now," I say, transferring boxes and gift bags over to a nearby table.

Chase and the dads come over to shake hands and say hello. When all the man business is done, Mama brings Ruby over and hands her off to me. Chase puts his hand on my back and we guide Emmett and Cooper over to a separate seating area, as suggested by the therapist. Coop's already been to see Ruby a few times—I seriously cannot believe how crazy that guy is over her; it's pretty damn cute—so he takes a seat in one of the chairs.

I sit down on the love seat and Emmett looks to me for confirmation before he sits down next to me.

"Are you sure you want to do this, Em? We can wait awhile longer if you need more time," I say.

He takes a deep breath and then says, "Lola, I need you in my life. I need to do this."

I nod and then shift over to place Ruby in his arms. He's so gentle with her, it seems so natural. I watch his face as he looks at her. When I see the tears start to fall, I put my hand on his arm and ask, "Are you all right? Do you want me to take her?"

"No," he says in a whisper. "It's—she's so beautiful, just like her mother."

He bends over and places a soft kiss on her

forehead, giving me flashbacks to another night that seems so long ago. It brings tears to my eyes.

"Ruby Ella Butler, I'm your Uncle Emmett. It's nice to meet you," he says, shaking her little hand. She gurgles at him in response. "I want you to know, here and now, that if you ever need anything, you can always come to Uncle Emmett. I might not be good at shopping for dresses, but I will show you how to bait a fishhook, climb a tree, tie a proper constrictor knot, how to execute the perfect wedgie, and how to throw a punch. I'm hoping you won't need to use the last two, but I want you to know them just in case."

We all chuckle. "Your mama is the most important person in the world to me, so you're very important to me, too," he continues. "And I promise that I will always be there for you. No matter what."

I can't swallow past the lumps in my throat. He kisses her a few more times and then she smiles up at him. It might just be her first non-gas-induced smile. He beams up at me.

"How are you feeling?"

"Honestly? At peace," he says. "She is very precious, Lola. And I want to be a part of her life; to protect her, teach her things, and spoil her rotten."

I look at Chase. He nods and says, "Well, then, you are welcome over here at any time. I like knowing my girls have other protectors when I'm away. Family is one thing, but I know that both of you would give everything it takes to keep my girls safe."

Emmett stands up to pass Ruby to Chase. They share a side bro-hug, taking care not to crush little

Ruby in between them. Coop stands up to steal Ruby away.

"Hey, I didn't get any Ruby time. You want to come and see your Uncle Cooper, don't you darling? You love your Uncle Cooper. Yes you do!"

I roll my eyes. "Dear lord, but you are done for, Cooper Forsythe!"

"Don't you listen to your mama, darling. I'm not done for. I just like to shower beautiful girls with attention. Yes, I do," he continues to baby talk, walking her over to look at the trees and flowers.

Chase sits down in the chair Cooper vacated. "Em, I'm proud of you. If you ever feel that you need help, just let us know. I know that things aren't as solid as they used to be with us, but they're getting there. Just know that you're family. Always have been. All right?"

Emmett nods, swallowing hard. "Thanks, Chase. I appreciate that more than you know."

"Can I get you something to drink? We've got water, soda, coffee, juice..." he trails off, not knowing what other non-alcoholic items we have to offer.

"A water with lemon would be great, thanks," Emmett replies.

"Will do. Back in a few," Chase says, planting a kiss on the top of my head before he heads into the house.

"Are you sure you're okay, Mutt?"

He smiles, "That's the first time you've called me Mutt in a long, long time. Too long, if you ask me."

I smile. "Yeah, well, I think you've finally earned

it."

"I have? I'm glad. It means a lot to me," he says, taking my hand. "I thought it was going to be difficult after what happened with Violet. But when I saw Ruby I realized she's an extension of you, and it made it easy. I meant every word I said, Lola. I'll do anything for her, for you."

I squeeze his hand, looking in his eyes for confirmation. "I know you would, Mutt."

# Chapter 34

## Emmett

Mmmm... I like waking up to my dick in the mouth of a beautiful woman. It's honestly the best way to wake up. The only thing that would make it perfect is if that beautiful woman was Lola.

Lola. Crap! What time is it? I look at the clock and groan as I pull Denise's head off my cock. "I'm sorry, but I have to be somewhere."

"At 11:00 on a Sunday morning?" She looks appalled. That's what I get for picking up a 22-year-old.

"Yes. It's incredibly important. Not that I didn't enjoy last night. Or this morning, for that matter. But I really need to get showered and dressed and run before I'm late," I say. I'd invite her to shower with me, but I've tried that before. It always ends with me running behind.

"Fine," she huffs, as she gets off the bed and starts

digging around for her clothes. "Do you think we can see each other again?"

"I don't think so, Denise. I'm not that guy. I told you that last night," I say, grabbing some boxer briefs from my drawer.

"You did. It was just so good, I want more," she says, eyes downcast and a small smile on her lips.

"It was, but that's my rule and I don't have time to explain it to you," I say, walking over. I give her one of my heartbreaker kisses and escort her to the front door, planting another one on her before I open it. "Thanks for everything."

She looks positively livid as I close the door.

I have had no problem telling women up front exactly what the deal is: I only do one night stands. It's not that I'm a dick. I just don't trust women after what happened with Whitney. The only woman I truly trust is Lola. I'm not willing to even try with anyone else. It's not worth it.

My therapist has a lot to say about that, but I don't care. I have too many women trying to dig their claws into me. I'm not going to let it happen again. It can't happen if I don't let it.

I hop in the shower and quickly rub one out before washing, needing to do something with my raging hard-on. I don't have time to shave, so I leave the scruff on my chin. "So manly," I laugh as I scratch my stubble in the mirror before heading to get dressed. I grab my wallet, my phone, my keys and then I grab the bags on the console table before I head out to my car and race to Druid Hills, pulling up in front of the Butler household right at noon.

I know better than to ring the doorbell so I let myself in, heading out to the backyard.

My God. I can't believe Ruby is three today! Where has the time gone?

Chase is as big a name as Bill Gates or Steve Jobs. Lola's the person to call if you want to restore a historic property. Cooper and I own a good chunk of the rental and commercial properties surrounding Atlanta and some in-town. He recently asked Tiffany to marry him. Kevin has made a name for himself as District Attorney. And Deedee is now pregnant with baby number two. Frankly, I'm surprised she wanted to have another after hearing stories of her delivering Cady; it wasn't rough by any stretch of the imagination but she was such a princess about it!

Lola and Chase hired Alma to come and run their house and look after Ruby, so I have been able to reconnect with her. And Dad's back in Georgia, over in Macon.

I stop at the edge of the patio and just take it all in. These wonderful people are all my family, related or not. Even Chase's folks and their respective significant others have accepted me as one of their own. I smile and step outside.

Ruby spies me and runs over to hug me around my knees. "Uncle Mutt! Are all of those presents for me?"

I put the bags down on the ground and scoop her up, giving her a bear hug and smothering her with kisses, as I always do. "I don't know. Is it someone else's birthday today?"

Slapping my shoulder she says, "No, silly!"

I can't help but laugh; she truly is her mother's daughter. "Well, then, I guess they're all for you!"

She squeals in delight as I tickle her and then put her down. I pick the bags back up, grab her hand and we walk over to the gift table where I am accosted by Alma.

"There's my boy!" Alma says, squeezing the breath out of me.

"Alma," I whine. "I'm a grown-ass man!"

She smacks my back. "Language! You'll always be my boy."

"Yes, ma'am," I say. I love getting a rise out of her. Always have.

Lola spots me and comes over, shaking her head. "Nick of time, Mutt. Who kept you distracted this morning?"

I laugh. "Come on, I overslept!"

"And *why* did you oversleep?" She arches an eyebrow at me.

"Okay, you got me," I say, planting a kiss on her forehead.

"Ewww! I don't know where those have been!" She wipes her forehead while I laugh. "Seriously, if we ever have a son, you're not allowed to 'foster him' when he's older. That shit ain't right, Mutt."

"What shit ain't right?" Chase comes up, giving me a handshake before handing me a Solo cup of seltzer water with lime.

"His love life, that's what," Lola says, looking

disgusted. I know she's joking. We've discussed my lack of trust and intimacy before. She may not like it, but she gets it.

Chase hoots out a laugh. "Petal, you know you ruined him for all others. You did the same for me." He may be joking, but it's the truth.

"Oh, stop it! Is the big surprise ready?" She asks, suddenly serious.

"Yup!" Chase says, popping the 'p'. "Are you sure you're okay with it?"

"It's too late to back out now. But you might not like having to buy new furniture in a few months," she says.

"Mama! Mama! Can I open my presents yet?" Ruby tugs on the hem of Lola's dress.

"Of course! Let's get going!"

We all sit and ooh and ahh while Ruby tears through the wrapping on each of the hundred presents she got. One might assume I am exaggerating, but not by much. That child is spoiled rotten, but you'd never know it. She's just as gracious and kind and caring as her mother. I don't even think she went through that terrible stage everyone talks about. I don't know if that bodes ill for the future, but I think this kid is very well rounded and is going to go places. Of course, I'm biased.

When she gets to one of mine, she comes over and sits on my lap. "Uncle Mutt, will you help me with this one?"

"How did you know that was from me?" I ask, looking at her through narrowed eyes.

"It says 'Mutt' right there," she says in a 'duh' voice, pointing to the tag. She's only three and she can read. Seriously going places, this one.

"Oh, silly me! Let's see what's in here, then," I say, holding the small box out to her. She rips the wrapping paper off and opens the box.

"I love it, Uncle Mutt! Will you please put it on me?" She turns her little back to me and moves the curtain of her auburn hair aside. I place the necklace around her neck and then she turns back to me, holding up the pendant.

I help her open it up. On one side is a picture of Coop, on the other, me.

"This is so you never forget your two favorite uncles," I say.

"I heard that!" pipes Carlyle.

She gives me a big hug and a kiss. "Don't tell anyone else, but you're my favorite," she whispers in my ear.

I kiss her on the cheek and whisper back, "I know."

Chase brings out a box with a big ribbon on the top. Judging by the scratching noises, there's something desperately trying to get out.

Ruby runs over. "What is it, Daddy?" A soft bark gives it away before Chase sets down the box and the top flies off.

"Oh my goodness! Daddy! Thank you! Thank you! Thank you!" She tackles him and kisses him before turning her attentions to the black and white Boston Terrier pup, who licks her without even thinking twice.

She hugs him tightly. "What are you going to name him, Ruby?" Lola asks.

"I'm going to call him Mutt," she says proudly.

No one can control the laughter. "Why Mutt?" Chase asks, barely able to get the words out.

"Well, I love my Uncle Mutt. And this puppy is going to be my new best friend. Mommy calls her best friend Mutt."

I can't contain my smile. I love this little girl.

Chase is still howling with laughter, "Well, then, Mutt it is."

# Chapter 35

## Chase

Part of me always knew that getting in bed with the government would not lead to good things. But the opportunity to do the work I have been doing was too big to pass up. Annals of history big. But now I know it's not worth it.

I look down at the photo of my beautiful girls that I keep in my wallet, a tear rolling down my cheek.

"I love you, Petal," I whisper. "You, too, Ruby. Daddy loves you."

# Chapter 36

*Viola*

Work has been non-stop lately. I don't know where all this money is coming from, but it seems everyone is buying up historic properties and bringing them into the now. I'm traveling all over the state, sometimes into others, too. It is just crazy.

I'm currently down in Savannah, working on a townhouse that hasn't had its walls opened since the 1940's. It's a far cry better than the abandoned antebellum home I've been working on outside of Macon, but it's still pretty horrible. I'm desperately trying to wrap things up with the foreman so I can head home. Poor Ruby's been without Mama and Daddy for a few days. She loves staying with Grandma Lu and Grandpa Jack, but I know she misses me something fierce. And I return the sentiment.

My phone rings. I see it's Mama, so I send the call to voicemail. It rings again immediately. I do the same thing. She needs to not bother me when I'm working. On the third call, I know this isn't something that can't wait.

I excuse myself and answer. "What's going on, Mama? Is everything all right?"

"Vi—baby girl—can you get someone to drive you home?"

"What's going on, Mama? Is Ruby all right?" I can feel the bile start to rise in my throat. I've never heard Mama sound like this.

"Ruby's fine, baby. It's Chase. The plane he was on went down," she says before letting out a sob.

My knees give out and I crumble to a heap on the floor. "What do you mean it went down, Mama?"

I hear Daddy take the phone from my mom. "Vi, baby. We don't have much information yet. All we know is that the plane went down after the pilot mentioned something about low oil pressure. They were heading over the Rockies at the time. It's not looking good."

I can't even cry right now. I'm in complete and total shock. The foreman sees me and races over to get me before my head smacks the floor as I pass out.

I wake up at home. I'm not sure what time it is. Ruby and little Mutt are curled up beside me. I see Daddy asleep in the comfy chair.

"Daddy?" I whisper. "Daddy?"

I see him slowly wake up and then stand to walk

over to the bed.

"How did I get home? How long have I been here? What's going on?"

The tears in Daddy's eyes tell me that they've had more news about Chase's plane.

"Your foreman, Joe, grabbed you as you passed out. He picked up the phone and I told him what was going on. He drove you home in your car. I hired a car service to take him back to Savannah. You were in and out of consciousness during the drive. I called Pete and he had a friend come meet you here when you got home. You're in shock and you need to rest. Dr. Reynolds will be back tomorrow to check in on you."

"Tell me," I say, swallowing hard.

Daddy shakes his head no.

"Tell. Me."

"They found the wreckage, Vi. No one made it," Daddy says.

I can't stop the violent sobs that escape me. My love—my life—is gone. Daddy picks up Ruby and takes her out of my room, not wanting me to wake her up. A few moments later, Mama comes in and holds me while I cry.

I don't remember falling back to sleep, but evidently I did. I wake up to little Mutt licking my face. I cuddle him to me for a few minutes. And then I hear the bedroom door open. Ruby quietly walks over to the bed and climbs on. She comes over to me and wraps her arms around me and starts to cry.

"Mama? Where's Daddy? Why is everyone so sad? I want my Daddy," she sobs.

I start to cry, too. I do my best to keep it in check, smoothing her hair away from her face before kissing her forehead. "Daddy's with the angels now, sweetling. Daddy's going to watch over us from heaven now."

Ruby and I cry together for a while until she falls back to sleep, her little body curled into my torso, head on my shoulder.

Dr. Reynolds finds us like this about an hour later. He attempts to help Ruby and I discuss the accident. My parents are in the room with us while this is going on. When Ruby asks why she won't be able to see Daddy at the funeral, I lose it. Mama and Daddy take Ruby out and I sit with Dr. Reynolds. He hands me a tissue, and after a few minutes, I manage to calm myself down.

"How do I go on? How do I find the strength, the will to get up every day? How do I... I don't know how I can live without him." I burst into tears again.

Dr. Reynolds says, "You get up every day for your little girl, Viola. Ruby's going to need you as much as you need her. You lean on your friends and family for support. You cry when you need to. You talk to me—or another professional—as much as you need to get through this. It won't be easy, Viola. But day after day it will get less difficult. You're lucky to have a lot of love surrounding you."

He tells me to let him know if I feel the need for antidepressants or medication to help me sleep. I thank him and then head into the shower.

I think about what he said. I think we're just

going to have to take this hour by hour, day by day. I throw on some yoga pants and a t-shirt. I am not about to impress anyone today. When I get downstairs, I see Mama feeding Ruby a grilled cheese sandwich and some carrot sticks.

"Would you like something to eat, baby girl?"

"I think all I'll be able to manage is toast, Mama. Thanks," I say, going to grab a large bottle of water from the fridge. I take off the cap and have half of it in me before I sit down next to Ruby. I lean over and kiss her on the head and give her a hug.

"I'm sorry if I upset you, Mama," she says sadly. "I didn't mean to make you cry."

I squeeze her tight, "Sweetling, you didn't upset me or make me cry. Like you, I am still trying to figure out how to deal with what happened. I'm sorry if you thought that. I just didn't know how to get out what I was feeling, so I started to cry."

I can feel her nodding against me. "Is it okay to cry?"

"Of course it is, Ruby. Dr. Reynolds told me to cry as much as I needed to. And you should do the same thing. He also told us to take care of each other. If you need me, you come and get me, whether it be for a cry, a hug, it doesn't matter what. You just come to me— or Alma or Grandma and Grandpa, Uncle Cooper, Uncle Mutt—and you tell us what you need. Okay?"

"Okay, Mama," she says. I kiss her again and then loosen my hold on her.

"It's hard right now, but we will get through this," I say, with as much conviction as I can muster.

The doorbell rings. I hear Alma shout that she'll get it. A few moments later, Cooper and Emmett come into the kitchen. Emmett comes over to me immediately and pulls me to him, Cooper takes Ruby. I can't stop the sobs that come out of me. He walks me over to the sectional in the great room and sits down, pulling me into his lap. I grip his shirt and cry until I run dry. I'm not sure how long that lasts, but at some point Cooper brought Ruby over as well. She's fallen asleep with her head over his shoulder, still in the same position he likely carried her over in. He's kissing her head and rubbing her back. I smile at him.

Then I look up at Emmett. "Thank you," I say, my voice hoarse.

He kisses me on the forehead. "I'm here for you, Lola. Whatever you and Ruby need, just tell me."

I bury my head back into his damp chest and fall asleep.

It's night again when I wake up. Cooper and Ruby are gone, Alma's in the kitchen, and I'm still on Emmett's lap, feeling him stroking my hair and kissing my head.

"How long have I been out?" I stretch.

"About four hours," he says.

"Ruby?"

"Your folks took her back to their place for the night. They figured you needed some time. Don't worry, I told them I'd come get her if she wanted to come home. Alma's cooking up a pot of chicken noodle soup and some biscuits for you. Are you hungry?"

The last time I ate was lunch yesterday. Or was it the day before? I have no idea what day it even is.

We get up and head to the island to sit. Alma ladles big bowls of soup for both of us and puts a plate piled high with her cheese and herb biscuits on the countertop. She grabs two bottles of water from the fridge and places one in front of each of us.

"I'm going to head out for the night, honey. I'll be back in the morning to do whatever I can," she says, coming around the counter to hug me. "I love you, child."

"I love you, too, Alma," I say as I hug her back. She lets go, puts the soup in the fridge, and then gives us a sad wave as she walks out of the kitchen.

I push the soup around in the bowl with my spoon.

"Eat something, Lola," Emmett says softly. "I know you don't want to, but you need to. Just take ten spoonfuls and eat a biscuit and I'll let you off the hook."

I scowl at him before I pick up my spoon and slurp noisily. He smiles around the spoonful of soup he just put in his mouth.

"There's my stubborn girl," he says, as he hands me a biscuit. "I know how hard this is and I want you to lean on me as much as possible. You can hate me all you want. You can cry on me. You can beat me up. Do what you need to do, I'm going to be here for you. I just hope you don't shut me out because that means you're not dealing. You need to deal with this, Lola. If it's not with me, then let it be with Deedee or Cooper or Kevin or your folks or a therapist or whoever. Just deal. You don't want to end up how I did."

I take a sip of water before I say, "Thank you, Emmett. Thank you for being here for me. Thank you for your support. And thank you for pointing that out to me. I can see how easy it is to be consumed with grief and not want to deal."

He puts his spoon down and swivels his chair to face mine. He uses his feet to pull my stool toward his. He takes my hands and says, "We'll get you and Ruby through this. You don't have to worry."

I nod my head as I drop it to his shoulder. He removes his hands from mine and puts them around my back, rubbing gently.

"I know I've done nothing but cry and sleep all day, but I think I'm going to go up and have a bath and crawl into bed," I say, yawning.

"I'll stay in the guest room so you're not here alone. I'll look after little Mutt for you," he says, reaching down to scratch the little guy behind the ears.

"Thank you," I say with a weak smile.

I head upstairs, and, as I draw a bath, I think back to all of the baths Chase and I took together. I turn off the taps and slide down the edge of the tub, sobbing. Memories of our wedding night haunt me. He's everywhere I look. I see his bathrobe hanging up on the wall and I crawl across the floor and drag it down to me, inhaling his scent.

Oh, God. I miss him so much. I break down crying on the bathroom floor. I'm not sure how long I'm down there when Emmett finds me, picks me up, and carries me back to my bed. He digs around in the dresser until he finds a nightgown for me. He helps me get out of my t-shirt and yoga pants and then puts my nightgown over my head.

He turns back the sheets and then helps me back onto the bed. I see him take his shirt and pants off and turn the light off and crawl into bed with me. He pulls me to him and all of a sudden, I panic.

"No! You can't be in here!"

He immediately hops out of the bed. " Shit, Lola! I'm sorry. I wasn't thinking. I just remember how comforting it was when you stayed with me. I'm sorry." He gathers his clothes and heads out of the bedroom, closing the door behind him.

# Chapter 37

## Emmett

I can't believe what a fucking idiot I am! Why would I think it was okay to crawl into their bed with her? I knock on my head a few times.

That horrible night, feeling Lola's arms around me, her warm body curled around mine was the only thing that gave me comfort. Even with the Seconal, my head was filled with visions of the cold, lifeless body of my baby girl in my arms. I needed Lola's touch to ground me.

I even grieved for Whitney. She may not have been the best person, but she and I had made our peace during her pregnancy, both looking toward the common goal of raising a happy, healthy little girl. But I didn't think twice to ask Lola to comfort me in my bed.

Lola loved Chase. As much as I hate to think of it, they probably made love in that bed hundreds of times over the years. Many good memories in there. What the hell was I thinking?

I grab my *Sports Illustrated* and plump up the pillows behind me in the guest bed. I don't think I can sleep, but I want to be close by if she needs me.

I must have drifted off because I jolt awake when I hear the door open.

"Mutt? I'm sorry. I shouldn't have freaked out on you like that. I know you were just trying to be helpful," she says, making patterns in the thick carpet with her toe.

"No, Lola, I'm sorry. I didn't think. I just wanted to hold you the way you held me that night. I know how much it soothed me," I say.

"I know. I was wondering if I can stay here with you tonight? That room... it smells like him. I can't..." She chokes. "I can't stay in there."

I lift the bedding for her and scoot over. She turns off the lamp and burrows into me. I throw the covers back over us and hold her as tightly as I can, rocking her a little from side to side. Within a few minutes, she's sleeping.

I know the agony I felt at losing Violet. My pain for Whitney was fleeting. I try to imagine how painful it would be to lose Lola in an accident. Even in an imaginary situation, it feels like my heart has been ripped from my chest, still beating.

I kiss her lightly on the top of her head, making a big decision without even having to think about the pros and cons. I'm going to be here for her. And for my darling little Ruby. No more random women. My life is going to revolve around the two most important women in my life. Even if I never get to have her, I'm going to spend the rest of my life trying to make her happy again, trying to be the man I always should have been.

I wake up again to a light scratching sound. Poor little Mutt's eyes must be crossed he must have to pee so bad! I gently remove myself from Lola's embrace, throw on my jeans and sweater and let myself out of the bedroom.

I'm just grabbing his leash and a baggie when Alma lets herself in.

"I'm glad you stayed here with her, Emmett," she says, giving me a hug.

"She's up in the guest room; it was too difficult for her to stay in her room last night," I tell Alma. She nods her head. "I'm taking little Mutt out for a walk and I'll be back in a bit."

"I'll have some coffee ready and get started on some eggs and sausage and toast," she says warmly.

I do some thinking while Mutt's taking his sweet time doing his business. We walk about a mile before I turn around and head back to Lola's house. She's awake and sitting at the island when I get back. She gives me a small smile over the rim of her coffee cup. I smile back as I sit down and grab my mug.

"My folks are heading back with Ruby in a few minutes," Lola tells me. "We've got a long day of planning ahead of us. I don't know if you're able to stick around, but I know that Ruby would love it if you did. So would I."

"Whatever you need, Lola. I'm here for both of you. I'll just run home to shower and change," I tell her.

"Why don't you bring stuff for a few days," she suggests. She rests her hand on mine. "I... I need you to help me get through this, Mutt."

"Lucky for you, I already decided that I wasn't going to give you a choice in the matter," I say, picking her hand up to kiss it. "You are my two best girls. You're more important to me than anything."

She smiles and squeezes my hand, mouthing 'thank you' as we hear Ruby, Jack, and Luanne coming through the front door.

We all eat breakfast in silence and then I excuse myself to head back to my condo for a bit. I make a few calls, arranging to be gone from work for a little while. Then I pack and head out. I stop off at the bookstore on the way back to pick up books for Lola about death and coping. I am surprised to find a few for children, so I pick those up as well. I also grab bouquets of flowers for both my girls and then head back to Druid Hills.

When I get back, there's a car I don't recognize out in front of the house. I head inside and see Lola in her office with her father and a stranger. I go into the kitchen to grab a bottle of water, after depositing my duffle bag and laptop bag by the stairs. Alma's got a chicken roasting in the oven and is snapping green beans for a casserole. There's a pile of potatoes on the counter to be peeled. Ruby and Luanne are watching a cartoon. I grab one of the bouquets and the books I bought and I head over.

Ruby races over and hugs me. "I'm glad you're back, Uncle Mutt," she says.

"Nowhere else I'd rather be, darlin'. Now, I think you may want to go and have Alma help you put these in some water. And then come on back. I've got some books to read with you. All right?"

Luanne pokes through the book bag and looks up at me in surprise. "I didn't realize they wrote books like these! Thank you for being so thoughtful, Emmett."

"It's what I'm here for, Luanne," I say.

When Ruby gets back, we read *Life Is Like The Wind* and *Saying Goodbye to Daddy*. We're just finishing up the latter when I see Lola out of the corner of my eye. She's leaning against one of the columns that divide the great room from the kitchen, arms crossed, head tilted to the side, a look of awe on her face.

Ruby gets up and goes to hug Lola. "Uncle Mutt brought me some books."

"So I see," she says, smiling at her daughter. "Why don't you go and get washed up. Alma's going to need some help making the apple crumble for dessert."

"Yes, Mama!" And off she flies.

Lola comes over to sit down next to me.

"Thank you for those books. I got here halfway through the last one and I am amazed at how brilliant they are. I don't think I could have explained half of that to her as well."

"You're welcome. I'm glad I could help. Everything okay?" I ask.

"Yeah. That guy was from the FAA. Since the jet was a private charter, they're a lot more... involved with the families of the deceased. Particularly since on-site investigations have indicated tampering and some other inconsistencies. He also came to let us know that Chase's remains are here. Daddy and I have made arrangements to have him transferred to the funeral home. We'll go and have everything settled tomorrow."

I lean her against me and rub my hand up and down her arm. "Do you want me to come with you?"

"It might be better if you're here for Ruby. Not that I don't need you, I do. But Uncle Mutt always makes things better," she sighs.

"Who do they think would tamper with Chase's plane?"

"That's the big question. His most recent contract job had DOD written all over it—he couldn't tell me who he was working for, where he was going. I was given flight information for the planes they chartered and he got two calls to us a day—one in the morning, one at night. Normally he discusses his work with me a bit, but he was tight-lipped about it this time around. Couldn't get anything out of him."

"Why would he take a job like that?" Seriously, if I had two lovely ladies waiting at home for me every day, I would never agree to terms like those.

"When I asked him, he said it was groundbreaking and a huge honor to be singled out as the guy for the job. And that I couldn't ask him more about it. Literally," she says, frowning. "I have never told him what to do, but this job made me nervous because of all of the secrecy. When I told him about my concerns, he told me, 'Don't worry. Where I'll be, I'll be incredibly safe.' I guess he didn't take into account getting to and from there."

I hear Alma making a lot of noise behind us. I'm guessing she's trying to tell us there are little ears about.

"Well, let's get up and help set the table and do whatever Alma needs us to do. Then maybe we can all curl up on the couch in our pajamas and watch Disney movies." I turn and ask a little louder, "What do you think, Ruby?"

"I think that sounds like a great idea, Uncle Mutt."

And that's what we do. Luanne and Jack and Alma all stay for dinner. Cooper shows up a little later and eats a plate that Alma made for him. We all settle down in front of the TV and watch *The Little Mermaid* and then *Cinderella*. Ruby falls asleep in my lap. I take her upstairs and deposit her in her bed, Lola behind me to tuck her in and give her a kiss.

"I'm going to stay in the other guest room tonight," she says with a yawn. "It's been a long day. I think I'm going to head to bed."

"I'll be down the hall if you need anything. I'll take little Mutt out for a potty break before I tuck in for the night."

"Thank you, big Mutt," she says, smiling. "For

everything."

"You'd better stop saying that. I'm just looking after my best girls," I say, giving her a hug.

I'm not at all surprised when I hear my door open and close and feel Ruby slide in the bed next to me. Even less so when I feel Lola slide in on my other side about an hour later. I lie there and hug them, giving whatever comfort I can.

The funeral was tough. There were paparazzi everywhere. Like I said, Chase was a big deal. They even sat outside Lola's house, waiting to get a glimpse of the grieving widow.

After consulting with the police, we all decide it's best for the girls to get away for a bit. Chase's dad offers his little getaway in Bermuda, but Ruby refuses to get on a plane. Frankly, I don't blame her. So we decide to drive out to Washington and stay at the plantation with her folks. Every night, Ruby, Lola, and little Mutt share my bed.

# Chapter 38

*Viola*

It's been two years since Chase's death. Ruby and I have been able to move forward, thanks to weekly therapy and the help of our family and friends.

Government officials came to the house shortly after the funeral and boxed up everything in Chase's office, as well as his off-site servers. When they had determined he had only used the laptop he purchased specifically for that project (which went down with him in the plane) and the dedicated server at a government facility to do work or discuss the project, they returned the rest to us and released the other servers back to the companies whose projects Chase had them on.

Being a highly classified project, results of the investigation into Chase's plane crash became need to know. And, evidently, his family didn't need to know. To add insult to injury, shortly after the government came to confiscate everything in Chase's office, everyone close to him was questioned about what they knew about the project. Of course, the answer they got from each and every one of us was 'nothing.' But that didn't stop them from pushing.

All the government would tell us was that Chase was working on a special project for the Department of Defense. We received condolences from the President and a very large check, but not one word as to what was so important that someone would want to take Chase's life.

Living in the house was difficult. Chase was everywhere we looked. We ended up sleeping in the guest bedrooms all the time because neither of us could sleep in our own. So I found another house in Druid Hills a few streets over on Villa Drive. The renovations that had been done to it already were up to my strict standards, but I still needed to make it my own in the bathrooms and kitchen.

Emmett has been here for us every single day, so much so that I gave him his own suite in the new house. I feel bad for him, spending all this time with us and not getting his needs taken care of by random women. But he swears he wouldn't have it any other way. He usually comes to check in on us for dinner from Monday through Thursday, going back to his condo downtown so he doesn't have to deal with the commute in the mornings, and then stays over from Friday night to Monday morning.

My folks have taken the grandkids to Orlando for DisneyWorld and Universal Studios fun while Carlyle and Christine take a babymoon before number two arrives. I decided to take advantage of flying solo and booked the time off to relax. I head into Atlanta to my favorite spa for a manicure, pedicure, facial, massage, and a seaweed wrap. I stop off at Emmett and Cooper's office before I head back to Druid Hills to see if they want to have dinner. I can hear laughter from Emmett's office, so I head there, giving their executive assistant a wave.

"Hello, gorgeous!" Emmett's sitting in the chair behind his desk, one foot up on the other knee, head braced on his hands behind his neck.

"Wow! Spa day does a body good!" Coop says, holding his arms out for a hug. I head over and give him a hug and a kiss on the top of his head, and then head over to give Emmett the same treatment. He pulls me into his lap.

"I wanted to see if we could do an impromptu get together tonight," I say, looking at Coop.

"Sorry, honey. Tiffany and I have some boring charity event to attend tonight. I was just getting ready to head out," he says, getting to his feet.

"Oh. Well, hope you guys have fun. I'll message Tiffany and set up something for next weekend, then."

Coop says, "Sounds good. Have a good weekend, guys!" giving us a wink.

"You, too," Emmett and I say at the same time as Coop heads out the door.

I turn to face Emmett, "So, what now?"

"Do you want to get out of town?"

I look at him and raise my eyebrow. "What'd you have in mind?"

"Pack for somewhere warm and meet me at the condo. I'll take care of the rest," he says, rubbing his hands together.

I smile at him and then say, "You're on. See you in a bit!"

I head home and grab my Louis Vuitton suitcase out of the closet and stand there for awhile, figuring out what to pack. I throw in the usual warm weather gear: bikinis, sarongs, sundresses, skirts, shorts, t-shirts, and lots of sandals. I toss in some workout gear and cross-trainers, knowing that neither of us will be able to go more than a day without a workout. Last, but not least, I throw in some pajamas and undergarments and then head into the bathroom to grab my toiletries.

When I'm done with that, I grab my overnight bag and throw in a sundress, sandals, a bathing suit, a sarong, a change of underwear, and a set of pajamas. I toss in my makeup bag, my laptop, and a few books I'd been hoarding for such an occasion.

I grab my passport out of the safe, my camera, and all my chargers from my office and then grab my purse and head out the door, after making sure the alarm is set. I called Alma on my way to Druid Hills to make sure she could look after little Mutt. She picked him up before I even got home. I also called my folks and let them know I was taking off with Emmett for a week. All they said was, "Have fun!"

By the time I'm back at Emmett's condo building,

I realize he's had this whole thing planned. I call up and tell him to get his butt downstairs ASAP. He comes running down, grinning, and, after tossing his duffle bag into the back seat, shouts, "Drive! Drive!"

"When did you plan this?" I ask, looking at him through narrowed eyes.

He chuckles. "I planned it last weekend. Be mad later. We really need to get to the airport. Our flight leaves in less than 2 hours."

I hit the gas pedal with a grin, shaking my head. "How did you know I'd even say yes?"

"I didn't. But I figured whisking you away last minute would be much better than you having a staycation at home. You need the break, Lola."

"You're right. I do," I say with a sigh. "So, are you going to tell me where we're headed?"

"First stop is LA," he says. "And then, we're going to Maui!"

"Emmett Alan Davis! You're taking me to Hawaii?"

"Yup! We're going to do whatever you want. We can golf, we can just lie on the beach, we can snorkel, we can surf. We can take each day as it comes and do whatever we feel like."

"That sounds amazing," I say, reaching for his hand. "Thank you."

"Anything for my Lola," he murmurs, softly kissing the back of my hand.

I am not prepared for what his words and actions do to me. A shiver runs down my spine and my stomach feels like there are a million butterflies taking flight. My mouth goes dry. I clear my throat and then ask him to uncap my bottle of water from the console. He obliges, passing it to me, and I take several big gulps before handing it back to him. He puts the bottle to his lips and I watch his Adam's apple bob up and down with each gulp. My mouth goes dry again.

I shake my head to try and rid myself of the desire that came from nowhere. I realize I'm driving in two lanes and shift back into one.

"Are you all right? Want me to drive?"

"We're almost there. I am still zoned out from my spa day," I say, my voice really squeaky to my ears.

He shakes his head, laughing silently.

We park and haul ass to the ticketing agent. She checks us in, takes our checked bags, and sends us on our merry way. We scoot through security and make the plane just before they announce the doors are closing. I get comfy in my seat and grab my book and reading glasses from my overnight bag.

Emmett pulls out a *Sports Illustrated* from his carry-on bag. As I curl up in my seat, I feel him looking at me. I turn to ask him what's so interesting, but I stop when I see the look in his eyes. I know that look. It's pure hunger. And not for food. I swallow hard.

The flight attendant breaks the silence by checking to make sure we're both buckled in and have our cell phones and other electronics turned off.

After we take off, the flight attendant brings me the pillow and blanket I ask for.

"I'm going to try and sleep, since when we get to

Maui, it'll be morning and we'll have a full day ahead of us. I don't want to waste one moment in paradise," I say.

Emmett leans over and kisses me gently on the lips. "Sweet dreams, Lola."

"Night, Mutt," I say, before curling up and resting my head against the frame of the plane, running my fingers over the lips he just kissed.

I sleep the rest of the flight from Atlanta to LAX. We have a few hours to spend in the first class lounge and then board our flight to Maui. We both get some sleep on the second flight, even though we were bouncing off the walls prior to departure, excited to get to our destination.

I wake when the captain announces we're about an hour from Maui. The flight attendant comes around with mimosas, coffee, some fresh pastries, and fruit salad. I sip the champagne concoction and hum in delight.

Emmett starts picking through his fruit salad. "Do you want my papaya?"

"Yes, please," I say. He takes the single chunk out of his bowl with his fork and then lifts it to my mouth. I watch him watch me as I close my mouth around the juicy fruit and he slowly draws the fork back. I chew slowly, watching as he licks the fork clean. Oh. My. Word.

I pretend to read for the rest of breakfast, trying to ignore the lust I feel for him. But it's hard when my whole body is alive with it. Is this what I want? Am I ready for this? Am I ready to move on?

I try to figure out the answers to these questions—and many more—while starting out the window at the deep blue ocean below us. When I see the island approaching, I close my eyes. I picture Emmett coming out of the ocean, the hard planes of his body glistening, board shorts low on his waist, salacious smile on his lips. He slinks toward me like a lion stalking its prey.

The plane lands with a thump and my eyes snap open. *Oh my!*

We step off the plane onto the tarmac and get 'lei'd' before heading in to wait for our bags. I call to check in with Ruby and my folks while Emmett picks up our rental car. And then we're off.

"We're going on a bit of a drive. But you might want to have your camera out—we'll be making some pit stops for pictures."

I make sure my camera is at the ready.

"Where are we headed?"

"Haiku," he says with a smile. "Cooper's folks have a vacation property there. They were more than happy to loan it to me. There's staff to cook and clean, so we don't have to lift a finger."

"Wow! That sounds fantastic!"

"We have to drive the road to Hana in order to get there—you're going to love it."

We turn onto State Route 360 and I am absolutely mesmerized by the scenery. The bamboo forests, the coastline, the waterfalls—it truly is like Eden here. And I'm about to go and spend a week in Eden with Emmett. I blush at the thought.

After a leisurely drive with stops to take lots of pictures and lunch in town at Hana, we turn back and head to our final destination. It looks like we are in the middle of the jungle, thick foliage on either side of the road, when I spot a set of iron gates. Emmett stops and punches a code into a keypad on the stonework fence and the gates open slowly.

The road is lined by native vegetation and palm trees. It curves and goes on for a bit before coming to an end at a circular drive. I see several buildings, one of them being a four-car garage.

I turn to look at Emmett, as he parks the car. I raise an eyebrow.

"Cooper's folks own car dealerships in 6 Atlantic states," he says with a shrug. "They live pretty well."

I almost scream when my car door is opened for me.

"Welcome to Haiku, Miss Viola," says a large Polynesian man. "My name is Don Ho. Not that Don Ho, though."

I chuckle. "Hi, Don. Please, call me Vi."

"I am the caretaker and head of staff here. If there is anything you need while you are here, please do not hesitate to let me know. We can coordinate any island activities you may wish to do; I've left some literature in the living room for you. Just let us know and we'll make it happen."

"Thanks, Don," Emmett says, coming over to shake hands and pat him on the back.

"Emmett, it's been awhile! It's good to see you. Mr. Forsythe made my day when he told me you were coming. I'm hoping I can win back some of the money I lost last time we played poker," Don says.

Emmett throws his head back and laughs. "I don't know, Don. If anything, my game has improved. But you're welcome to try. Now, why don't we take Vi up to the house and see what she thinks?"

"Of course," Don says, bending over to strap my overnight bag onto my suitcase.

The property is oceanfront, but not beachfront. We are on a cliff overlooking the ocean, which is all you can see when you open the front doors. The back of the house consists of large, sliding glass doors that are currently open, allowing the salty ocean breeze into the room which is tastefully furnished in muted tones, lots of teak wood furniture, and hardwood floors.

I am led to a master suite with stunning ocean views and my own private balcony, complete with a sunken hot tub. Inside the bathroom is gigantic with a sunken marble tub and shower combination with marble pillars surrounding it in the middle of the floor. I spy another patio that leads to a private man-made lagoon, complete with waterfall.

I spend a few minutes getting settled in my suite before heading to the living room and sitting down to peruse the activities literature that Don so thoughtfully left for us. Emmett comes out a few minutes later.

"So," he says slowly. "What do you think?"

"I think I don't ever want to go back to Atlanta," I say with a laugh. "Let's just bring Ruby and everyone out here."

He laughs. "We probably could. There are a couple of guest cottages on the property, as well as the main house and the staff quarters. It's not on the beach, but there's one not too far away. And there's plenty of water and sun to soak in. It's nice and quiet, you don't have to worry about the tourists. And, if you want to be a tourist, all you need to do is drive to Hana or Lahaina."

"I love it here, Emmett. I've got to personally thank Cooper's folks the next time they're in town. This is heaven," I say with a contented sigh.

He comes over and kisses the top of my head and says, "Glad you like it. What do you want to do with the rest of the day?"

"I think I might just want to relax by the lagoon and read and nap and just soak up the sun," I tell him.

"Then that's exactly what we'll do. I'll let Don know to have dinner on the patio around 7:30 and where we'll be so they can bring us some cold drinks and snacks."

I head into my room and change into a black bikini and sheer black sarong. I put my hair up into a messy bun on top of my head and start to put suntan lotion on myself when Emmett knocks on the door.

"Are you ready?"

He's wearing a pair of navy blue board shorts that ride low on his hips. I've seen him with his shirt off a million times in the past few years, but today? Today I can't help myself. I bite my lower lip while I take him in. He works out every day and it shows: his broad shoulders ripple with muscle, his biceps bulge without even having to flex, he has perfectly formed pecs and has washboard abs and a deep cut v that I want to run my tongue over. I look up and see him eyeing me just as hungrily. My heart feels like it's about to beat right out of my chest.

I swallow and manage to say, "Yeah, I'm ready."

He opens the door to the patio and makes a 'ladies first' motion with his hand. I exit and walk the path down to the lagoon. There's a small beach area with a few chaises and a couple of beach umbrellas. I opt to spread a towel out on the sand under an umbrella. Emmett follows suit.

Don comes out with a small cooler and a little folding table that he places between us, under the umbrella. He pops two Solo cups in the sand and then sticks ice cold bottles of water in the cups so they don't get covered in sand. Then he sets out some veggies and hummus and a fruit plate. He places a mesh cover on top and places some linen napkins under two plates.

"Enjoy," he says before turning around and heading back to the main house.

I pick up my bottle of water and take a long drink, hoping it will help cool me down. I'm warm from being in a tropical location, and even warmer due to the company I'm keeping.

"I think I'm going to take a dip," I say, standing up.

"Right behind you," he says.

# Chapter 39

## Emmett

I sure as hell hope that water is freezing cold. I'm going to need something to get rid of the wood I'm sporting.

I don't think she has any idea how perfect she is. She took up running in high school and it has helped keep her lean. Twice weekly Pilates sessions help keep her tone everywhere. Even after having had a child, her body is made for sin and that bikini only emphasizes it, covering up just enough to make me want more. The two triangles barely cover her D cup breasts and the bottom covers only half her amazing ass before tying at the sides. I want to rip them off with my teeth. Combine that with her auburn hair done in a messy topknot and her stunning face, she could be on the cover of SI's swimsuit issue.

I watch her wade out into the lagoon and head over to the waterfall to stand under it. I take her obscured vision as the opportunity to get me, and my raging hard-on, into the lagoon. Cool, but not enough to do any good. I shift myself as best I can and wade over to where she is.

I swear I've had this dream before. She's standing under the waterfall with her back to me, head back, eyes closed, face tilting upward, pulling her hair out of the topknot, and running her fingers through it. The water runs over her front and sides.

I have dreamed about this woman every day of my life since I met her. She is my fantasy in the flesh. She is also my best friend—and I don't want to do anything to jeopardize that. We've come too far. But what if she's feeling this as much as I am? What if she wants me as badly as I want her? Will I be able to stop myself if I get daring enough to make a move?

"Take a picture, it'll last longer," she says, snapping me out of my reverie.

She's staring at me over her shoulder, auburn curls cascading down her back. Her green eyes sparkle, her lips tilted up in a smirk. I make my way over to her as she steps to the side to give me some room to join her under the deluge.

After getting myself good and wet, I make my way over to the little grotto behind the falls and find one of the underwater rock benches to sit on. She follows and stops just in front of me. Brazenly, I reach out my hands and put them on her hips, pulling her to stand in between my legs. I rub my thumbs up and down her sides. She rests her forearms on my shoulders and then starts playing with my hair, head tilting to the side.

"What are you thinking?" I ask, my hands getting a little bolder as I slide them a little lower on her rear.

"I'm trying not to," she says, breath hitching as I slip a finger underneath the string on the side of her bikini bottom. "What are you thinking right now?"

I watch her breasts heave as I lick my lips. "I think," I say, pulling her a little closer, "that it's time you and I had a talk."

"Oh," she says. Is that disappointment in her voice? I'd bet my last dollar it is. The thought makes me smile.

"Yeah. I want you to know that you are, above anything, my best friend," I start.

"Okay," she drawls, looking at me through narrowed eyes.

"And, over the past few years I have been able to talk to you about the women I 'see', for lack of a better term," I continue, running my hands down to cup her behind.

She gasps. "Uh huh."

"Well, there's this one woman I want to spend more time with," I say, gently squeezing. "Actually, I want to spend all my time with her. I do spend all my spare time with her, but I want to spend our time together... differently."

"Oh?" I watch her arch an eyebrow over an emerald green eye that glints with lust. "And would I happen to know this woman?"

"Very well. In fact, she's standing right in front of me."

"Mmmm, I see," she says as I knead her bottom. "And just how do you want to spend your time with her?"

I grin. "Naked." I pull one of the strings on her bikini bottom.

"And, do you think she wants this?" She's sliding her tongue along her lower lip.

"I'm pretty sure she does," I say, pulling a string on the other side and gently pull the bottoms away from her and place them on the rocks behind me.

"You're sure about this?" She's suddenly very serious.

"I love you, Lola. I've never been more sure about anything my entire life," I say, pulling her lips to mine.

I kiss her tenderly, just enjoying the way her lips move against mine. It's been a long time since we've done this and I'm savoring it, memorizing every last detail of this moment. How she tastes, how good she feels pressed against me, the scent of coconut from her suntan oil, the roar of the waterfall, the warm water, everything. I never want to forget this. I move one hand to her front and slide my hand down her seam, splitting it with my finger.

When she gasps, I take the opportunity to touch my tongue to hers, loving the whimper I get in response. I tease her tongue with mine while I'm teasing her pussy with my fingers and then I break our kiss, sliding my lips and tongue down her throat to her breasts. I pull the upper tie to her bikini top, and then the bottom tie. She takes her now untied, useless top and tosses it with the bottoms behind me as I take one of her nipples in my mouth. I feel the quiver in her pussy as I gently tease her perky tip that is now at full attention between my teeth.

"Oh God, Emmett," she moans.

I feel her grab my hair tightly and pull me closer to her. I smile and chuckle as I make my way over to her other nipple, rubbing lazy circles around her clit with my thumb. Her breath is coming out in pants and I can't say it's not affecting me.

I stop what I'm doing, eliciting a groan and a pout. I grab her ass in my hands and lift her up. She wraps her legs around my waist, and I wade over to a ledge across the grotto and place her on it. I kiss her again, this time with years of pent-up longing.

I break away, both of us needing to catch our breath. I start to make a lazy trail down from her mouth, over her chin, down her throat to her breasts. But I don't stop there. I head down and dip my tongue into her belly button, sending a shiver down her spine. I look up at her as I kneel down in the water and make my way to where I really want to be: praying at the altar of Lola. In all my years, I have never wanted to taste anyone so badly as I want to taste her.

I spread her legs a little further and close my eyes as I lay my tongue on her lower lips. Oh God, it's so much better than I had dreamed. I part her with my fingers and take my time getting to know her, feeling her move, and loving the noises she is making.

"More," she pants.

I oblige, sticking two fingers in her and moving

my tongue up to her clit. When I feel her walls start to tighten around my fingers, I close my lips around her mound and suck hard. I feel her hips start to rock against me, so I pump her harder with my fingers.

"Holy shit, Emmett! Oh God! Oh! God!"

I work her down from her orgasm, feeling her body turn to jelly. Then I kiss my way back up to her mouth. She kisses me with a passion I've never felt before. We stop, foreheads together, panting.

"I want to be inside you, Lola. I have never wanted anything as much as I want you. Can I make you mine?"

She nods, biting her bottom lip. I pull it out from her teeth with my thumb and then suck it into my mouth. She runs her hand down my chest, lower, and into my board shorts. My whole body jerks when I feel her fingers graze my cock. She makes a fist around me and gently strokes from top to bottom and then up again. She slowly pulls her head back, tugging her lower lip out of my mouth. She kisses across my jawline to my ear. After taking a nip at my earlobe, she whispers, "What are you waiting for, Emmett?" She strokes up and down again, licking around the shell of my ear while she does.

She gently rubs me up against her wetness. I can't contain the growl as I push my board shorts down all the way, take myself in hand and push into her entrance.

"Deeper, Emmett," she rasps.

I don't thrust, instead sliding my length inside her slowly. She throws her head back when I take it to the hilt. I have to stop. I'm almost dizzy it feels so good. She locks her legs around me and I lean forward to lick one of her nipples. I tease her rigid peak while slowly retreating, and then I suck it sharply into my mouth as I ram into her hard. She screams in response.

"Fuck, Lola! Are you all right?" I ask, scared I hurt her.

"Again," she says, looking at me with eyes filled with unadulterated lust.

I do, grabbing the other breast and teasing the nipple with my fingers. I slam into her fast and pull out slow. I continue my motions, going a little faster when I see her hips rising to meet me. I do a little grind when we come together.

"Yes," she hisses. "Just like that."

"Oh God, Lola. You feel so fucking good," I growl.

There is no going back after this. I can't, I won't. Lola is everything I have always wanted, always needed. And now that I have experienced her, I know without a doubt that no one else will ever compare. She is it for me. Always has been, now always will be. She. Is. Mine.

Our movements become fluid, working toward a common goal. I move my mouth up to hers. Her hands grab my hair as she tilts her head and moves her lips over mine, moaning. I grab her hips and help her grind into me, loving how good it feels. Her moans become more and more intense until finally I feel her walls clench me.

"Emmett!"

I pump once more then succumb to the strength of her orgasm, murmuring her name over and over.

I lean my forehead against hers as I catch my breath, looking into her eyes.

"I love you, Lola," I whisper.

"I love you, too, Mutt," she whispers back.

# Chapter 40

*Viola*

Ohmigod. That just happened. And it was... life altering.

"Lola, tell me what you're thinking. I need to know," he says, cupping my face in his hands, his voice desperate. "I love you, Lola. So much. I want you to know right now that I will not fuck this up. You are it for me. You and Ruby are my life now."

I pull back and look at him. I know this to be true. I know how hard he worked to earn back my trust and my friendship. I know that he completely devoted himself to Ruby and me after Chase's death. I know that he hasn't slept with another woman in all that time. I know that he loves Ruby more than life itself. And I know without a doubt that he'd die for me.

He finally did it. He made something of himself. He came for me.

"Lola?"

I smile. "I think that I love you, Emmett Allan Davis. And I think that we should go inside and have a shower and get dressed so we can enjoy whatever Don Ho and his minions are cooking up for us."

He laughs. "That's it?"

"Hardly," I chuckle. I wrap my arms around his neck. "I know that there was a reason that we weren't meant to be together until now. I'm not sure what it was, but it doesn't matter."

"I know what that reason was. I had to lose everything, including you, in order to make myself into the man that you need me to be. I've only ever loved one woman in my life, Lola. It's always only ever been you. And while you always had faith in me that I'd become that man, I don't think I ever did. I took for granted the fact that you'd always love me."

I cock my head to the side. "Did your dad ever tell you what he whispered to me the day you two left for Albany?"

He shakes his head no.

"He told me, 'No matter what happens, Viola, don't stop loving him. Love conquers all.' Even when I was upset with you, I never stopped loving you, Emmett."

"Who'd have thought the cranky bastard had such a soft heart?"

I shrug. "I'm guessing your mama taught him that lesson first-hand. Maybe we can ask him one day."

After finding our discarded suits and grabbing our towels, we head inside and I start the shower.

Emmett grabs his bags from the other room and brings them into mine. He joins me in the shower and we have a bit of fun getting clean together. We're late for dinner, but that's all right. We spend the night sitting on the patio, cuddling and talking. And then he takes me to bed and shows me just how much he loves me.

The rest of our week is pure bliss. We snorkel a few times—I got to feed a reef shark—we swim in the Seven Sacred Pools, we take a private helicopter tour around the island, we watch the sun rise on top of Haleakala Crater and then bike down the volcano. It isn't all about exploring the island, though. We spend as much time exploring each other.

All too soon, it's time to face reality. But reality is pretty darn cute, and I really missed her. As soon as she sees us come through the doors at the airport, she races over and leaps at me. I catch her, barely managing to keep myself upright.

"Mama! Mama! I'm so glad you're home! Grandma Lu and Grandpa Jack and Connor and I had so much fun in Florida! I got to have a princess makeover! I chose to be Ariel!"

"Good choice," I laugh. "You've got the right hair color! I want to hear all about your adventures at DisneyWorld, sweetling."

I put her down and she goes over and climbs up Emmett. He smothers her with kisses and hugs her to him like he can't get enough of her. "I missed you, my precious gem!!"

"I missed you, too, Uncle Mutt! Wait until you see

what I got you!" She is so giddy, it's the most adorable thing I've ever seen.

"You got me a present?" He kisses her on the cheek. "Thank you! I can't wait to see it! Should we go home and exchange presents?"

She nods her head. Mama and Daddy help us gather our suitcases and usher us out to the car. I can see Mama's knowing smirk, looking at our joined hands.

When we get home, we give Ruby all of her presents: a tin of chocolate covered macadamia nuts, a pukka shell anklet, a grass skirt and coconut bra, a floral print dress, a lei, a stuffed sea turtle, and a pink ukulele.

And then she gives us our gifts. I got a set of Minnie Mouse ears, including big bow with *Mama* embroidered on them. I also got a necklace with a pendant that says *Dreams Do Come True*. I smile at how appropriate this is.

And then I howl with laughter when I see what she's given Emmett. Not only is he proudly wearing his Mickey ears with *Uncle Mutt* embroidered on them, but he's hugging a stuffed animal: Tramp from *Lady and The Tramp*, the ultimate mutt.

She shows us the entire collection of stuffed animals and dolls she got—I told my folks not to deny her anything. They had to buy two suitcases just to lug all of the extra stuff home. But she's worth it. And, from the pictures and videos we watched, she had a very special time with her cousin, getting spoiled rotten by Grandma Lu and Grandpa Jack.

We show them our photos and videos and gobble up the chicken pot pie and spinach salad Alma makes for dinner. Finally, it's bedtime. We tuck Ruby in and then head downstairs to say goodbye to my folks.

"Soooooo," Mama drawls. "Anything you might like to tell us?" She raises an eyebrow.

"Evidently there's something you think you know," I say dryly, crossing my arms.

Daddy pipes up. "We just want you to know that we support this," he says, pointing to the two of us; Emmett's arm is wrapped around my waist. "It's been a long and difficult journey, but we've been watching you two over the past couple of years and we see the love between you, platonic and otherwise. I think Chase would be happy knowing that you're looking after his girls, Emmett."

Emmett steps over to give Daddy a hug. "Thanks, Jack. I just want to make them happy."

"I know you do, son," Daddy says, clapping him on the back a few times before letting go.

"Well, goodnight you two," Mama says with a smile. "Don't do anything I wouldn't do!"

"God, Mama! There are things you can't un-hear!" I shout.

Emmett bursts out laughing. Mama and Daddy chuckle as they shut the door behind them.

I go over and lock the door. "Well, I'm ready for a nice hot shower and then bed. Care to join me?"

"You go warm up the shower, I'll take little Mutt out to do his business and join you in a minute."

I turn on the steam shower and then put my hair

up in a messy bun. I take off my clothing and toss it in the hamper, then step in the shower, savoring the warmth. Momentarily, I feel a cool breeze and I know Emmett has joined me. Kisses on my shoulder confirm it.

"You're so beautiful," he whispers. "I honestly don't know how I even function around you." I feel his erection pressed up against my rear. I wiggle into him. "You're playing with fire, Lola."

"I know," I murmur, raising my arms behind my head to run them in his hair.

He runs one hand up to my breast and the other down lower, gently caressing my sex. I arch back against him. "Mmmmm..."

He nips me just below my ear and then licks with his tongue and finishes with a gentle kiss. "Tell me what you want me to do to you, Lola."

I tilt my head back as he runs a finger lazily over my clit. I turn my head back to his and say, "Make me yours, Emmett Allan Davis."

He accepts the challenge, kissing me fiercely. He leans me forward and I brace myself against the shower wall, knowing I'm going to love everything he plans to do to me. He kneels down on the floor, lifting one of my legs to rest on the bench before me. And then he pulls me back onto his mouth, eating me hungrily until I cry out at the intense pleasure. He doesn't allow me to pleasure him, instead he goes straight to thrusting into me from behind.

He murmurs sweet somethings into my ear with each thrust. *I love you, Lola. You're finally mine, Lola.*

I feel my orgasm building inside of me, electric sparks jolt through my belly. I push back into him. He moves a hand from my waist to my front, rubbing my clit, taking me to where I need to be. I cry out as the orgasm explodes throughout my body. He comes with me. Pumping hard, I feel him spill into me.

He pulls out of me after kissing me senseless and then grabs a bath puff and my shower gel. We wash each other, taking time to kiss and explore. When we're done, we dry off, and then crawl into my bed naked. We make love again, this time tenderly.

Although I'm exhausted, I make sure we put on pajamas of some variety. I know without a doubt that a little auburn haired beauty will be jumping into bed with us first thing in the morning.

True to form, at 7:05 a.m., we hear the door creak open and then we're attacked by Ruby and little Mutt. I watch her to judge her reaction at us being in bed together.

Emmett tickles her and she squeals. When he stops she says, "Mama? Are you and Uncle Mutt dating now?"

"Yes, sweetling. Is that okay?"

She thinks about it for a minute, scrunching up her nose. And then she nods. "Yup. It's all right with me."

I chuckle. "Do you want to talk about it?"

"Nope. Uncle Mutt has always been around since I was born. He's always been like another dad to me," she says, shrugging. "It makes sense."

He looks up at me, smiling as a tear rolls slowly

down his cheek. I can't stop the ones flowing from mine.

"Ruby, darlin', I'm so happy you think of me like that. I couldn't love you more if you were my own. I don't want to replace your Daddy; he was a very special man and I could never fill those shoes. But one day, I hope that we can be a family."

She gives him a big hug. "I'd like that." He kisses the top of her head and motions for me to join them. We all cuddle together for a bit and then I hear Alma making breakfast downstairs.

"All right. Let's get up and have some breakfast. And then what should we do with the rest of the day?" I ask, untangling myself from my two favorite people.

"I think we should go buy a pony," Ruby says seriously.

"Think again," Emmett says, ruffling her hair, walking her out of the room.

I shake my head and smile, following them downstairs.

# Epilogue

## Emmett

Given how big of a day today is, I am all kinds of calm. This is the day I've waited for every day since I was 7. This is the day I marry my Lola.

Our wedding is a small affair, only immediate family and extremely close friends. As I look down at the wedding site, I smile. I'd always pictured us getting married there. It was the place of our first kiss. It was the place where I asked her to marry me. Our tree.

I know she's a couple of doors down the hallway getting all dolled up. I can't wait to see her. We slept in the same house but in different rooms last night. Our family has taken great care to keep us out of view of each other, letting me know when I can go downstairs to eat, go into the bathroom to shower.

I'm just finishing buttoning up my dress shirt when I hear a knock on the door. "Come in!"

"Papa? Mama asked me to give you something," Ruby says, coming into the room. She looks absolutely adorable in her dress. The top is white satin with spaghetti straps and the bottom is a voluminous pink chiffon skirt with embroidered flowers here and there. She picked it out herself and she looks like a little princess in it.

"What'd your Mama send me?"

She puts a small box in my hand.

"Should we open it and see what's inside?" I ask.

She nods, so I take the wrapping paper off and open the small jewelers box. I can't help but laugh. Inside the box are platinum cufflinks in the shape of dogs. They have onyx eyes. There's a little note tucked into the lid of the box.

*For my Mutt. Love you, forever and always, Lola*

Ruby smiles when she sees the cufflinks.

"Mama had those specially made for you!"

"I can tell. Can you give her a message for me?" After she nods, I pull her over and give her a big hug and a kiss on the cheek. "Tell her that for me."

"Okay, Papa. See you soon," she says excitedly as she closes the door to the guest room.

I pop my cufflinks in, shaking my head and smiling. Coop opens the door while knocking, Kevin and Carlyle following behind. I see four tumblers with ice and a bottle of Laphroaig. Today being a special day, I'm going to nurse a drink or two.

Kevin pours the scotch while Carlyle passes out the glasses. When we each have one in hand, we clink and then sip.

"You really are a lucky bastard. You know this, right?" Kevin asks.

"Believe me, Kev, I am well aware of how lucky I am."

"I don't think you do. Every time you'd upset her, Chase and I swore we were going to find you and beat the living shit out of you," he says in all seriousness.

"And I would have deserved it," I say, stone-faced. "Each and every time."

Carlyle pipes up. "You're lucky I was oblivious. I would have ripped your dick off and shoved it in your ear."

"Pleasant thought, Car. Thanks," I say, slapping him on the back. We all have a little chuckle and then sip our scotch.

"I know that I've done her wrong in the past, guys. But she is my future. All I want to do is make her and Ruby happy and keep them safe," I vow.

Carlyle gives me a big hug and says, "We know you do, man."

I pat his back a few times and then wipe a tear from my eye when we part. Kev comes over and gives me a hug, too.

"I know that Chase is up there smiling. On Ruby's third birthday, he told me that he hoped you would step up to the plate if anything happened to him. He knew you'd love them as fiercely as he did," Kev whispers to me.

I can't do anything but nod and let more tears fall. He finally releases me, grabs the bottle of Laphroaig and pulls Carlyle out of the room.

Now it's Coop's turn. "Well, here we are. This is the day you've been waiting for since you were a kid. Are you ready?"

"I was born ready to marry her, man," I declare, with every ounce of conviction I feel. "She's the one. It's only ever been her."

He nods. "I know it, Em. Now, get your tie and jacket on and we'll all see you downstairs." He doesn't go in for a real hug, instead going for a side hug. I think it's because Tiffany's very pregnant and he's in 'don't crush the baby' mode.

I start doing a Windsor knot in my black tie when Dad walks in. Since we announced our engagement, I haven't seen him without a smile. Mind you, it might also have something to do with the thing he's got going on with Alma. But I don't want to think about that on my wedding day.

"I can't believe this day is finally here, son. I'm so proud of you. For everything. You've had to overcome so much, but I knew you'd get through it. She would be your beacon of hope, showing you love to get through the dark times."

I smile. "Dad, she told me what you said to her when we left for Albany. What brought that out?"

"I think you know, son: your mama. You know we met while I was in college. I was a quarterback and I was being scouted by NFL teams and then I messed up my shoulder so bad that I had to quit. You know it still aches every time it rains. I got so down in the dumps and started drinking. But your mama—she let me have a few months and then she kicked me in the ass and told me to stop wallowing and get on with life; that she wasn't going to wait around for me forever.

"So, I started looking for jobs in football and got a job as assistant coach at my high school. I married your mama and, after a year, I was head coach of the football team. They were doing horribly. I had seen a lot of things I didn't like while I was assistant coach, so I changed them when I finally had my turn. And a few years later, we went to the state championships and won.

"Another team hired me to do the same. And that's how my career started. Your mama got jobs at the schools where I worked, teaching part time or as a substitute. Until the day we found out she was pregnant with you.

"She would have been so proud of you, Emmett. And she would have loved Viola and Ruby to bits," he says, choking up a little.

"Come here, you big softie," I say, opening my arms. He squeezes me tight, pats my head, and then pulls back, smiling.

"Let's get you downstairs and get you married."

I grab my jacket and follow him down to the tree.

The organizers did a great job. There's a white runner littered with pink and white peony petals. The white folding chairs all have giant sheer pink bows on them and a pillar of pink and white peonies, tied with the same fabric as the chairs at the end of each row. There's a white pergola where the minister stands, flowing with white fabric. Dad and I take our places and wait patiently for the bride.

When the string quartet starts playing, I focus on the end of the aisle, heart pounding in my chest. I see my darling soon-to-be daughter, holding her bouquet and smiling brightly, skipping along. And then I look a little higher. I'm thankful that I arranged myself for maximum retention because I cannot control the reaction in my pants when I see Lola. She looks absolutely stunning. Her hair is down and curly, a pink peony holding some back behind one ear. She's wearing the necklace and earrings Chase and her folks gave her at her first wedding; I insisted on it. Her gown is white silk. The straps tie at the top of each shoulder, the fabric coming down the front in a deep v. It's fitted to her waist and then flows freely to the tips of her bare feet. She is absolutely glowing.

And she's all mine.

I'm man enough to admit that I'm crying a little right now. It has been a long and difficult journey to this moment in time. But it's finally here and I am just so thankful that it's happening at last.

It's happening in the place where we spent so much of our time when we were younger. The place where our friendship grew, the place where I fell in love with her.

As I stand under the oak tree, waiting for my Lola to come to me, I can't help but feel that, even with all the bad that has happened over the years, this was how it was meant to happen. I needed to lose her, lose everything, so I could see what was truly important. And the two beautiful angels walking toward me are the most important things in my universe.

She and Ruby make it down the aisle. I give Ruby a hug and kiss before she takes her Mama's bouquet from her, like a little maid of honor should, and then I take both of Lola's hands in mine.

She squeezes my hands and I squeeze hers back, smiling, eyes glistening.

"Dearly beloved. We are gathered here today to join this man and this woman," the minister starts.

I can hardly hear him over the beating of my heart. I truly am the luckiest man alive. This woman has loved me for close to all of our lives. Her love helped me through some dark times, even when I pushed her away. I don't think it's possible for anyone to love someone more than I love my Lola.

"Emmett?" she says, looking at me with her head tilted. In my musings, I had tuned out the minister.

The minister repeats, "Do you take this woman to be your lawfully wedded wife?"

"I really do, sir," I state, earning a chuckle from our family and friends.

Before I know it, it's that time and I can't wait to kiss my bride. When I'm allowed, I pull her face to mine and kiss her with everything I've got, although I try to hold back and not maul her or use too much tongue because Ruby is standing right there!

Our reception is perfect. A long table is laid out with Lola and I at the head of it. We're sipping sweet tea and lemonade out of mason jars and having some good old-fashioned, home cooking: roast chicken, mashed potatoes with gravy, biscuits, beans, collard greens, and all kinds of fixings. I've got Lola's legs up in my lap and I'm rubbing her bare feet. She gives a contented sigh.

"Today was perfect," she says, running a finger along my jawline, a lazy smile on her lips.

"Mmhmmm," I murmur. "It doesn't get any better than this."

I look down the table and all I see is love. Dad and Alma, Luanne and Jack, Carlyle and Christine and their two kids, Kevin and Deedee and their three kids, their folks, Cooper and Tiffany, his folks, Uncle Pete and Aunt Polly, and our little Ruby. It is perfection.

After cake has been served and we've danced until my feet hurt, I turn to my beautiful wife. "How do you feel about saying our goodbyes and heading to the hotel?" I ask.

"That sounds wonderful," she says, stifling a yawn.

"Am I boring you already?" I ask with a laugh.

"No. Just a little tired. But never too tired to let you do naughty things to me," she whispers into my ear before kissing it.

That's all it takes for me to stand up and say, "Well, we'll be heading out now!"

We spend some time with Ruby, giving her lots of hugs and kisses and telling her how much we'll miss her, then say goodbye to the rest of our guests and then hop into my Land Rover to head back to the bed and breakfast we booked for the night. We're flying down to Jamaica for our honeymoon tomorrow. Ruby's going to stay with Luanne and Jack at the plantation until we get back.

When we get to the hotel, I carry her across the threshold and up the stairs to our room. I set her down and kiss her and then say, "I have a present for you."

She takes the box I give her and opens it up. Inside is a charm bracelet.

"Each charm represents something about us. The tree is for, well, our tree. The heart is for our love. The football is for Dad and how I came to be in Washington. The palm tree is for our trip to Hawaii. The dog is, well, me," I smile. "The L is for Lola. And the ruby is for our little gem."

She wipes tears away from her eyes and says, "It's perfect, Emmett. Put it on me?"

I fasten it around her wrist and then give her hand a kiss.

She heads over to our bags, grabs something and then comes back to me. "I have a present for you, too."

"The cufflinks were perfect. And I got the best gifts of all: you and Ruby," I stand shaking my head in surprise at Lola.

She says, "Oh, I think you're going to like this gift a lot."

She holds out a small picture, a sonogram of my baby in her belly.

"I'm about two months along. I didn't realize it until earlier this week when my breasts started getting tender. I had forgotten to go and get my birth control shot, I was so busy with work."

I stare at the little speck on the paper, my mind reeling. I immediately feel panic, as one would, having lost a child during birth. But Lola didn't have any problems at all during her pregnancy. She was healthy. She was strong. She has always been that way. I think back to all that we have been through, both the good and the bad. And through it all, she loved me. Dad was right: love does conquer all.

And now I have my Lola and my darling little gem. And my baby growing in Lola's belly. I'm not sure what I did to get so lucky, but a man knows when he is truly blessed. And I am. I blink away a few tears before I look at her.

"I didn't think it was possible for this day to get any better, but you just made it happen. I love you so much, Lola!"

I pull her to me and kiss her with everything I've got.

When we come up for air, she rests her forehead against mine and whispers, "I love you, too, Mutt. Forever and always."

# Acknowledgments

My first thank you goes to **Isabelle Richards.** Thank you so much for convincing me to try my hand at something new. Thank you for your words of encouragement and your sage advice. Thank you for talking me off the ledge all the time. I love you so much! zpzp

Thank you to my 'alpha' reader, **Aja Sinesky**. Not a day goes by where I am not thankful for your response to my post looking for beta readers. Meeting you truly changed my life. Your faith in me, in my writing, keeps me going. Your friendship means the world to me. I loves you, boo!

**Kari Nappi**, thank you so much for taking my vision of the cover for *Time Will Tell* and making it come to life! Thank you for all your advice over the years. But most of all, thank you for your friendship. You are a beautiful soul – don't ever change.

**Amy Donnelly**, girl, thank you so much for being an amazing editor, for guiding me through this process, for holding my hand, for believing in my words. You rock (and roll)! \m/

Thank you to my girls at **Talk Nerdy To Me Book Group**. From admins, to OGs, to newbies, you ladies rock my stilettos.

**Susan Carswell**, my graphic goddess. Thank you so much for your amazing designs and ideas for my swag! You deserve a medal for putting up with my crazy ass for the better part of two decades. Love you, girlie.

Thank you to my wonderful family. Mom, I'm still not letting you read the naughty bits.

To my husband, **Bob**, thank you so much for supporting me in this endeavor. Thank you for not raising an eyebrow any time the Amex bill came in. But most of all, thank you so much for loving me and putting up with me.

To my baby girl, **Rowan**. I know I tell you this every night, but you are the best thing that ever happened to me. Thank you for your patience while I am writing and social networking. Thank you for giving me all the hugs I could ever want or need. And thank you for being my shining star.

And finally, thank you to you, dear reader. For taking a chance on me.

xoxo,
Scarlett

# About *The* Author

Scarlett Wells has been a voracious reader since she was a toddler sitting in the laundry basket she used to move her library from place to place. Her love of reading has been a constant in her life and ultimately led to her sharing her own stories.

Scarlett is a stay-at-home mom to a sassy, precocious 5-year old, wife to a software engineer (read: geek), and slave to two cats. If she's not reading or writing, she can be found at Target, trapped under an avalanche of laundry, guzzling wine while she's cooking dinner, or playing with her munchkin

## Follow Scarlett

**Website**:
www.scarlettwells.com

**Facebook**:
Author Scarlett Wells

**Instagram** :
@author_scarlett_wells

**Twitter**
@Authorscarlett1

**Email**
AuthorScarlettWells@gmail.com

# Sneak Peek

Tag: An ST3 Security Novel
by
Scarlett Wells

## Chapter 1

*Cami*

I've been in some scary situations in my life. I've had some close calls. I've definitely known fear. But this time? This time I'm fucking petrified.

I'm sitting in one of the wingback chairs in Daddy's home office, my knees to my chin, arms wrapped around them. I'm listening to Daddy yell at my security team.

"I'm having a problem trying to understand how this asshole got so close to her, Jim. So close he was able to slip these," he shakes a plastic bag containing the offending items, "into her pocket. It wasn't like the barista casually handed them over to her. She had no clue they were there until she came home, emptied out her pockets only to find a death threat and a bullet with her name literally written on it!"

Jim, my head of security for the past two years, has the decency to look sheepish. I have to feel for the poor guy. I mean, he is almost literally glued to my ass any time I leave the house. He drives my car. He sits next to me in my classes at UCLA (I major in Art History; I imagine it can't be incredibly stimulating for him). He's there when I go out to eat. He's there when I go out to socialize. He's even there when I spend hours wandering around the stores on Rodeo Drive shopping.

I put this guy in some pretty uncomfortable situations. It's bad enough that he has to clear out and 'hold' restrooms for me so I can do my business. But he's stood in the room while I've had my annual women's exams. He's also stood sentry while I've gotten my freak on at a frat party or two. I mean, he's on the other side of the door, but I'm very vocal when I'm enjoying myself. Not to mention the fact that he's had to frisk the dudes I've been with when I've already got them sporting some serious wood. Can you say awkward?

All that said, he's a good guy and I know he

wouldn't intentionally let anything bad happen to me. But the fact that this creep managed to slide his hand in the pocket of my jacket without me feeling it? Means the guy got too close. And that's not good.

Still, I try to calm my father down. "Daddy, don't take it so hard on Jim. It was an absolute zoo at Starbucks in between classes today. Mid-terms are coming up - you know how badly we students need our caffeine to study."

"Camille," he says, taking a deep breath in and out in an attempt to contain his utter rage. "What if the guy had had a knife, or a gun, or a syringe instead of a note and a bullet? We were lucky this time. It was a warning. And one I'm not going to take lightly."

I close my eyes and start to rub my temples, hoping if I rub hard enough I can transport myself into an alternate dimension where I'm not a walking target for kidnapping and death threats, where I am just a regular girl. I open my eyes. Nope. No such luck.

Daddy sighs. "Darling, I'm afraid we're going to have to take the necessary precautions."

"No, Daddy. Please not that! I'll do anything you ask of me. I'll stay at the house. I'll get my professors to let me finish my courses online. I'll do anything. Please," I plead.

"They know where we live, Camille. They've... They've been in the house, darling. It's not safe for you here," he says softly.

This is news to me.

"What do you mean 'they've been in the house'?"

Daddy sits back down in the leather executive

chair behind his desk and rubs his hands over his face just as his security guys open the door. My godfather, Bill Hansen, walks in.

He immediately comes over to my chair and puts his arms around me.

"Are you okay, sweetheart?" he asks, his head resting on top of mine.

I nod as he's pulling away from me. He puts a hand on either side of my face and kisses me gently on the forehead. It's not until that point that I feel my throat get thick and the sting of tears in my eyes.

"Don't cry, sweetheart," Bill murmurs. "I'm going to make sure you're safe."

I take a shuddering breath in and dash the tears from my eyes before giving him a weak smile. "I know, Uncle Bill."

He stands up, turns to face Daddy, and puts his hand on my back, rubbing soothing circles on my upper back.

"I've already set the plan we devised in motion. Troops are rallying as we speak, George," Bill informs.

Daddy nods. "Good."

"Tell me about them getting into the house. How is that possible?" I ask.

Bill looks at Jim and his team and motions his head toward the door. The guys all stand up and throw me apologetic looks before they turn and walk out of the room. There's just me, Bill, Daddy, and his long-time bodyguard, Tony.

Bill sits down in the chair Jim just vacated. "We're pretty sure there's someone on the inside."

I gasp. "How is that possible, Uncle Bill? I thought all your guys were thoroughly vetted and given the rubber glove treatment before they came to work for you."

He chuckles. "For the most part, that's true... except for the rubber glove thing. There are always ways for things to slip through the cracks. We're putting some more in-depth protocols into place in HR as we speak. We're looking into financials for all the guys on the teams assigned to you and your father, their families, friends... Anything that could give us a clue into who may have done this."

I nod my head. And turn to Daddy. "Tell me how you know someone was here."

He looks pained as he says, "The picture of you, your mother, and me in St. Moritz that was on my dresser is missing."

I press my lips together, barely able to hold back a sob. That was the only copy of that picture. It was the last picture taken of my family before my mother died. I turn my head away from Daddy and Bill, letting my tears fall.

"I would not be able to forgive myself if anything happened to you, Camille. I've already lost your mother. I can't lose you, too," Daddy whispers.

I nod my head, swallowing loudly before I respond. "I know, Daddy."

"Donna is going to be over in a little bit to help. And I've called in a team I've had on retainer since the last incident. These are good guys, Camille. If they weren't so stubborn, wanting to work for themselves, they would have been the ones I'd have handpicked for your detail. They were my go-to guys when I was their CO. I trust them with my life."

I look back at Bill, using my tongue to swipe a tear that hit my lip. "Did they pass the rubber glove inspection?"

Bill laughs and smiles at me. "They did. Every one of them."

I take in a deep breath and let it out, then push myself out of the chair.

"Well, I guess I should go upstairs and start packing, then."

Daddy comes around the side of his desk and pulls me into a bear hug.

"I love you so much, Camille. I don't want to do this. I hate having you out of my sight. But this is our only option right now."

I hug him back just as tight as he's hugging me. "I know, Daddy."

We stand there hugging for a while before I whisper, "I'm scared."

I feel him nod. "Me, too, darling. Me, too."

*Tag*

"Ramsey Taggert," I snap into my cell phone. I turn off the treadmill and hop off, sweating like a whore on nickel night and breathing just as heavy.

"Tag? It's Bill Hansen."

"Lieutenant Commander, Sir!"

"At ease, Chief Petty Officer," he chuckles. "I hope

to God you didn't stand at attention."

I laugh. "No, sir. Just surprised to get your call."

"Enough of the 'sir' business - we're civilians now. You can call me Bill," he says.

"Fair enough. What can I do for you?" I ask.

"I'm calling you boys in. How quick can you get your team up to Topanga?"

I look at my watch. "Give us 90 minutes."

He gives me an address, tells me to pack heavy, and then hangs up. I immediately call Tito and tell him to get the boys in gear and pick me up in 15 minutes.

Like clockwork, the horn honks 15 minutes later and I head out the door with my large duffel and my backpack. I set the alarm and lock up the house, not knowing when I'll see it again. But that's part of the job.

I open the passenger door of the Humvee and hop in. Tito grins at me.

"Another damsel in distress?"

I snort. "Bill's calling in his marker."

"This the job that the Lieutenant Commander has us on retainer for?" Gus asks.

I nod. "Yup."

"Have we been given a brief?" Gunner asks.

"Not updated, no. We'll get what we need when we see him."

We're all silent for the remainder of the drive, listening to Led Zeppelin like we did when we were driving around Iran, Iraq, and Afghanistan while we were doing contracts.

We pull up to the gates of the estate in Topanga. After showing our IDs to the guard and waiting for clearance, the gates slowly open and Tito drives us up the long, winding road to the main house.

This place looks like a Tuscan villa: limestone brick facade, terra cotta tile roof, cypress trees lining the walls and a bubbling fountain in the middle of the circular stone-work driveway.

Jett lets out a low whistle.

"You can say that again," I tell him.

Tito parks the Humvee and we head up to the wrought iron and glass front doors. Bill pulls a door open before I can even ring the doorbell. He looks at his watch.

"Two minutes early," he says, giving me a smile and holding his hand out.

I take his hand in mine and grip it firmly. He gives me a nod and then gives each of the guys a handshake and a slap on the shoulder as we enter.

"Follow me, boys," he says, heading deeper into the house.

I focus on his back, knowing that if I look around I'm going to be floored by the opulence of this place. We're walking for about 2 minutes before Bill knocks and opens up a set of intricately carved solid walnut double doors and leads us into a giant office.

Floor-to-ceiling windows overlooking a courtyard line one wall, built-in bookcases on the other, complete with one of those rolling ladders. There is a large conference table with a dozen chairs around it in the middle of the room, followed by a giant mahogany desk with leather wing back chairs in front of it. Behind the desk is a large fieldstone fireplace, over which is hanging what has to be an original Monet.

What? I may be an ex-Navy SEAL but I'm fucking cultured.

My eyes finally settle on the gentleman sitting behind the desk, rubbing his eyes with the heels of his hands.

"George, I'd like you to meet Ramsey Taggert and his team. Guys, this is George Montgomery," Bill announces.

George Montgomery: shipping magnate, net worth in the tens of billions. I know this guy's got hardcore security - Bill personally recruited a bunch of guys we trained with in Coronado. Guys who would have been us if we hadn't decided to hang out our own shingle.

Bill directs us to sit at the conference table. We take our seats and gladly accept the bottled water given to us by George's secretary. Bill asks George's bodyguard and secretary to give us the room. They both exit quickly and quietly. George takes a seat at one end of the table, Bill the other.

"This morning, George's daughter, Camille, was threatened. This isn't new to them, but this one was different. A .44 Remington Magnum hollow point with her name etched on it was wrapped in a note containing a death threat and placed in the pocket of her jacket. No prints. We think it happened while she was grabbing a coffee in between her classes at UCLA.

She was with her bodyguard, a team close by. No one has been this bold before - mostly they get threats via email, mail, or even called in. But this time they wanted George to be aware of just how close they could get to her. They also managed to get into the house - stole a family picture from the dresser in George's room."

I close my eyes and shake my head. "So, when we discussed this a few years ago when you put us on retainer, you wanted her sequestered. Is that still the case?"

Bill nods. "Yes, but we're taking it a step further than that. My group has been working on logistics since then, planning heavy diversions so we can get her out and safe. I personally selected and made arrangements for the safe house - no one has the address but me. I need you to get her there and guard her for as long as this takes."

"Where's the safe house?" I ask.

"You boys ever been to Greece?" Bill says.